Books by Phyllis A. Whitney

The
Ebony Swan

Phyllis A. Whitney

DOUBLEDAY
NEW YORK
LONDON
TORONTO
SYDNEY
AUCKLAND

The
Ebony Swan

PUBLISHED BY DOUBLEDAY
a division of Bantam Doubleday Dell Publishing Group, Inc.
666 Fifth Avenue, New York, New York 10103

DOUBLEDAY and the portrayal of an anchor
with a dolphin are trademarks of Doubleday,
a division of Bantam Doubleday Dell Publishing Group, Inc.

Book design by Anne Ling

Library of Congress Cataloging-in-Publication Data

Whitney, Phyllis A., 1903–
The ebony swan / Phyllis A. Whitney. — Large
print ed.
p.   cm.
I. Title.
[PS3545.H8363E26   1992]
813′.54—dc20]   92-4384
                                                 CIP

ISBN 0-385-42443-4
ISBN 0-385-42444-2 (large print)

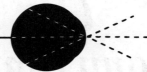

**This Large Print Book carries the
Seal of Approval of N.A.V.H.**

Printed in the United States of America
1   3   5   7   9   10   8   6   4   2
FIRST EDITION

For Leona Nevler

Thank you for believing in my books when few others did, and for helping me to achieve my first "best seller." Because of your support, beginning nearly thirty years ago at Fawcett, my books now appear everywhere in paper. Equally important has been your friendship for all these years.

Foreword

My thanks to Virginia Adcock and the volunteer staff of the Lancaster County Library in Kilmarnock for as warm and helpful a reception as I've ever received.

Ann. L. Burrows, of the Mary Ball Washington Museum in Lancaster, helped to launch me on my journey of discovery when I visited Virginia's Northern Neck—that peninsula that viii reaches down the map for a hundred miles between the Rappahannock and Potomac rivers, with its toe in Chesapeake Bay. My thanks as well to F. W. Jenkins, Jr., director of research at the museum, for reading my novel in manuscript and helping me with local details.

Mimi Beckwith, executive director of the Foundation for Historic Christ Church, and a number of docents at the Carter Reception Center, were helpful in introducing me to that remarkable edifice, which so affected me that it became a powerful influence in my story.

I am grateful to Stanley Shelton, Louise Denegre, and Katharine Dunton for showing me their beautiful homes, so that I could "build" the Montoro house in my story and give it a proper setting.

Eleanor Friede, a gifted freelance editor and my good friend and neighbor, first told me of Tangier Island and set me off on my search. I first visited the island—that speck of land out on the Chesapeake between the two shores of Virginia—by tourist boat. Months later, Eleanor (herself a flyer) arranged for friends to take me back to Tangier by small plane. My thanks to James and Heidi Kramer for flying me there in their wonderful "bamboo bomber," so that I could further explore the island. By that time I had met my characters and knew what they were doing there.

I am indebted to Bette Nohe, of Hilda Crockett's Chesapeake House on Tangier, for inviting me into her hundred-and-fifty-year-old home, and answering my many questions about the island.

Tanya Dickenson, of the *Rappahannock Record*, not only interviewed me for her paper, but supplied me with clippings that provided endless sources of information about the Northern Neck and Tangier Island. All of this provided me with a setting like no other I've ever found for one of my novels.

My deepest thanks go to Dr. Robert Atkins for his radio programs and books, which have helped me to better health, and have given me a basis for what is said by the young doctor in my story.

The
Ebony Swan

One

*A*lex slammed the car door as hard as she could, the sound venting some of her irritation. For a moment she leaned against the hood, stretching her right leg so it would lose its stiffness and take her weight more comfortably. At seventy-two she scorned the use of a cane except when absolutely necessary, and resented her in-

2 ability to walk with the long, easy stride of the dancer she had once been.

As she approached this unwanted meeting with Gilbert Townsend, she knew she must not give him the satisfaction of sensing her physical weakness. She must be in control of her body— she needn't worry about spirit. She still had plenty of that.

With careful steps she walked along the brick path, the afternoon sun of August hot in a clear blue sky. At least the building she approached would be cool inside, with no concession to air-conditioning. Still, it displeased her that Gilbert had chosen this place for their meeting, even though the choice was not illogical, since they were both trustees of Christ Church, which had been designated a Virginia landmark.

The great building was like no other church in Virginia. This was no white-steepled edifice, and its red brick dignity still inspired her with a certain awe. She was thankful that it stood well out in the country, without a town crowding around to detract from its solitary distinction.

Gilbert was nowhere to be seen, and she was grateful for further time to fortify her resolve in order to resist whatever he wanted of her. The peremptory demand of his note had been so disturbing that she'd angrily torn it up. No one took that tone with Alexandrina Montoro. Unfortunately, tearing up his note had not erased his words from her mind, and she felt more vulnerable than she had in years.

I must see you at once, he had written. *I have just learned that your granddaughter is arriving today. You must listen to me, and send her away as soon as possible.*

That was all, except for asking her to meet him here. His very secretiveness was troubling, and she'd begun to feel both annoyed and alarmed in spite of efforts to reassure herself.

Her mirror had given her some comfort when she'd dressed for this meeting. She had been tall for a ballet dancer, and she had lost none of her height to age. Her back was still straight, and if there were imperfections of figure, they were hidden by the white Chinese jacket—one of several she had had made for her in Hong Kong—which sported a delicate spray of blue embroidery over one shoulder. If all her once-famous young beauty had vanished, she was still a handsome woman, and the heavy coil of hair at the nape of her neck was not yet entirely gray. As a girl it had been her pride—long and gleaming black—her Spanish heritage from Peru.

Whatever pain she had suffered over her daughter's death, with her husband's death following a few months later, nothing from that time could hurt her now. She had steeled herself against being upset by many things, including an

4 impending visit by a granddaughter she had not seen since that time of tragedy—twenty-five years ago.

Perhaps she could quiet her inner spirit with an old ritual that had served her well over the years she had been visiting this church. She began by fixing her eyes upon the bricks at her feet, allowing her gaze to follow the path slowly, seeing only what was small and easily encompassed; then lifting her eyes a little to reach the open gate set in low brick walls that stretched away on either hand—walls that had been built onto the original three-hundred-year-old foundations. Beyond the gate, the walk led to two shallow steps up to the door. All this was earthbound and immediate—small realities she took for granted, but which helped to still her inner turmoil.

She moved toward the gate, allowing her eyes to lift to the simple, gracefully framed doorway, then upward to the arch above. Still higher, her gaze reached a white-spoked oxeye window where the peaked roof began.

Now was the moment. She tilted her head back and let the full dramatic impact reduce her to a tiny human speck that hardly mattered. This perspective was good for her much-too-human soul. She could shed vanity and pride, and put aside the protective shield that shut out all emotions that might hurt her.

Massive red brick glowed in the sun. The

church, built in a shortened cruciform shape that
looked almost square, possessed a marvelous balance that pleased the eye and raised the spirit.
Tremendous gray roofs slanted into the sky, their
tipped-up corners suggesting the Chinese, though
the architecture was entirely English. There were
authorities who claimed that the design was pure
Christopher Wren, with a balanced grandeur that
was forever satisfying to the beholder. Even
though Alex Montoro was no longer on speaking
terms with God, in this spot she could not deny
some mysterious power that strengthened her.

As she stood at the gate, deliberately releasing
tension, anger subsided, and new strength flowed
through her. She had every reason to dislike the
man she had come to meet, but he could not
touch her now. She was her own strong self
again. For that little while when she'd been very
young she had danced as prima ballerina in the
capitals of the world. "Drina," they had called
her. She had been showered with applause and
love and praise. Such memories still gave her a
certain manner that she could summon when it
was needed. Stage presence, perhaps, and there
were those who found it intimidating. Unfortunately, Gilbert never had.

As she moved up the walk, a man appeared
through the church door, and stood staring down
at her from the steps. She had not expected him

6 to be inside the building, and for a moment she was disconcerted.

He was a big man, still broad-shouldered and good-looking. Men aged more successfully than women, she thought ruefully, and he had developed an impressive, authoritative manner. Sheer theatrics, of course. When young, he had once aspired—unsuccessfully—to the stage. His gray hair, which used to be a shining blond, was still thick, and he wore it brushed back in a style that showed his wide forehead. Younger, more supple flesh had given way to a sculpted, stony look, making his profile sharp.

She had no need to be afraid of him, she told herself. He was of no more consequence than he'd ever been. It was only some sixth sense that warned her that he might now be a threat to the peaceful life she had so painfully achieved.

The smile he flashed had lost none of its dramatic quality. "Alex!" he cried. "How marvelous you look!"

He didn't exactly leap down the steps—she noted that he, too, had a knee problem—but he came down quickly, and before she could draw back, he caught up her hand, bowing over it, touching it lightly with his lips, then raising his head to look deeply into her eyes. All mockery, of course.

She snatched her hand back impatiently.

"Don't perform, Gilbert. Just tell me why I've been summoned here in this ridiculous way."

He didn't seem to mind her tone. Nearly fifty years ago, when she and Juan Gabriel Montoro had first come here from Peru to escape the dangerous political situation at home, Gilbert had tried to ingratiate himself, undoubtedly impressed by Juan Gabriel's fame as a distinguished novelist. Her husband had been thirty years older than Alex, and that, she supposed, had made her seem fair game to a dashing would-be young actor. She had been unfaithful to Juan Gabriel only once, and that had not been with Gilbert Townsend.

"I thought we might talk inside," he said, and turned to open the door for her, not waiting for agreement.

Historic Christ Church was one of Virginia's treasures, and open to visitors only during the warmer months. Unheated and unlighted, it was closed when the weather grew chilly, though congregations in the past must have attended bundled in winter clothes. She was not pleased that Gilbert wanted this conference to take place inside. This was not the church of her youth—she had followed her husband in turning away from that—and she had never made her peace with whatever it was she felt when she stepped within these walls. Sometimes she needed that spiritual life, yet at the same time resented it. But unless

8 she held back, she had no choice now. She must know what this meeting was all about.

Thankful that the steps were shallow, she went up easily and stepped into the lower nave. At once she felt the chill of limestone flags beneath her feet. The interior was always cool, no matter how warm it grew outside.

There were no open rows of seats for the congregation, only the high pine-paneled walls of pews on either hand. Gilbert motioned her on and she walked toward the transept aisle. Below the chancel, set opposite each other, were two pews larger than the rest. Of course Gilbert would choose one of the pews that had been reserved for the use of Robert Carter and his family. "King" Carter, they'd called him, and he had owned a good part of Virginia in early days. Carter had built this church, and his stone tomb, along with the tombs of his two wives, stood in the churchyard at one side.

Gilbert probably sensed and enjoyed her reluctance to hold their meeting here. They both knew the rules very well. Signs asked visitors not to touch or enter the pews, in order to preserve old wood. But, arrogant as ever, Gilbert opened the door of Robert Carter's pew for her, and reluctantly she stepped up to the higher wooden floor that had protected the feet of worshipers from cold limestone. Until she understood the urgent purpose behind his demand to send Susan away, Alex would go along with what he wished.

Hard wooden benches ran around the rectangle of the pew, though history reported that Robert Carter had placed his own comfortable chair in this particular pew. When seated, none of the congregation could see the members of any other family, and only the minister in his high walnut pulpit, set centrally, could look down upon his flock—every sinner in view. Narrow circular stairs led up two levels of the pulpit, the top level placed beneath a handsome canopy that formed a sounding board for the stern sermons that must have echoed through these spaces. In spite of her anxiety, when Alex looked up she felt once more the mystery and wonder within these walls. It had been years since she had been able to pray, and she had long ago discarded those Catholic prayers taught her by the nuns when she was a child. Now, however, as had happened before, some wordless petition seemed to fill her, asking for help from—somewhere. Perhaps asking for a shield against trouble to come.

"Please sit down," Gilbert said. At least he spoke softly in this hushed place.

She lowered herself carefully to a hard bench, her back straight, her long, dancer's feet in flat-heeled slippers placed neatly together. Vanity had rejected all efforts to get her into "sensible" shoes.

"I'm waiting to hear your explanation," she

10 said. "I have other things to do today. Why are we here? There are a hundred other spots where we could have met privately—if that's what you wanted."

"My sister Hallie suggested that we meet here. Besides, I know you have a special feeling for this place, Alex. Maybe you're even afraid of its invisible power. I thought you might be more amenable to reason if we met here."

Hallie! She might have known. There were few pies into which Hallie Townsend didn't poke with her curious, nimble fingers.

"Explain what you mean by *reason*," she said.

She'd grown increasingly aware of a nervous quality behind the bluff of his assured manner. He was worried about something, and she had no idea what his sister Hallie had to do with this. Except that Hallie worked as a docent for the Carter Reception Center connected with the church, and if they met here, she might be able to meddle.

For a moment Gilbert moved about the enclosed space without speaking, his back to her as he gazed upward at the pulpit. Perhaps the pulpit was a symbol of whatever he wanted to conceal from Alex's penetrating look.

When he spoke again, his naturally dramatic manner fell away. "I never told you before, Alex, since it seemed pointless, but I visited Juan Gabriel a month or so before your daughter's death.

We'd had a—a disagreement—and I simply wanted to make my peace. But since he'd suffered a stroke it was difficult for him to talk. Everyone else was out of the house and I saw him alone. He managed to tell me that he didn't want to live—that life meant nothing to him anymore."

The chill of the building seeped into her bones, but Alex kept very still to prevent emotion from surfacing visibly.

"I don't believe you, Gilbert. I was very close to my husband, and he never lacked courage. If it hadn't been for the shock he suffered when Dolores died, I know he would have recovered. What are you driving at?"

"Hallie told me yesterday that your granddaughter is coming here. If she stays for long she will begin to ask questions. Can you risk what she may recall during this visit? Do you want anything of what really happened to surface?"

The trembling started at the pit of her stomach, but she held herself still, betraying nothing. "My daughter died in an accident—a fall down the stairs. She tripped. I don't know what you are implying."

His eyes seemed to deny everything she was saying. "As I recall, when you returned home that day to find your daughter dead at the foot of the stairs, Juan Gabriel had struggled from his

12 wheelchair and lay unconscious in the upper hall."

"That's true. We believe he tried to come to Dolores's aid. We found him in a coma from which he never recovered, except for regaining consciousness a few moments before his death."

In those final moments, he had managed a few words as he struggled to speak. Frightening words. Now Gilbert was thrusting her back into that time of anguish and fear.

"I still have no idea why you brought me here to talk about this," she told him coldly.

"Don't you? Think about it, Alex. There's still time to send the child away before anything surfaces in her mind. What she might remember could destroy your peace forever."

"That's nonsense! In any case, why should you become involved in my affairs?"

He had turned to face her as he spoke, and now he made a helpless gesture. "My sister Hallie cares about you, Alex. I'm here because she felt that I should talk with you. Emily agrees. She thinks you would never listen to Hallie."

Gilbert had two sisters—Hallie a few years younger, and Emily as many years older. A long time ago, before she moved away, Emily had been Alex's good friend. Friends parted and changed, and she hadn't seen Emily in years. An even older pain lay in that direction. And, after all, Emily had nothing to do with the present.

Over the years Gilbert's full lips had thinned, 13
and they twisted now unpleasantly. "There's another reason for our concern, Alex. Lawrence
Prentice was my good friend, as well as being
Dolores's husband, and Susan's father. Hallie was
fond of him too, and we both grieved to hear of
his death in New Mexico a few months ago. He
never wanted his daughter to return to Virginia,
and Hallie and I respect his feelings."

Anger stirred. Hallie had always had crushes
on unavailable men, and she'd been more than
fond of Lawrence Prentice. Of course, Lawrence
had detested her—as he'd detested Alex as well,
blaming her unreasonably for Dolores's death.
Afterward, he had taken Susan away to punish
her grandmother.

She spoke sharply. "I never had any respect
for Lawrence Prentice. He was the wrong husband for my daughter. I remember Hallie's crush
on him very well."

The moment she spoke, she recognized the
unkindness of her words. She might not have
much affection for Hallie, but she had always felt
sorry for her, and tried to be kind. Gilbert was
probably equally moved to this action by his own
long-held malice toward Alex Montoro. Right
now all she wanted was for him to go away.

"Since Lawrence is dead, Gilbert, all this is
water under the bridge. It's because he has died
that Susan is free of his restraint and can come

14 here. She's never understood what she thought was my long silence, and we need to talk face to face."

He rejected this dismissal of all he'd been hinting at. "Do you really believe the past exists in some closed-off compartment, Alex? That it doesn't grow into the future and affect everything that happens later? You may be lifting a barrier that is better left down."

One thing she knew. While Susan was here she must keep her away from Gilbert Townsend at all costs.

He came abruptly to sit beside her, and when she stiffened, he laughed slyly.

"Don't worry, Alex. You still matter to me, and I don't want to see you hurt."

It was hard to contain her indignation, but she ignored the falsity of his words. Whatever his reason for what he was doing, affection for her played no part in it.

"You called Susan a child, Gilbert. She's hardly that. Her father took her away from me twenty-five years ago, so she is thirty-one. Old enough to make her own decisions. I shall welcome her and try to make her visit a happy one. I don't suppose she will stay very long."

Before Alex could rise to leave, the nearby transept door opened, and footsteps sounded on the flagstones. Alex and Gilbert sat very still. Undoubtedly some sightseer had wandered in, but they couldn't see over the walls of the pew to discover who it was. In a few moments the visitor would probably go away.

Instead, a woman's voice called out to them. "Gilbert? Alex? Are you here?"

Alex recognized the high, rather querulous voice of Gilbert's sister. His reaction, however, surprised her. He looked as though his sister's presence alarmed him. "Tell her nothing of what we discussed," he cautioned in a whisper.

As Hallie opened the door of the pew, he got to his feet, staring at her. Hallie didn't step up to the wooden floor to join them, but stayed outside —a tall, thin figure in a shapeless tan dress that hung nearly to her ankles. There had always seemed an immaturity about her. She was the youngest of the three, and some aspect of her had remained a child. An inquisitive child. Her eyes were bright and much too eager.

"Well!" She sounded pleased. "An assignation?"

"Don't be foolish, Hallie. You knew I was meeting Alex here. Alex, we'll talk another time, but do think about what I've said. I'll leave Hallie to you." He went through the door past his sister and out of the church, moving hastily, as though eager to be away.

"Now what was that all about?" Hallie asked.

16   "You'd better ask your brother. He told me that meeting me here was your idea."

"It was."

Alex was silent, waiting for Hallie to continue or leave. Not that she'd ever been one to take a hint—and she didn't now.

"Susan was such a darling little girl. I can't wait to see her again. It was sad that she had to leave under such unhappy circumstances."

"Let's give her time to catch her breath, shall we, Hallie? She'll be tired after a long trip."

"Of course. Well—I'll get back to work, though it's been a slow day. I just wanted to look in on you two since I knew you were here. I'll see you later on, after Susan has arrived." She went clattering away over the flagstones, and it was a relief to have them both gone, though Alex felt more bewildered and anxious than ever. The last thing she wanted Susan's coming to do was to dredge up the past. At the time, the horror of what had happened to Dolores seemed to cause a loss of memory on Susan's part. She had been unable to tell anyone what had happened, and questions had sent her into bursts of hysteria. Alex could only hope that nothing of that experience had remained with her over the years.

Remembering where she was, Alex wondered if some help might come to her in these surroundings. She looked up into the vast, vaulted

spaces overhead. There were no cross beams,
nothing to interfere with that airy expanse. Space
soared thirty feet above her head, with the roof
rising another ten feet higher. Light glowed
through three oxeye windows set in deep eaves,
while high, arched windows along the outside
walls added more formal lighting. The effect was
softly subdued and quieting to her troubled spirit.

Somehow she must find the courage to deal
with all the concerns that Susan's arrival would
bring into her life. But for now, Susan was on her
way, and Alex wanted to be home when her
granddaughter arrived.

Outside, in the warmth of the afternoon, she
followed the walk to her car, passing ancient
gravestones where other members of the Carter
family were buried. She must not allow Gilbert's
silly notions to worry her. He was, after all, what
he had always been—a frustrated actor. Unsuc-
cessful on the stage, he had turned to a second
profession—teaching early American history at a
small local college. He had used his acting ability
to dramatize his subjects, and his classes had been
enormously popular. He had managed to teach
even his more unmotivated students to appreciate
history. Now that he had retired, he claimed to
be working on a definitive history of Christ
Church, though no one had seen any pages of his
manuscript as yet.

To everyone's further astonishment he had

18 purchased an old mansion on the Rappahannock River and turned it into an inn he called The Mulberry Tree. It had recently received several stars in a highly regarded guide. An innkeeper could benefit from being an actor too.

Ironically his son Eric also wanted to go on the stage, and Gilbert was opposing him at every turn, perhaps because he knew the hardships so well. As usual, Eric had his Aunt Hallie's support —which must have added to Gilbert's displeasure.

Back in her car, Alex drove to Kilmarnock and turned east toward home. The Northern Neck of Virginia—a peninsula that lay between the Rappahannock and the Potomac rivers, with its toe in the Chesapeake—had offered a safe haven to Juan Gabriel when they had fled from Peru. Because of its position between two rivers, the Northern Neck was almost an island, and had been isolated from the rest of the state. Even when bridges were built, things didn't change a great deal.

Along the road loblolly pines thinned occasionally to make room for fields of soy beans or healthy stands of high corn. Away from Kilmarnock a side road led to Sawmill Creek and the house Juan Gabriel had bought for them when they'd first arrived in what was to be their adopted country. Virginia's history and pleasant climate had interested him, so they had come here. Having lived in Virginia most of her life, Alex took pride in being an American, and had managed to rid herself of all but a trace of her Spanish accent.

The ragged coastline of the peninsula was etched with dozens of Tidewater creeks, and it was at the head of one of these that Juan Gabriel found the house he wanted. Victorian architecture had fascinated him, and since there were many such houses, he had bided his time and found just the gem he had hoped to acquire.

The move away from Peru and the danger that country held for him had been good for Juan Gabriel's writing. Already a distinguished novelist whose books were read in translation everywhere, he had found new perspectives in the United States and his creativity had thrived.

Alex had loved each and every one of his books, except *The Black Swan,* which had left her troubled and unhappy—though she'd assured herself that it was only fiction.

He had continued to write until he had his stroke. After that there had been nothing. He hadn't wanted to live as he was. She knew that, so she quickly dismissed Gilbert's implications. She mustn't think about his words. She was eager now to be home.

When she turned into her driveway, George Dixon came around the house to open the car door and help her out. George and his wife,

20 Gracie, had been with her almost since the Montoros' arrival, and both were dependable friends. George was part Indian and not as dark as Gracie. Almost all the Indians were gone from the Northern Neck, but here and there one saw the high cheekbones and long noses that signified Indian blood.

George conveyed his news quickly. "Your granddaughter phoned, Miss Alex, and Miss Theresa took the call. She'll tell you."

Alex thanked him, and when he'd taken the car around to the garage she stood for a moment on the front walk looking up at the house. Fanciful nineteenth-century whims prevailed, with gables, a flat, cupola-topped tower, peaked roofs at different levels—all impractical and delightful. These days, Alex seldom climbed the stairs to the upper floors. A comfortable suite had been arranged for her on the first floor and she lived in it happily.

When she and Juan Gabriel had bought the house, it had been painted yellow, but she much preferred the present white with gray trim. Soft gray roofs blended with white clapboard and white veranda railings. Here people said "porch," but Alex loved the word "veranda," and felt that it better suited the generous expanse that embraced the front of the house and curved back for a distance on either side.

To the right of the white wooden steps a

flamboyant blooming of crape myrtle pleased her with its startling pink. Green shrubbery, carefully trimmed by George, grew beneath the veranda rail, and had been kept just as Juan Gabriel would have wished. Behind the house a wide lawn sloped to the water. Only a few well-spaced houses occupied this street. Alex enjoyed living on the outskirts of a village that was so tiny it didn't appear on most maps.

She looked up at the tower with its narrow encircling balcony, and found that its eccentricity still delighted her. She planned to put Susan in the tower room, and she hoped it would please her. All those many years ago, Susan had carried her dolls up there to look out windows that must have seemed majestically high to an imaginative child.

The thought of Lawrence disturbed Alex all over again. The fact that he had died recently didn't lessen the pain of the harm he had done. She planned to be cautious around Susan, since she had no idea how close her granddaughter might have been to her father, or what lies about her grandmother he might have fed her. At least Susan had wanted to come, and it was she who had written the first recent letter.

Alex's examination of the house was only a delaying tactic, a postponement of what lay ahead. Right now she felt too weary to deal with

22 the events of the rest of the day, yet none of them could be avoided.

When the screen door opened and her niece Theresa Montoro came to the head of the steps, Alex stiffened. She knew she ought to feel grateful to have Theresa in her life. For years the young woman had dealt capably with whatever crises arose, and had managed all the business connected with Juan Gabriel's books. She had come to live with them as a little girl, when her father, Juan Gabriel's nephew, had died a political prisoner back in Peru, and her mother succumbed to a long illness soon after.

Theresa had been twelve when Susan was taken to New Mexico by her father, and Alex knew instinctively that she didn't welcome the idea of Susan's return.

Theresa waited on the veranda, unsmiling, though that meant little, since she seldom smiled. She was a stunningly beautiful woman, with huge dark eyes—eyes that looked out at the world with habitual distrust from under thick brows. She wore her heavy black hair wrapped around her head in a high coiffure. The only lively thing about her was the long amethyst earrings she always wore, which danced when she moved her head. She could be animated enough when she was angry, but fortunately her temper was usually under control.

Theresa wore a smock the color of crape

myrtle blossoms over slim black trousers. As usual, a splash of paint streaked the smock—today it was aquamarine. Theresa was a gifted painter, but at present her choice of eggs as a medium seemed strange to Alex. She had chosen to paint dozens and dozens of intricately detailed eggs in the "Russian" style.

"You didn't tell me where you were going, Alex," Theresa said. A statement of fact, rather than a reproach.

Nevertheless, it made Alex testy. "I needed to get away. And I haven't been gone long." Her meeting with Gilbert Townsend was none of Theresa's affair.

"Susan Prentice called," Theresa continued, her disapproval clear.

"Yes—George told me. When will she arrive?"

"Peter should be meeting her at the library soon. You needn't have taken his time. I could have gone."

Alex didn't answer. She hadn't wanted Theresa to be the first person Susan met when she arrived. Peter Macklin was a few years older than Susan and they had played together as children. Peter was Alex's most trusted friend, as well as her doctor, and he had been quick to offer this small service, since Alex preferred to meet her granddaughter on home ground. Susan had writ-

24 ten that she was a nurse, so Alex felt they would have something in common.

Alex climbed the steps with the aid of the railing, wishing that Theresa weren't there watching her slow movements.

"Susan may arrive at any minute, so I'll go and change," she said.

"Don't hurry," Theresa said with a slow smile, "I'll be here to meet her."

"*I* will meet my granddaughter," she said, and Theresa shrugged.

In her own big, pleasant room, which was comfortable in spite of the August heat, she bathed her face in cool water, and then regarded herself in a long mirror. Her white jacket and trousers hadn't wilted too much: they would do. Her courage began to return as she studied her reflection. The woman in the glass *looked* confident. If any weakness or vulnerability hid behind her façade, no one ever need guess. This woman could deal with whatever was to come. Sometimes it was an advantage to be intimidating.

She touched soft rose lipstick to her mouth, and renewed the black of her long eyelashes. Not too much eye shadow. She didn't care for the pale faces of older women, but she didn't want to look made up either. "Drina" had been lost long ago, but she still had herself—Alexandrina Vargas Montoro—a woman to reckon with. And she still possessed that mysterious quality that had drawn audiences to their feet when she was young. Rudy Folkes, who had discovered her, taught her, loved her, had once said, "It's not only that you are a great dancer—it's the magic you bring to a stage that is endlessly fascinating." Well, she mused, some men had found her fascinating even when she no longer danced.

She lifted the crystal stopper from a bottle of perfume and touched it behind her ears, and at her throat and wrists. The scent had been her "signature" for more years than she cared to recall and it brought back memories she couldn't afford to think about now.

She went out to what Juan Gabriel had called the drawing room, or sometimes the sala—though neither term seemed suitable here in the States. As she sat in her favorite chair—a tapestried wingback, from which she could look out the front windows toward the street—she was glad that Theresa was nowhere in sight. She wanted to be alone when Susan arrived.

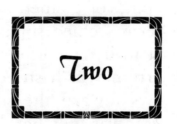

Two

In the library in Kilmarnock the volunteer at the front desk had been watching for Susan. When the young woman introduced herself, the older woman held out a friendly hand, regarding Alex Montoro's granddaughter with open interest. Susan's grave expression made her resemble her grandmother, though she seemed far more apprehensive than Alex ever did. Her brown hair had been trimmed into a smooth cap, and her dark eyes were wide and serious. She looked tired, which was natural, but when she smiled her face was warm and attractive. Alex must have been more beautiful when young, but her granddaughter's prettiness had a disarming appeal.

"My grandmother wrote that someone would meet me here in the library," Susan began.

"Yes, of course. It's Dr. Macklin you're expected to meet. He phoned to say it may be another half hour before he gets here. Would you like to call your grandmother?"

Susan nodded, all her uncertainties about this trip rising in a wave of new anxiety. She had yet to speak directly with her grandmother; they had only exchanged letters. Now, however, the inevitable seemed upon her. She picked up the receiver and dialed. Theresa Montoro answered, and that was even more disturbing to Susan. She hadn't thought of Theresa in years, and a vague, unsettling memory returned of someone who had enjoyed teasing her in an unkind way—someone she had disliked and feared. Susan sensed that Theresa felt as uncomfortable as she did. Their exchange was brief. Her grandmother would be told of her arrival, Theresa said, and they would expect her when Dr. Macklin could pick her up. Susan found a corner of the library where she

28 could sit at a table near a window and look out at the grass and bushes.

Bookshelves were close by, but she was too tired to open a book. Tired, not only because she'd left Santa Fe early this morning, but because of a deep anxiety that wore her down emotionally. Nothing her father had told her about Alex Montoro had been reassuring.

Nevertheless, there were questions about her mother that needed to be answered. She needed to know why her father had hated her grandmother so deeply. She knew nothing of his years in Virginia—something he refused to talk about —and when he married again, her stepmother had been the only loving presence in her life.

Her work as a nurse had been satisfying to a great extent, but in the last year her own problems had become a pressing issue.

During this time she had taken only terminal patients, since she felt they were the ones who needed her most, but the inevitability of death had begun to destroy her peace of mind. Falling in love with Dr. Colin Cheney hadn't helped.

When she was a young nurse in training, she'd been warned that while she must use her own humanity to enhance her nursing skill, she should never allow herself to become emotionally involved with patients who were going to die. Some nurses managed this detachment, but Susan's response had become one of indignation against a profession she found too narrow in its views. Whatever protective skill she had started out with had worn thin during Gina Martin's illness.

She'd grown to love the frail, courageous little woman in whose home she had lived for the last few months. She had watched the destructive ravages of chemotherapy and despaired of a profession that offered nothing better. It hadn't helped that Susan was engaged to marry Colin— not when her indignation was directed against him as Gina's doctor.

"There *are* other ways!" she'd protested more than once. "Why can't you at least look into them?"

Colin had dismissed such alternatives as quackery and told her she was being unprofessional. He'd been so arrogantly sure that he knew all the answers!

At the memorial service, Susan sat with Gina's family and felt all the more guilty and miserable because of their gratitude for the little she'd been able to do. Colin, of course, was a busy doctor and hadn't been there. The next time she saw him they'd argued more heatedly than usual, and she had returned his ring. The following day she wrote to her grandmother in Virginia. It was time to turn her back on nursing and reexamine what she wanted from life. It was also time to discover who she was and that meant delving

30   into the past. She wished that her grandmother hadn't sent this Dr. Macklin to meet her. She was weary of the whole medical profession.

Dozing in her chair, she looked up suddenly to find a man studying her from across the table. His gray eyes, set beneath straight, dark brows, seemed disconcertingly intent and, oddly enough, a little amused.

"Hello, Susy," he said.

In confusion her thoughts tumbled back to when she was six and there'd been a dark-haired boy she'd called—Petey? He had been all of ten years old, and she'd followed him around when his family came to visit, always his eager and adoring slave. As memory returned, she began to smile.

"I wondered if you'd remember," he said.

The boy's face had developed wide cheekbones and a rather craggy look that was unrecognizable. The young mouth had grown straight and a little stern. Only his dark forelock had a tendency to flop over his forehead as it had done when he was a boy.

"I do remember," she said, and held out her hand. "You're Dr. Macklin, of course, though I remember you only as Petey."

He shook her hand and then examined it carefully. "You seem to have survived pretty well, in spite of me. All your bones intact? I wanted to be a doctor even then, as you may recall, and you were willing to be my patient—so I spent a lot of time mending your shattered bones and saving you from dire illnesses. You often had galloping pneumonia because I liked the sound of that disease even though broken bones—my specialty—weren't involved."

"Your treatments were pretty imaginative," she said, laughing with him and feeling wonderfully relaxed for the first time since she'd left Santa Fe. "You were always putting my arms into splints and bandaging my hands!"

He sat down across the table from her. "So now you've come home. It's the right time—I think your grandmother needs you."

His words brought back her misgivings. "How can she need me? We don't even know each other. She's never been in touch with me."

He let that go. "Perhaps you're both worth knowing." The slight smile that had reassured her was gone. "Your grandmother hasn't been well lately. It's nothing serious, but she gets easily upset. I hope you'll keep that in mind."

"Why should I upset her?"

"I'm sorry. I'm sure you won't, but she's been anxious about your coming."

"I've been anxious too. My father died a few months ago, and my stepmother encouraged me to get in touch with my grandmother."

Peter Macklin looked at her for a long moment and then stood up abruptly. "Perhaps we'd better get started. I know your grandmother is eager to see you."

She rose to follow him, noting his informal dress—a short-sleeved blue cotton shirt, worn outside his light cord pants. Hardly the clothes a doctor would wear in his office. She wondered that he should be taking time off in mid-afternoon.

They thanked the librarian and walked outside together.

"I'm sure I could have found the way myself," she said as he opened the door of the car she'd rented at the airport in Richmond. "It wasn't necessary to call you away from your patients."

"My office is closed," he told her, and she noted that he hadn't said "today," or "this week," which seemed puzzling.

He went on. "It's not far to Mrs. Montoro's house, but there are a number of turns, so it's simpler if I show you the way the first time."

When she was behind the wheel, he leaned in to touch her arm lightly, and his faint smile returned. "Besides, Susy, I wanted to see how you'd turned out."

For just a moment the boy she remembered was teasing her. Then the look was gone, and in contrast he seemed even more remote than before.

She waited as he walked to his own slightly

battered Chevy and pulled away from the curb. Instantly, she thought of the Mercedes Colin enjoyed so much—almost wearing it like a second skin.

Peter drove slowly and it was easy to follow him. At this hour of the afternoon Kilmarnock seemed a busy little town, its main street lined with shops and shoppers.

They were quickly out on the highway, and as she followed Peter's car, Susan tried to register the turns for future reference. In only a few miles he pulled into a driveway, and she drew in behind him. For a moment she sat viewing the big gray and white house that seemed to have gone whimsically erratic in its architecture. Crape myrtle bloomed gloriously at one side of the steps —a delight to eyes more accustomed to the earth colors of New Mexico.

A black man came from behind the house to greet her with a warm smile. "Welcome home, Miss Susy."

He was an older man, so she must have known him long ago. He saw the question in her eyes and reassured her quickly.

"I'm George Dixon. Guess maybe that little girl was too small to remember."

She smiled warmly and held out her hand. "I'll need a little time to remember everything."

He shook her hand and went to take her bags from the trunk. Peter left his car to join them,

34 waiting while Susan stood looking up at this house that must be more than a hundred years old.

Behind the peaked room over the entrance, rose a tower with windows and a gallery running around the outside. Here was something she remembered.

"I remember that tower," she told Peter.

"How old were you when you went away, Susan?"

"Six, I think. Or close to seven. I can only remember snatches of that life."

One of those snatches had to do with a loving, comforting woman and another with crying when her father took her away. When she was older he told her that they were no longer welcome in her grandmother's house and that it had been necessary to leave when they did.

A woman walked onto the porch, and Susan moved toward her. Though she seemed very old to Susan she still looked proudly handsome, with wonderful facial bones that age couldn't touch. She held herself tall, her shoulders straight in her white Chinese jacket, her legs long in slim white trousers. Her manner was grave and somewhat intimidating, so that Susan felt even more uncertain.

Peter ran up the steps ahead of her. "I'm sorry we're late, Alex, something came up that I had to take care of. I've brought your grand-daughter."

As Susan stepped onto the porch, the old woman moved forward and held out a formal hand in greeting. "Welcome to Virginia, Susan. I hope your journey hasn't been too tiring."

She shouldn't have expected an affectionate welcome, Susan thought. Long ago this woman had held her on her lap, and they had cried to-gether because her mother had died—a flash of brief memory told her that—but this stiff formal-ity made her wish she were elsewhere.

"Thank you for helping us out, Peter. I hope you will stay for tea," Alex said, then turned to the black man, who was waiting. "George, will you carry Miss Susan's bags upstairs, please."

Miss Susan? But, of course, this was the South.

Peter opened the screen door for the two women, and Susan walked into a hall that ran from the front to the back of the house. On her right an open double doorway revealed a long, beautiful room with pine-paneled walls and a flowered Chinese rug, faded to softly luminous colors.

Her grandmother gestured and Susan stepped into the room. A fireplace, set almost flat against the wall, caught her eye. The protrusion of mantelpiece formed a narrow ledge, on which

36 stood several ceramic cats. One cat was only a head, with a huge grin that ran from ear to ear.

"The Cheshire cat!" Susan cried. "I remember him."

"Yes." Her grandmother spoke softly. "Your mother used to read you *Alice in Wonderland,* though you were much too young for that book. You are the one who dropped him on the hearth and took a piece out of his ear."

A smile touched her grandmother's face—a wonderful, warming smile that lasted for only an instant, before the guarded expression returned. A long-fingered hand, beautiful in its grace, invited Susan to a chair. Then she seated herself regally in the center of a sofa, disdaining the supportive damask cushions behind her.

"I've ordered tea," she said. "I thought you might need refreshment after your long trip, Susan. And you will stay, won't you, Peter?"

There seemed a faint entreaty in her voice, and Susan suspected that, for all her assurance, this woman did not want to be left alone with a granddaughter she barely knew.

Peter agreed to stay, though he sat down a bit stiffly on a delicate chair—a chair that might have come from some French salon.

Tension seemed to fill the room, and Susan's feeling that this was never going to work increased.

Peter made an effort toward conversation.

"How long has it been since you two saw each other?"

"About twenty-five years," Alex said, and added with an emotion she couldn't control, "All those senseless years!" At once she suppressed her feelings. "Did your father tell you much about us here in Virginia?"

"He didn't talk about you very much," Susan admitted. "He never told me what happened, but his views were pretty prejudiced. I never knew what to believe. Perhaps that's one reason why I'm here."

Her grandmother made no response to her words, changing the subject quickly. "I can't think where Theresa is. She promised to join us for tea. Susan, do you remember your cousin Theresa?"

Before she could answer, Theresa Montoro came through a rear door, her arms filled with sprays of crape myrtle, the pink blossoms lending a glow to her cheeks. Her big dark eyes were luminous, offset by black, dramatic eyebrows. Susan remembered her instantly.

"Hello, Susan," Theresa said, nodding, and then turned to Alex Montoro. "I'll put these into water and tell Gracie to bring in your tea. Everything is ready, I'm sure."

"In a few minutes," Alex told her. "There's no hurry. Run along and take care of your flowers. Peter, perhaps you should take Susan up to

38 her room before we have tea, so that she can freshen up."

"Of course," he said.

Susan was glad to escape the increasingly uncomfortable atmosphere.

Peter led the way into the hall and toward a flight of stairs rising against the wall. Susan paused at the foot of the stairs, looking upward, arrested. Some frightening twinge of memory had stopped her, only to evaporate before she could grasp it.

"Is something the matter?" Peter asked.

She shook her head, unable to explain, and went past him to the floor above, where a second flight climbed to a long hallway. They followed this to the tower room, built a few steps up from the hall level.

The door stood open and Susan walked in, while Peter waited in the doorway. She remembered this room. A curving wall followed the outside shape of the tower, though the room was not a complete circle, since a portion of it had been partitioned off, forming the shape of a half moon. A door in the outer wall opened on the balcony. All this she recognized uneasily and without joy.

"Perhaps you'd like to settle in a bit," he suggested. "Your bathroom is next door, and if you want to rest a little, I can tell your grandmother."

"No, no. I'll come down soon, thank you—I don't need to rest."

When he'd gone she stood looking around, studying the room's detail, trying to quiet the tugging of something ominous that seemed just out of reach of her consciousness.

The room was simply furnished. A highboy with brass pulls stood against the flat wall, and a comfortable armchair sat in the open, with a lamp on the table beside it. A small, straight-backed chair had been pulled up to a desk with cubbyholes. The faded wallpaper, with sprigs of violets in the pattern, seemed familiar. She smiled, recalling that she'd tried to smell those tiny flowers as a child. On the wall above the bed a bright square of wallpaper stood out, as though a picture might have hung there until recently.

Farther along, a framed watercolor of a lighthouse caught her eye—circular and squat, built on pilings out in the water. Gulls soared around it, and she knew she must have sat fascinated before this painting as a child. A name flashed into her mind—though she wasn't sure it had any connection with the painting: Tangerine Island. Was there really such a place?

The next painting was of a little girl, and she stopped in recognition. The face was hers. It must have been painted only a little while before she left Virginia. By her mother? she wondered.

40 She seemed to remember watercolor paints, and a room where they'd painted happily together.

The artist had shown a dreamy quality in the young face—wide eyes and a mouth almost ready to smile. This must have been the way she'd looked just before her mother's death. Just before her father had taken her away from Virginia forever. No details of that time remained—only a heavy sense of tears and pain. This was why she had come—to find all the memories that had been shut away from her for these many years.

The tower door to the balcony drew her and she stepped outside to look down on a wide green lawn at the rear of the house. Grass sloped to the lapping waters of the creek, reaching to the edge of a small beach. She could remember running down there to paddle at the water's edge, though it had been forbidden unless a grownup was with her. Sometimes Theresa had served in that capacity, young as she was.

A few memories stirred and she recalled the stories Theresa used to tell. One was about a time when she was a princess in a palace high in the mountains of Peru. She had been born in Peru, and clearly looked down on Susan, whose birthplace was Virginia's Northern Neck. But there was no time for this now, much as she wanted to remember.

She went into the delightfully old-fashioned bathroom and washed her face and hands, feeling better immediately. Then she returned to put on a blue cambric shirt. Her gray slacks would do for now, and she would unpack properly later. Just as she brushed her hair into its smooth cap, Theresa appeared.

"Your grandmother would like you to come down for tea now. Peter has to leave in a little while."

"Thank you, I'm ready," Susan told her, and added curiously, "Do you remember me, Theresa?"

"Of course I remember you. And I remember your father very well—a dark, angry man who frightened me a little."

That sounded like Lawrence Prentice, Susan thought. She followed Theresa down the stairs. "Perhaps you can tell me about my parents sometime. I remember so little about the years when I lived here."

"Sometimes it's better not to remember," Theresa said and went busily ahead as though she wanted no more talk. Susan hurried after her down to the long room where Alex Montoro sat before a dropleaf table that had been opened to serve them tea. When Peter had brought chairs for Susan, Theresa, and himself, he sat down with them. He still seemed absent at times, as though his focus lay elsewhere, and Susan wondered what it was that troubled him so deeply.

Tea with lemon was refreshing, and short-

42 bread from Scotland unexpected and delicious. Alex smiled and explained that imported shortbread was a little luxury the family had always indulged.

"The Montoro family boasted a stray Highlander who turned up in Peru in his wanderings during the last century, and stayed on to marry a Montoro girl. Perhaps that's why Kilmarnock, which was named for a town in Scotland, appealed to Juan Gabriel."

This was the first time her grandfather had been mentioned. Susan had no memory of him at all, but was eager to absorb every scrap of information about the family that came her way. She felt closer to that long-ago Scotsman who had wandered out of his ken, than to her Spanish ancestors in Peru.

Peter continued to seem preoccupied, and Susan made an effort to pull him back into the conversation.

"Are you a family physician, Peter? Or do you specialize?"

Theresa made a small sound of dismay, as though Susan had said something inappropriate. Alex set her cup down carefully, waiting.

Peter didn't seem to mind. "I suppose I'm still in family practice, though I've closed my office for the time being."

The silence that followed seemed awkward, and Peter asked a question of his own.

"I understand you're a nurse, Susan?"

"That's what I'm trained for, though I'm not sure it's a profession I want to follow."

"Why is that?"

She tried to speak evenly. "The last four private patients I've nursed have died. Perhaps needlessly—as much from their treatment as from their disease. But when I challenge and ask questions, I'm cut off, dismissed." There was challenge in the look she turned on Peter.

"You're quite right to ask questions," he said gravely. "I'm inclined to agree with you."

Alex Montoro moved quietly away from what Susan sensed might be an uncomfortable topic.

"How much do you know about my adopted land of Virginia, Susan? This Northern Neck? It was given that name by the English back in the 1600s."

"Not very much. I've looked at maps and there seem to be three peninsulas extending along Virginia's northeastern shore."

"Those are the Necks. Tidal rivers have carved them out of the mainland. Ours is the northern peninsula, between the Rappahannock and the Potomac. It's almost a hundred miles long, but only fifteen or twenty wide at various points. And it's sliced into by hundreds of tidal creeks, which give it a good deal of coastline. Up near Fredricksburg the rivers almost meet. Peter

44 —you're a native—tell her about the Northern Neck."

Here was a subject he could warm to. "In the old days there were no bridges and few roads, so this area was almost an island. Our little towns, especially in the south, are still pretty isolated. People who live in one part of the peninsula may not see much of those in other parts. And there's an opposite shore of Virginia, across the Chesapeake, that we seldom get to at all."

"There are two little islands as well, out on the bay. One belongs to Virginia, the other to Maryland," her grandmother put in.

Susan smiled. "Did I used to call one of those islands Tangerine?"

"I had forgotten that," Peter said happily, "but you're right, Susan. You could never remember Tangier." He went on with his account. "A good deal of history was made in this area. The Algonquins were here first, of course. Then Captain John Smith came along—he was brought here as a captive. According to his own account, this is where Pocahontas saved him. Jamestown was settled in the northern county of Northumberland. English kings began to take an interest in Virginia's rich prospects—tobacco growing, for one thing."

Alex brightened. "Tell her how Virginia came to be called the Old Dominion."

"It's a good story. When Cromwell was dead

and his son had abdicated, Charles II returned to England in 1660. Because Virginia had been loyal to his cause, when he became king, he had coins struck commemorating the dominions of 'England, Scotland, Ireland, and Virginia.' So we Virginians are still proud to call our state the Old Dominion."

Peter seemed to have relaxed as he talked, and he smiled at Alex. "There's no Virginian more patriotic than a come here who stays, like you, Alex. Will you excuse me if I run? There's someone I need to meet. Let me know if there's anything I can do to help."

Alex gave him her hand, and old woman and young man looked at each other with trust and affection. The apparent bond was somehow reassuring to Susan.

As Theresa walked Peter out to the porch, Alex's eyes followed him thoughtfully.

"Is Peter in some sort of trouble?" Susan asked. "Why has he closed his office?"

Her grandmother was silent for a moment. "He is in very serious trouble. But I'd rather not talk about it, since it's his affair. I'll just say that it concerns his wife, who died under mysterious circumstances nearly a year ago. I'm sure Peter will choose to tell you all about it, at the right time."

This sounded alarming, but Susan let it go.

"There are a great many things we need to

46 talk about," Alex added. "Some may be off limits to start with—we need to get to know each other first—but tomorrow we must begin."

By now, Alex Montoro seemed a little less austere and forbidding, and Susan was willing enough to wait.

"We'll have a late supper tonight, so, if you'd like to rest for awhile, you certainly have time."

Susan accepted the suggestion and thanked Alex for the refreshing tea. Out in the hall she found Theresa waiting for her at the foot of the stairs. As Susan approached she began to speak softly, with a hint of malice in her words.

"That's where she fell—from right up there at the top of the stairs. Your mother, Susan. Do you remember?"

The shock of something like terror flashed through her and frightened Susan badly. "I don't remember anything about that time," she told Theresa quickly.

The dark, young woman seemed oddly intent as she went on. "You were home alone with your mother, and too young and frightened to understand what happened. At least, everyone said you were too young when you couldn't tell them anything. They decided that Dolores must have tripped on the top step, tumbled all the way down and struck her head at the bottom. She was dead by the time they found her, and you were sitting beside her crying.

"Alex came home before I did, and by the time I arrived, she was taking hold with her usual strength, even though your mother's death shattered her. It was a double tragedy, of course, because your grandfather was found lying in the hall up there, near the top of the stairs. He'd had a stroke earlier, so it was a wonder that he managed to get out of his wheelchair. When they found him he was in a coma and could never tell anyone what had happened. Since you couldn't tell them anything either, how Dolores met her death has always remained a puzzle. Alex believes there was more to what happened than a mere fall, although the police called it an accident and made nothing of it."

Susan couldn't bear to hear any more. Her trembling made it difficult to speak. "All I remember is a feeling that something terrible happened."

"Your father didn't tell you anything about it? That seems pretty odd."

She couldn't deal with Theresa or any of this now. "I'm very tired; I'm going upstairs to rest for a while."

She hurried past Theresa and up the stairs, wanting only to be alone. The whole atmosphere of this house was wrong. The answers she'd wanted might be too frightening to bear. Perhaps she should leave as soon as she could.

When she reached the tower room, she

48 kicked off her shoes and flung herself full length on the bed. All she wanted was for this shock of pain and fear to stop. She didn't know why she was afraid, but only that a deep sense of loss that belonged to the time when she'd lived here as a small child filled her. Her memory of Peter seemed clearer in her mind than anything about her mother and grandmother. It was as though all that was most important had been blanked out. She tried to tell herself that it was only the present that mattered. It might be necessary to let everything else go.

She was still curious about her grandfather, however. He had hardly been mentioned since she had come, but her father had admired his books, even though he'd seemed to disapprove of the man. There'd been English translations of his novels at home, and she'd read them in high school. She'd always tried, unsuccessfully, to find some connection to herself in his writing.

Though she had no wish to, she began to think of Colin Cheney again. Perhaps the very fact that her father—with whom she'd disagreed on most points—had liked Colin should have warned her that she had made a mistake. She knew now that she'd trusted Colin too soon; perhaps even fallen in love with her own idea of what a doctor should be.

She tried not to think about this now. She needed to rest and let emptiness take over. Deep

breathing sometimes helped. She lost track of 49
counting her breaths and fell asleep.

When she opened her eyes the tower windows reflected the dramatic beauty of a sunset sky. Feeling refreshed and more alive, she slipped on her shoes and went out on the balcony. The rear of the house faced west, and the creek waters shone like crumpled gold. Tremendous folds of color washed across the sky making it look like a great canopy.

Angel wings, she thought—like some vast Michelangelo painting. Streaming color swept outward, with bits of blue shadow showing through, forming the convolutions that reminded her of wings.

Below the tower the lawn had brightened in the glow of light, and across the creek a few lamps had come to life in windows. Within her closer range of vision something moved, and looking down she saw that a woman stood near the water, her face lifted toward Susan's balcony. She wore dark jeans, and a shirt washed colorless by the brilliance of the sky. When she realized that Susan had seen her, she waved a hand, then, mysteriously, put a finger to her lips and gestured that she was coming up.

Susan watched as she disappeared around the house. Perhaps there were outside stairs? She

50 walked around the circling gallery to where the steps began, and waited. The woman came up too fast, and paused near the top, breathless, a hand pressed to her heart. Again she put a cautioning finger to her lips as she came up the remaining steps.

She was a tall woman—though not as tall as Alex Montoro—and thin to the point of being bony. In her hurried movements her long arms seemed to have an uncontrolled life of their own, swinging away from her body. It was her face, however, that caught Susan's interest. Triangular in shape, and wide at the cheekbones, it tapered to a pointed, cat-like chin. Her short hair was fluffed around her face in a youthful style, though she must be in her sixties, and her eyes seemed bright with curiosity as they rested on Susan.

"I had to come and see for myself! I'm Hallie Townsend, an old friend of your parents, and I just can't believe you're here," she cried. She went around toward the door to the tower room, where she stood waiting to be invited in. Once she'd stepped into the room she regarded Susan with an eagerness that was embarrassing.

"Let's sit down," Susan said, feeling awkward and at a loss.

"Let's do. I remember you very well as a little tyke, and I liked the way you laughed at my silliness. You knew how to get around your mother, but you met your match when it came to Alex, and you behaved yourself when she was around."

Thinking of the handsome, rather intimidating woman she had met downstairs, Susan could easily imagine that to be true. Hallie, at least, might prove a source of some of the things she wanted to know.

"I have no relatives in Santa Fe," she said, "and I was so young when I left here. I'll enjoy hearing your stories."

"My brother Gilbert was real fond of your papa. I'm the youngest Townsend, though I've looked out for my brother and sister so much that sometimes I feel like I'm older. Gilbert is the middle one, and our sister Emily is a few years older—around Alex's age." Hallie looked suddenly sad. "Emily married and moved away— out to an island in the bay, and I hardly ever see her anymore." Hallie paused for a moment. "Susan, why have you come back?"

The question came so suddenly, after all the skipping around, that it seemed startling. Susan offered a simple answer. "My father died, and I know none of my family, so I wondered about my Virginia relatives."

"I don't think your gramma's too happy about your coming here."

Perhaps that was true, but Susan said nothing. Clearly Hallie Townsend would love to gos-

52 sip, and Susan didn't want to discuss Alex with anyone. Her questions lay in other directions. If she was unwelcome here, then she wanted to know why, but not from this eagerly curious woman. She countered with a question of her own.

"Why didn't you want anyone to know you were coming up here to see me just now?"

Hallie made a face, answering readily. "Theresa doesn't approve of me. She thinks I upset Alex. And you'll find out how much Theresa runs things around here. Your gramma's too tired to pay enough attention."

"Why does Theresa disapprove of you?"

"Lots of reasons, but, as of this moment, because even though I was older, I was your mother's friend when we were young. I might tell you more than they'll want you to know. How much do you remember, anyway? About when you were little."

"I don't remember anything," Susan said flatly.

Hallie's smile showed relief as she stood up, her thin arms reaching out as if to embrace the room. "I haven't been up here since your mama died. I used to come often to visit her."

"This was my mother's room?"

"Your mother's, but not your father's. He preferred to climb fewer stairs, and he liked the front of the house." Hallie dropped into a chair again, crossing her sharp knees, "You don't know much about your mother, do you?"

Susan had no desire to offer confidences to this rather strange woman, so she merely shook her head.

Hallie went on. "Your father was a brilliant man. I admired him a lot. He and my brother were good friends. Juan Gabriel used to like him and respect him, but that was before they had a terrible fight. Your gramma never took to him, though. She hated it when Dolores married him. And, of course, he never did care for Alex Montoro. Dolores was a lot more gentle—his kind of woman." Hallie sighed, her oddly shaped face turning wistful.

Susan waited for this welling up of disconnected information to continue. As it did.

"Your gramma would have been very happy when Lawrence went away—except that he took you with him. Maybe now that you're back, she's afraid of what tales he may have told you over the years."

Her father had told her very little, though his prejudice against her grandmother had always come through.

The light outside the windows had faded to black, and Susan rose to turn on some lamps. She still waited for Hallie to reveal the real purpose behind her visit.

Over one arm Hallie carried a straw hand-

54 bag, which she now opened. "I've brought you something you might like to have." She took out a tissue-wrapped package that she handed to Susan. "Dolores gave me this years ago, but I think you should have it now."

Unwrapping the paper, Susan found a color photograph set in a silver frame, and she studied it eagerly. Dark hair swept back from a delicate forehead. Dreamy dark eyes looked away from the camera. Dolores had possessed a gentle beauty quite unlike Alex's more dramatic quality. In the photograph her mother looked as though she might be listening to some faraway music.

Gazing at the picture, Susan knew that she had never forgotten her mother's face. Tears came into her eyes as a feeling of total love and trust filled her. This was a recognition she had not felt with her formidable grandmother. Pain and loss ran deep.

"What do you remember?" Hallie asked with sudden intensity.

"Only her face. If you were her friend there's so much you can tell me about her and about my grandmother."

Hallie answered cheerfully, though Susan sensed evasion in spite of her seeming openness. "The Montoros knew everyone, but they were always a bit exclusive. Juan Gabriel valued his privacy, and your grandmother did as he wished. She involved herself in local affairs but didn't develop many close friendships. Dolores was shy and reserved. Well, I'm rattling on. We'll talk sometime, Susan. Maybe it's just as well you don't remember much. It might upset your gramma to dig up all those old times. I'd better go now. I left my skiff tied up at your dock. Our house is just a little way down the creek, so it's easier to come by water. But I want to get home before it's too dark. I'll see you again, Susan. Before you leave." There seemed an emphasis on her last words.

"Thank you for the picture, Hallie."

Susan went with her onto the balcony. At the top of the outside stairs, the older woman paused. "I reckon it might be better for everybody if you don't stay too long, Susan."

With that she hurried down the stairs and ran toward her boat. Feeling a sudden chill in the night air, Susan returned to her room. From the direction of the dock she heard the sound of an outboard motor.

It must be time to join her grandmother and she hurried down to the long front parlor.

Alex Montoro sat at the cleared tea table with several glossy photographs spread before her. As Susan approached she saw that they were photos of a ballet dancer.

Alex looked up gravely. "Come and sit down, Susan. I want to show you something."

Three

*A*lex was not sure exactly why she had brought out this box of old photographs to show Susan. Perhaps, she thought, as she sorted through, picking out a special picture here and there, these might give Susan a glimpse of what Alex Montoro had once been like. Proof that an old woman had once been young? Often the young looked at older people as though they had never been anything but what they were now. Perhaps the photographs would provide a bridge over the years. She wanted to think that it was more than vanity that made her bring these out for her granddaughter to see.

Back in Peru her own mother had wanted her to place all of these in albums, but after Rudy Folkes's untimely death, Alex had no heart for that.

Looking at them brought back memories of sorrow and joy—and the knowledge that this young dancer, posed in frozen moments of time, was a stranger to her now. For all these years, since the last time a spotlight had followed her on a stage, she had been growing into someone else. "Drina" belonged to several lifetimes ago. Still, she wanted Susan to see who her grandmother had once been.

A step sounded in the hall, and Alex watched as Susan came into the room. She was as slender as a dancer. Not as beautiful as Dolores had been, but with a small, graceful head, and a face that made one look twice. Intelligence could be more arresting than beauty. If only she could forget all the things Gilbert had said in the church. But now that Susan was here, she was afraid to forget.

"Please come in and sit down, Susan." Her words sounded formal and without emotion. That was as it should be, and far safer than

58 showing what she might feel. She gestured to the sofa beside her, and Susan sank into soft cushions that Alex disdained, her back as straight as she'd been taught to hold it.

Her granddaughter glanced at the photographs. "Who is the dancer?"

Alex experienced an unexpected shock of dismay. So much for fame! "You don't know? No one ever told you?"

"Told me what?"

"I was nineteen, twenty, twenty-one, when these pictures were taken. But I suppose my dancing meant nothing to your father, so he would never have mentioned it."

With new interest Susan picked up a print that showed the black swan of *Swan Lake,* long of neck, with a sly smile and a glint of wickedness in her eyes. She looked from the photograph to her grandmother's face and smiled.

"I believe you could still look like that. I'm sorry I didn't know that you'd danced. Were you famous?"

"For a few years. A very great choreographer named Rudolf Folkes created several ballets for me, and I helped to make them known in European and South American capitals." She couldn't help boasting a little to her own granddaughter.

"I've heard of Folkes, and I've always loved ballet. Why did you stop dancing?"

Alex began to stack the pictures, returning

them to the box. "I stopped dancing when Rudy died. Perhaps I'll tell you about it one of these days."

The device of showing Susan the pictures had caught her interest, at least. Her eyes were shining over what she probably regarded as a romantic discovery.

"I'd love to know about your life as a dancer. There's so much I don't know about you—and about my mother. I know about my grandfather, of course. My father was impressed by his writing. He collected his books in translation, so I've read some of them. But he would never talk about Juan Gabriel Montoro the man. Or why he wrote about such disturbing violence."

"My husband wrote about the times in which he lived, Susan. But now I'd like to know what made you write to me after such a long silence?"

"My father always opposed my getting in touch with you. And, of course, I never heard from you in all those years."

That wasn't true, she had written many times and sent gifts on Susan's birthday and at Christmas, but Alex remained silent. She didn't dare allow her own anger to surface. How could Lawrence have hated her so much that he would deny his child gifts from her grandmother?

"My father made it clear that he didn't like you, but everything he said about you made me curious. So after he was gone and I came to a

60 place in my life where I needed a change, I wrote to you. In fact, my stepmother, who practically raised me, encouraged me to write."

"I'm glad she did." Part of Alex was really glad, but another part remained cautious and not ready to trust. There seemed something muted about Susan at times—as though some damage had been done to her spirit. That was troubling. But Alex was no mender of spirits—she'd suffered enough damage to her own.

"Do you remember this house, Susan? Do you remember anything of your life here?"

"I was so young, but I do remember Peter Macklin. I remember Theresa a little. And I remember the tower room—even the wallpaper. What I recall most is a feeling of unhappiness. I didn't remember my mother's face until Hallie Townsend gave me a picture of her. Then it was as if I'd never forgotten."

This was startling. "Hallie—when?"

"She came over to your landing in a boat, and when she saw me out on the balcony, she climbed the outside stairs. Tell me about her. She seems a strange woman."

"The Townsends are longtime friends," Alex said with a sigh. "But you mustn't pay too much attention to anything Hallie says. Her weakness is mixing into other people's affairs. Sometimes she creates fantasies that she believes herself."

"She and my mother were friends?"

"Of a sort."

"At least she brought me a picture. I'd never seen one before."

Damn Gilbert, Alex thought, somehow resisting the waves of emotion that kept wanting to rise in her and throw everything askew. "I have a great many pictures I can show you," she said stiffly.

"Why did my father hate you?"

The question came point-blank and was the one question Alex feared. "I can't answer that. I'm not sure I know." She knew, but these were matters she could never talk about.

"He seemed to blame you for my mother's death, though he would never talk to me about how she died. I didn't even know about the accident on the stairs, until Theresa showed me where my mother fell."

Theresa was as bad as Hallie. Alex hadn't expected everything to burst into the open so quickly.

"What did Theresa tell you?"

"She said that, except for my invalid grandfather, I was alone in the house with my mother when she fell. You'd think I would remember that, even though I was small. But I can't recall anything. I suppose I shut it away because it was too terrible to remember."

"There are matters we must talk about, Susan, but, for my sake, let's take it slowly."

"I can wait," Susan said. "I've waited all my life. But I don't want to leave until I understand all you can tell me about that time."

Could anyone be made to understand, Alex wondered? She herself never had, and this granddaughter belonged to another time, another generation. The things Gilbert had said today carried a warning, but Susan need never know about any of this if she left in a few days.

Alex carried the box of photographs to a bookshelf and replaced it beside other boxes. Susan's reaction had been more than Alex had expected, and she felt a little frightened. Dolores's daughter had begun to break through the protective shield her grandmother had tried to raise against her. But for everyone's sanity, and safety, the status quo should be preserved. First, however, Alex must be rid of her own uncharacteristic indecision.

Woven into all these threads from the past were Peter Macklin's own tragic problems. She hoped that Susan would never need to know how close he had come to going to prison, or about the cloud that still hung over him. She had been sure from the first that what happened to Peter was somehow connected directly with the past—perhaps even with herself and Juan Gabriel. She had never been a coward about facing trouble, and this was no time to start.

As she returned to her chair, a plump, middle-aged black woman appeared in the doorway, and Alex smiled at her. "We'll have supper whenever you're ready, Gracie. We've held you up longer than usual tonight. Susan, do you remember Gracie Dixon? She and George were here before you were born."

"I would like to remember," Susan said, "but I was very little. Hello, Gracie."

Gracie, who was never given to beating around bushes, fixed Susan with an interested look that carried a hint of criticism.

"It's time you came home to Virginia, Miss Susan. You stayed away too long. I'll get supper on the table now. Just a few minutes, Miss Alex."

Before Susan and Alex could continue their conversation, Theresa joined them, and the three women moved into the dining room.

Alex had always loved this room and she looked about with a familiar sense of satisfaction. Juan Gabriel had found it too dramatic for his taste, preferring quiet surroundings that were not distracting. Nevertheless, he'd indulged her wish for excitement, when that quality had mostly disappeared from her life. Her young years as a dancer had taken her to the cosmopolitan centers of the world, so she had been eclectic in her choices.

A Kurdish rug from Istanbul was still her pride, its fiery colors muted only a little by time. Kilim rugs had once been scorned, but in recent

64 years they had become more widely appreciated. She had always loved this one—magnificent, with its great central oblong woven in a strong, earthy red, and marked down the center with diamond forms in black and white. A stylized pattern of flowers, woven into the wheat-colored border, softened the effect.

The long, oval table had been made in Virginia's plantation days, and Alex had placed red leather chairs around it—chairs she had found long ago in Richmond. Red napkins lay beside each woven grass placemat.

"What a beautiful room!" Susan exclaimed, sitting down at the table next to Alex and looking around, her interest caught by a tall glass cabinet in which tiny wood carvings had been collected. "What are those?" she asked.

"Carving was a hobby of Juan Gabriel's. He made nothing of his accomplishment, but I've saved all those pieces."

All, Alex thought, except the one which had so upset her—that ebony piece that had been long since packed away and lost. She went on quietly, testing Susan.

"Do you remember this room at all? Do you remember that painting on the wall?"

Susan studied the large framed painting that dominated the oyster white space of wall. The scene was of a mountain village in the Andes—small houses with red tiled roofs perched along a steep hillside street. In the foreground two women in triangular ponchos, with distinctive hats tied under their chins, led a train of llamas burdened with loads of wood.

"I seem to remember—something. A red room that made me feel warm and happy. And I loved watching those llamas and the women in tall hats. I do remember!"

This, at least, was safe enough.

Theresa seemed indifferent to such talk, and Alex realized that she wore an expectant air, as though she listened for something. Or someone? Alex could guess well enough who it might be, and she wished she could forestall his coming.

Theresa had changed to a yellow silk print that flattered her dark coloring, and she wore a strand of amber beads that Juan Gabriel had given her one Christmas when she was a young girl. Her long gold and amber earrings caught the light from white candles, and she looked as beautiful as ever. Alex was pleased to note, however, that Susan was not overshadowed. Her granddaughter's more natural look contrasted agreeably with Theresa's flamboyance.

Gracie served her special potato salad, with thick slices of Virginia ham, and hot biscuits. Alex was pleased to see Susan eat hungrily. A little fattening up wouldn't hurt her, though most young women these days preferred to be thin. She smiled to herself, remembering that Juan Ga-

66 briel had never approved of "skinny ballet dancers," and had been pleased when she'd put on a little weight. Just a little, since she would never allow herself to be heavy.

"I saw Hallie Townsend scurrying off to the dock earlier," Theresa said. "I suppose she couldn't wait to satisfy her curiosity?"

Susan smiled. "I suppose she was curious. Though it seemed strange that she didn't want anyone to know she'd come to see me."

Theresa raised graceful shoulders in a shrug. "She likes to play secretive little games. Of course she's always welcome here, isn't she, Alex?"

Theresa also liked to play her little games, Alex thought. "Of course Hallie is welcome," she said carefully. "I just wish she could have waited a little longer. I saw her this afternoon."

"Oh?" Theresa was immediately interested. "Where did you see her?"

"I stopped by Christ Church," Alex said quietly, turning to Susan. "Hallie works as a docent at the Reception Center."

"You went to the church? Again?" Theresa asked with obvious disapproval. "You know that place upsets you."

"You're mistaken, Theresa. Whenever I take some disturbing emotion there, I am likely to experience a calming effect." Alex turned to Susan again. "Historic Christ Church is a remarkable old building—one of our Virginia landmarks. I must take you to visit it before you leave."

This led to a discussion about other places Susan might visit. No one spoke of the past, and every possibly treacherous subject was avoided.

Gracie had just cleared the table for dessert when Alex heard a car door slam out in front of the house. A moment later a cheerful male voice called out, asking if anybody was home. Theresa jumped up to run to the door, and Alex sighed. She'd had enough of the Townsends for one day, but there'd be no way to avoid inviting Eric to join them—not with the way Theresa felt about him. Eric was Gilbert's son, and Theresa was almost ten years older than he, which might not have mattered with some men, but Alex didn't trust Eric to make Theresa happy. She disapproved of their involvement, but she had only the instrument of her own legal will to stop the two if they decided to marry. She was reluctant to use such a weapon, but she felt she owed it to Juan Gabriel to look after his grandniece. It had been Juan Gabriel's writing that had left Alex a wealthy woman.

Theresa brought Eric Townsend back to the dining room and introduced him to Susan. Alex noted that he took Susan's hand much too warmly. Like father, like son, she thought impatiently. Eric even looked the way his father had when he was young—his hair as fair as Gilbert's

68　had once been. And he was good-looking enough for the actor's career he aspired to in the face of Gilbert's opposition.

"Welcome to Virginia," he said, kissing Susan's hand gallantly, amused that he'd flustered her.

Gracie came into the room with a dessert tray and Eric flashed her a grin. "Hi, Gracie. I see I'm in time for your key lime pie—if I'm invited."

"Do sit down, Eric," Alex said, suppressing her growing annoyance. He was, in a sense, one more test for Susan to pass.

As Gracie served them, Eric's full attention centered on Susan. "Hallie says Peter Macklin drove you over here this afternoon. Did he say anything about the latest development in our local scandal?"

Alex spoke quickly, firmly. "I'm sure Susan has no idea what you're talking about, Eric. And this is not the time—"

Eric's bright blue gaze dared her to stop him. With anyone else, she might have accepted the challenge, but Eric could be unpredictable and she didn't want to make matters worse.

He went right on. "This *is* exciting! You haven't heard the news?"

Gracie set a serving of pie before him with a thump of disapproval, and Alex gave up. Whatever news he had collected, she had better let him tell it.

Eric's look of wide-eyed innocence continued to be focused on Susan. "Do you mean that no one has told you about our Dr. Macklin? What are they protecting you from?"

Before Eric could say anything more, Alex straightened in her chair. "Susan, Peter was called before a grand jury just a few months ago. He was acquitted of all charges." She flashed a look at Eric. "Completely acquitted! So there's really nothing to discuss."

"How can you say that?" Eric demanded. "We still don't know who murdered Marilyn Macklin."

Susan looked so startled that Alex could have shaken Eric.

"There's a new complication that's just come up," he continued brightly, enjoying himself. "I think you'll be interested, Alex. In a way, it concerns you. You remember that the manuscript of Marilyn's biography of Juan Gabriel disappeared at the time of her death? Now it's turned up again. Somebody left it on the front steps of the library in Kilmarnock today. This makes for quite a mystery, don't you think?"

"Poor Peter," Theresa said. "Just as he was beginning to put this behind him. Now everything will be stirred up again."

Alex felt more upset by this news than she wanted anyone to guess. At the time of her death, Marilyn Macklin had indeed been working on

70 Juan Gabriel's biography. Alex had respected her talent as a journalist and had been willing to work with her. It had been disturbing that the manuscript had disappeared after her death. Not that there was anything in it to worry the living. Or, at least, that was what Alex wanted to believe. She had gone over this issue in her mind a good many times, without being sure of anything. Marilyn had been uncharacteristically canny about what she planned for the conclusion of the book, and Alex had never seen her notes for the unwritten chapters. If they were included in the manuscript that had just turned up, she wanted very much to see them.

Alex was about to reassure Theresa, when Susan spoke her own surprising words.

"I've just remembered something. My father received several letters from a woman in Virginia before he died. Connie, my stepmother, told me that this woman had wanted to come to talk with him because he had known Juan Gabriel Montoro, and because Juan Gabriel's daughter had been his wife. But my father wouldn't see her. I don't remember her name; it didn't mean anything to me at the time."

Alex found this all the more disturbing. Marilyn had never told her that she'd tried to see Lawrence Prentice. She would have heard only lies if she'd gone to Santa Fe. But Marilyn hadn't consulted her, and if Peter had known, he'd said nothing.

Susan broke into her thoughts. "How did Mrs. Macklin die?"

There was no point in holding back now. "She was poisoned," Alex said. "Poisoned with a prescription drug that Peter happened to be holding in his office. I've always thought that someone wanted to see him blamed. Fortunately the grand jury didn't feel there was a case against Peter. There was nothing but circumstantial evidence."

Before Susan could put her obvious dismay into words, a telephone rang in the front parlor, and Theresa went to answer it. She returned looking puzzled.

"It's for you, Alex. Tangier Island is calling."

Alex set her napkin beside her plate and rose calmly from the table. She must not let them see how shocked she felt, how near panic. It was ridiculous to be so shaken by a phone call. Of course it was not her present well-under-control self that was reacting. It was that long-ago young woman she had once been, a girl she'd believed safely buried in the past, but who could apparently still spring into quivering life at the mention of communication from the island.

"Excuse me," she said and went into the parlor. The phone stood waiting on a small table and she sat down beside it. When she picked it up her

72 hand was steady, and so was her voice. She heard a long-distance operator speaking with a woman.

"Hello. This is Alex Montoro."

"Yes, Mrs. Montoro, I have a call waiting for you. Go ahead," and the operator clicked off.

"Alex! It's been a long time since I've heard your voice. This is Emily Gower. How are you?"

Relief strengthened her. This was not the voice she'd been afraid to hear. "I am doing very well, thank you, Emily. And you?"

"I'm fine. We read in the paper that your granddaughter would be arriving for a visit. We remember when she was little, and John wondered if we might coax you over to the island while she's here."

There seemed something not quite right about Emily's tone. Something artificial, and Alex knew she was, as always, just doing what John wanted.

No! she cried to herself. John had no right! Or—he had every right. For Alex the past was many lifetimes ago, and she never wanted to set foot on the island again. She'd always been a little afraid of Tangier and its strange spell, and she didn't want to take Susan there.

She spoke quietly, with careful control—perhaps sounding artificial herself. "I'm afraid that won't be possible, Emily. Susan will be here for only a few days—and we have so many plans." She had no plans at all. It wouldn't be easy to get to Tangier and she would simply crowd their time with activities to prevent their going. Perhaps she would send Susan away even sooner than she'd intended. She couldn't bear to have the past explode into the present. All that pain was long over and—

"Please think about it," Emily was saying. "John sends his best and we'd love to see you and Susan. Do fit us in, Alex."

When they were both young, before Emily had married John Gower, she had been Alex Montoro's close friend. She had undoubtedly made a good wife for a waterman who'd spent most of his life on Chesapeake Bay.

"Thank you," Alex heard herself saying. "Let me call you back in a day or two and we'll see what's possible."

They rang off and she returned to the table, where Eric was finishing his key lime pie. She felt confidently sure of her rigid self-possession as she took her seat, but they all stared at her as though there had been some visible change, and she knew the shock she had experienced must show in her face. John had wanted her to come. Why? But of course she knew why.

"That was Emily Gower," she said quietly. "It's a long time since I've heard from her—quite a surprise. Susan, she was a friend of mine when I first came to the Northern Neck. She knew your mother. She was hoping to see you, but it's a

74 long trip by water to Tangier Island, and we won't have time."

Theresa shivered. "Don't ever go there, Susan. Tangier's a horrid place. I'm sure it's haunted. I went there once and I've never wanted to go back."

Theresa, Alex thought impatiently, believed in all sorts of strange spirits that had nothing to do with the spiritual. She even applied this negativity to Christ Church in her own peculiar way.

She spoke quickly, suppressing her annoyance. "To the islanders it is a beautiful place."

"Tell me about it," Susan said.

Eric, too long away from center stage, answered her. "Legend has it that Captain John Smith gave it that name. He'd spent some time in Tangier when he was in Morocco, and something about our Virginia island is supposed to have made a connection for him. Emily Gower is my aunt, so maybe I'll take you there, Susan, if your grandmother doesn't have time."

"Thank you, but we have other plans," Alex said, sounding sharp.

Susan nodded in agreement and smiled at her grandmother. Alex's heart twisted. Her smile was Dolores's smile, and it was as if old grief had never lessened.

Eric shrugged. "Okay. I'll be back. We'll do something soon—you and Theresa and I. Thank Gracie for the pie, Alex. I've got to get going. I'm working for Dad now at The Mulberry Tree, and he doesn't look lightly on employees who arrive late."

He was gone almost as suddenly as he'd arrived, and the air seemed to vibrate with energy in his wake. Eric really made her very tired, Alex thought. And she didn't at all like what she saw in Theresa's eyes when she looked at him. There was no stability in Eric, and even though Alex had never been able to love Theresa, she deserved better than Eric.

Susan folded her napkin. "This has been a lovely dinner, but do you mind if I go up to bed now? I'm a little tired."

Alex was contrite at once. "Of course you are. We've kept you too long. Sleep as late as you like in the morning. Run along now."

When she had gone, Theresa and Alex sat at the table for a few minutes longer.

"How do you feel about your granddaughter?" Theresa asked.

It wasn't how *she* felt that mattered most, Alex thought. Some unexpected longing to love Dolores's daughter had risen in her. But she rejected this weakening in herself, because there was too much pain in loving and she was too old for disappointments.

"I like her," she said, and let it go at that.

Theresa raised winged eyebrows. "I'm not sure she likes us. She'll always be her father's

76 daughter first, and *you* sent her father away, didn't you?"

Alex pushed back her chair and rose to her still regal height. "I don't know where you get your ideas. Anyway, all that is past history. It no longer matters, and I think Susan will make up her own mind about us."

"Perhaps the past is easier to retrieve than you imagine if Marilyn Macklin was trying to see Lawrence out in New Mexico before he died. What do you think about that?"

"I don't suppose we'll ever know."

Theresa glanced at her watch. "Perhaps I can get hold of Peter and find out what's happened. You never saw the whole manuscript, did you, Alex?"

"I saw all except the notes for the last chapters that were to bring Juan Gabriel's life up to date. Since the book will never be published now, this reappearance doesn't matter."

It would be safer if she could make Theresa believe that it didn't matter. Marilyn had wanted to use the details of that final terrible episode that had driven them from Peru—and which had reverberated in her husband's writings to the end of his life. Alex had been adamant in her refusal to talk about this, but of course Marilyn could have written to Lima and obtained old newspaper clippings. Whether she had or not, Alex didn't know, but she'd been aware that her own control over what Marilyn wanted to write had grown weaker toward the end. Marilyn had seemed excited about something, and her very eagerness had alarmed Alex.

Theresa was watching her, clearly unconvinced. "Perhaps now is the time to find out what Marilyn meant to say."

"It's none of your affair, Theresa. I will talk to Peter when the time is right."

"Yes, but I want to talk to him now," Theresa said.

It was hard to deflect Theresa from any project that stirred her curiosity. Alex let the conversation drop without further objection, unsure of what beehive Theresa was about to excite.

When Theresa had gone, Alex slipped on a sweater against the cool breeze that could blow in from the bay, even on a summer evening, and picked up a flashlight and a cane to keep her steady on uneven ground. She went down the back steps to the lawn that sloped to the water.

Little waves broke against the dock pilings with repeated sighs, while the August insects were busy with their own orchestra. The creek always seemed to breathe with the tide, so that stars reflected in its surface were never still. Due to the creek's turnings, the bay was distant. Across the water a few scattered lights shone in windows, and the night seemed close and dark.

Her mind began to replay what Gilbert

78   Townsend had said at the church. What was it that he so feared from Susan? What had happened during his exchange with Juan Gabriel that she had never known about? He had seemed alarmed by Hallie's sudden appearance, but what could he possibly fear from his dim-witted sister?

She was weary of questions she couldn't answer, and she turned her flashlight beam to pick out the shape of the old boathouse. There was no boat there now; she didn't even keep a rowboat. The closed door at the land end of the building drew her—within was the room where Juan Gabriel had liked to work. Gracie and George still kept everything clean and in order, no matter how many years it had been since her husband had used it. Alex had promised to show Marilyn where Juan Gabriel had worked, but she had never gotten around to it.

She walked slowly up the slope and placed her hand on the door. It swung open easily as she turned the knob. The smell of a closed-in space, faintly scented with the ghost of old pipe tobacco, assailed her as she stepped inside and reached for a light switch.

She had furnished this big room for Juan Gabriel and he had never wanted anything changed. There were no dramatic touches here, no distracting colors. She knew what he liked. To be a good wife to her husband, and to help nurture his talent, had been her goal and her pleasure. He had rescued her from despair after Rudy Folkes had died, and he'd loved her deeply, with an old man's love that had revived him and helped to keep his creativity alive.

Looking about in the lamplight, she found everything clean, dustless, unchanged. There were overhead fans for summer heat, and electricity when it grew cold. She had come here only a half dozen times since his death, because it was too painful to be reminded of all that happened during those last months of his life. But now, because of Susan's coming, the ghosts must be faced and dealt with.

The room's furnishings were simple—suited to a writer's needs. Behind the great mahogany desk from the West Indies stood shelves that held books and notes. Against the opposite wall stretched more shelves that held the complete collection of Juan Gabriel Montoro's works, in all their editions and translations. The small tea table and two chairs had been for the afternoon break he sometimes enjoyed taking with his wife. Though more often the tea table had been heaped with manuscript pages as they came from his hand.

Several large closets had been built into the room, and one held his sturdy safe. Every writer dreaded the loss of a manuscript in the making, and the safe had protected Juan Gabriel's work until it reached an editor's hands.

She had opened the safe for him just once during their first year in Virginia. She still felt chilled at the memory of what she had found on the top of the stacked manuscript pages—the loaded Spanish pistol he had brought from Peru. The gun had belonged to his father, and she could remember the gleam of the antique silver mountings. She'd known all too well how that gun had been used, and Juan Gabriel must have seen her shock, for he had come at once to hold her tenderly in his arms.

Strangely, after his death, the pistol had not turned up in any of his possessions, so he had probably disposed of it long ago.

She touched more switches so that lights came on and the room glowed with soft radiance. She looked around, in spite of herself, remembering—too much.

He had seldom used the covered typewriter that rested on a separate stand, for he loathed all machines. The pencil, with soft lead and a good eraser, was Juan Gabriel's chosen medium, and he believed strongly in the connection between brain and fingers. Alex, who was able to read his handwriting as no one else could, had been his secretary, answering the mail and typing his manuscripts. Sometimes he would ask for her suggestions, respecting her opinion. Perhaps that was one reason why she had loved him—he allowed her to be a person in her own right, suc-

cessful and intelligent. When she thought of him
now, she still felt that warm sense of loving protection with which he had surrounded her always. He had been kind, and he had trusted her
—a fact that still broke her heart. At least he had
never known about Tangier Island.

Alex moved to his worn, comfortable chair
and sat before the tilted writing table where he
had worked. A ceramic jug from the Andes stood
on a table beside his chair, filled with pencils
ready to his hand, all sharp points upward, so he
need never hesitate when he discarded, point
down, one that was dull. Alex had helped
sharpen all those pencils for him year after year,
and she'd sent to New York for the particular
variety that he'd liked to use.

She had come here once, while he was ill, and
sharpened every dull pencil, as though by keeping them sharp she could assure his return to this
room. She picked up a black pencil now and
tested the point with one finger. Holding the
shaft of wood was almost like feeling his touch
again. How strong the affection had been between them. How deep and lasting. He had been
her hero, teacher, idol. Her admiration for him
had never faltered.

But he had not been all she needed—Tangier
Island awaited her, as inevitably as fate. It was an
island possessed by a mystique that had both attracted and at times frightened her when she be-

82 gan to realize how deeply bred John Gower had been to that place. Even though he had grown up on the mainland, far away from Virginia, under circumstances that had seemed romantic to her in those young and foolish years, he had turned as a man to the old, rather fierce traditions that belonged to the island's centuries of isolation and the need to survive against high odds.

It was strange how happenstances had brought about her first meeting with John Gower. She had stopped at the local bookstore in Kilmarnock, where Emily Townsend worked in the days when she and Alex had been close friends.

After she and Emily had said hello, she wandered the aisles looking for a book for the weekend. John was there browsing as well, and even before Emily introduced them, they had looked into each other's eyes with unexpected intensity —a seemingly casual glance, but each had recognized something in the other that was startling and unasked for. Alex's grandmother in Lima had believed in second sight and she might have said that Alex and John had known each other in some former life. In spite of that strange sense of recognition, nothing further had developed at the time.

Later she learned a great deal more about John and the dramatic events of his childhood and teenage years. He had told her about his

lovely, gentle, mainland mother, who, nevertheless, had found in herself the spirit to stand up to
the Tangier Island man she had married and
come to fear. She had died when John was only
seventeen, but there had been money on his
mother's side to see him through college, and
friends to help. In the twenties, when his mother
had run away and taken her three-year-old son
with her, they might have been followed and the
boy taken back to the island, so it had been necessary to hide, and she had managed their escape.

John had been told about his heritage, and
when he was grown, the blood of generations of
men who had fought the sea for survival spoke to
him, drew him back. He had gone to the island
out of curiosity and to meet his many relatives,
but that speck of land, barely floating above water, held him and he had become a waterman—
with, however, an ambivalence that set him a little apart because of the heritage from his mother.

When Alex first knew him, she had never
dreamed that the island aspect was stronger than
the gentle-seeming side of the man she'd loved.
By the time she recognized this, it was already
too late. Fate had moved its pawns again.

Juan Gabriel Montoro had read about Tangier and he wanted to use a scene from the island
in a book he was writing that would touch on the
early history of Virginia. When he learned of
Alex's chance meeting with a "native" of Tan-

84 gier, he was delighted and couldn't wait to take a trip out on the bay, so he could learn more first-hand. John, still unwary, had fallen in with his plans, proud to show off the place of his birth.

The island, set out in the water between Virginia's two shores, was only twenty nautical miles away, and John Gower took them across in his fishing boat. This was in the forties, before the present influx of tourists had opened the island to the outer world. Not a woman had been in sight for a stranger to glimpse, and Alex had sensed a guarded suspicion in the few men they passed on the long hike to the beach that Juan Gabriel wanted to visit. He'd always sought first for the *feeling* of a place, his own reactions to it, before he looked for factual details. By the time they reached that long, clean stretch of shell-strewn sand, Juan Gabriel was ready to rest.

Alex could close her eyes now and see the beach again clearly. The sun had been about to set—John Gower had arranged for them to spend the night on the island—and colors of burnt orange and crimson stained the sky. She could remember Juan Gabriel urging them to go off together across the sand.

"You two have young legs—so go! Walk along the water's edge for me and I will sit here on the sand and go with you in my story-dreaming."

How young she had been! She'd worn a full

skirt that blew against her slender body, her long black hair free about her shoulders, and John hadn't changed from his waterman's gear, his face as brown as his arms in their rolled-up plain sleeves. They had walked together on hard, wet sand, and hadn't touched each other by so much as a finger. Yet they'd moved close in spirit, and they both knew very well what was happening.

For Alex this had been nothing like her feelings for Rudy Folkes, or for Juan Gabriel. This was her first *young* love—totally abandoned, without caution or forethought. The acceptance, each of the other, had been complete as they walked together on the sand. Something utterly magical had taken hold of them that evening. Something dangerous.

For her, there had been no choice. It had not been difficult to see one another. They had found delicious, secret places along the Tidewater shores for their lovemaking—never anything as mundane as a room or an ordinary bed. Sometimes it was a field where wildflowers bloomed, or perhaps the russet ground beneath pine trees. And how they had talked, opening their hearts to each other. The stoicism of island men had broken down in John. It seemed that each had understood the other as no one else ever could. That belief, of course, had been their greatest mistake.

Curiously, she had felt no betrayal toward Juan Gabriel. Not then. She knew that nothing

86 could change the special devotion she felt for her husband, but this new love, that she'd never before experienced, had risen in her so strongly that it swept all else away. There'd been no thought of the future, or of who might be hurt. How could this much happiness hurt anyone?

Only one insurmountable problem existed between John and herself. John wanted to marry her and she already was married. Juan Gabriel was an old man—in John's eyes—and he felt she deserved a young man's love. Someone with whom she could build a life, with whom she could have children. Her marriage to Juan Gabriel had brought only one child—a boy who had died as a baby before they had come to this country. There had been no more pregnancies, though they'd tried. What she hadn't understood was the deep island tradition of morality that governed John, even though the part of him that was like his mother could throw off such restrictions for a time.

In some strange way, Alex's relationship with John seemed to exist in another dimension that had nothing to do with her everyday life. In this way she avoided thought, avoided the truth of what was happening, even the truth about herself. John was sure about *his* life. He wanted to go on with the old ways of the men of his family and be a waterman on Chesapeake Bay out of Tangier Island. He found the dangers and uncertainties of that life to his taste. So, he pleaded with Alex to divorce Juan Gabriel and come to live on the island as his wife. The fact that divorce would never be possible for Juan Gabriel meant nothing to John. He had the arrogance of a young man and the rock-hard immovability of all his island-bred ancestors. He could never understand Juan Gabriel's principles, or that Alex Montoro had lived an entire lifetime as a ballerina before she even turned twenty-one. Even his mainland upbringing had not touched that fierce, hard core. He was a gentle man, whose hidden, inner fierceness came to frighten her. At first, time spent with John existed on a different plane. An unreal plane, perhaps. Something deep within Alex knew she could never leave Juan Gabriel, never go to live on that tiny, bleak island, burying herself forever. Perhaps she had buried herself in Virginia, but at least she had done so with someone who understood who she had once been, someone who valued her in ways John could never understand. So her refusal wasn't entirely cowardice on her part. An unexpected strength had risen in her—a will strong enough to overcome the emotions she felt in John Gower's arms. Perhaps it was a newly awakened sense of herself, of John, of Juan Gabriel. And she made her choice.

In dark moments, when she was being honest with herself, she knew there had been another reason for her decision not to leave Juan Gabriel. His terrible burst of violence back in Lima was something she could never forget. It was always there at the back of her mind as a warning, and more frightening than the same element in John. Perhaps something in Alex herself had attracted passionate, loving, possessive men, with a depth of violence in their nature.

Juan Gabriel had not been young—even then he was already in his fifties—so it was not the violence of youth that had betrayed him. A hot Spanish anger existed just beneath the surface, ready to explode. When she looked back now she could not be sure that her motive had been one of loyalty to her husband, or fear of what he might do. If she had followed John Gower, they both might be long dead by now. The gun she had seen in Juan Gabriel's safe had been a warning.

After she made her choice, there had been times when she wasn't sure she wanted to go on living. Times when she'd cried herself to sleep because John had married Emily. She was unable to be friends with Emily any longer, and there was loss for her there, too—something Emily, in her innocence, had never understood. Alex could not have endured seeing them together and hearing how happy they were in their marriage, since Emily could turn herself into a proper Tangier wife.

Alex had dealt with pain before, and she

dealt with it again, carrying on with her life so that Juan Gabriel was never hurt. The only time she had ever doubted Juan Gabriel's love—so many years later—had been when he had shown her his ebony carving of the black swan. She winced at the memory, and was glad that the carving had been misplaced over the years since his death. She remembered packing it away, but she couldn't remember where. It was just as well, she never wanted to see it again.

Strange that she had loved two men named John—two high-spirited men who could hide their deepest feelings.

When Dolores was born, Juan Gabriel had been exultant with pride, and he had not questioned this sudden miracle. He had wanted this daughter, and from the time she was a baby Dolores had given him an equal love. Sometimes Alex recognized John in Dolores, but Juan Gabriel never suspected, and she could be grateful for that.

John Gower never saw his daughter, nor did she ever tell him it was his child she bore. Nevertheless, with some sixth sense, she felt that he knew. Perhaps, that was why he now wanted to see his granddaughter Susan. Perhaps he had a right to see her? *The child of the child of his young love.*

To break the spell of her thoughts, Alex reached out to a pad of yellow paper upon which

90 Juan Gabriel had written a few lines. The pad had remained here on his writing table, untouched since he'd left it there. Oddly enough, the lines he'd written were about Tangier Island —only snippets of information. He had never written his novel using the island. Yet he had been picking up the idea again all those years later, shortly before he became ill.

She read the words:

> Indians occupied the island before the white man came. Perhaps a thousand years before John Smith sailed into its harbor.
>
> 2½ miles long. 1 mile wide. 7 feet above sea level. Fragile, vulnerable to hurricanes.
>
> Residents are of English descent. Elizabethan English can still be heard. The men catch crabs, oysters, fish of various sorts, clams. They are called watermen.
>
> The island has a strange beauty of its own and is peopled with men and women inbred and strong enough to survive all that is asked of them.

Alex stopped reading because Juan Gabriel had started to set down a hint of the island's eerie magic. He'd remembered the sunsets, and he had imagined a storm and written words of tense description. John had belonged to those generations of survivors, as Alex could never have belonged.

She set down the pad, not wanting to be drawn back—unable to help herself.

John! His ruggedly handsome young face was as clear in her mind as though she'd seen him yesterday. There'd been times when she'd forgotten how he looked—but every feature was there now, breaking her heart all over again. To her he would remain always young and strong and passionate. And he would remember her as the girl he had loved so desperately. She *had* been beautiful then. She had the photographs to prove it. So how could she bear to destroy his memory of her with the reality of old age?

She'd continued to hold Juan Gabriel's pencil in her fingers, and she set it back in the jug, pricking her thumb with the sharp point as she did so. She regarded the lead mark as though it was somehow important—a link between present and past.

There was still a question she didn't know how to answer. What if Susan had a right to know this story, and to meet her grandfather before it was too late? How was she to decide?

It was always, so quickly, too late.

Four

Susan climbed the two flights of stairs to the tower room, finding that the last steps took a special effort. She felt utterly weary, yet wide awake, her thoughts whirling in confusion. What she needed now was to be alone in a quiet space, so that she needn't think at all.

In a little while she would take a hot, soaking bath to help her fall asleep, but for now she

wanted only to lie down and rest. Without un-
dressing, she lay full-length on the bed and closed
her eyes. At once the faces and incidents of the
day began to flash through her mind, and there
was no way to dismiss them.

What did she think of her grandmother, now
that she had met her? The young pictures of her
as a ballet dancer had been fascinating, and Susan
wanted to know more about that time. Yet the
beautiful young girl in the photographs seemed
to have little connection with a woman grown
weary and remote from life. How could she hope
to feel any affection for a woman so old and austere?

The encounter with Theresa at the foot of the
stairs haunted her. Why could she remember
nothing of what had happened when her mother
died? There had been moments, in the past,
when some glimmer of memory had risen, only
to escape when she tried to grasp it.

In the end, unwillingly, her thoughts turned
to Peter Macklin. The small, adoring child who
had loved him still existed in some part of her
mind—perhaps more vividly than anything else
from the past. She felt unhappy and concerned
because of the things Eric Townsend had revealed so carelessly—perhaps maliciously—but
she must not get involved. In a few days she
would have all the answers she needed and she

94 would be gone. Nothing that existed here in Virginia need ever affect her again.

Deep in her subconscious a faint voice was laughing. *It's already too late,* it seemed to be saying, and she told it to be quiet.

Lying down wasn't going to work. She couldn't rest while her mind was so active. She threw a sweater over her shoulders and went outside to the small balcony that circled the tower. The sky was dark except for millions of stars. A few clouds covered the moon.

She let the balcony rail guide her as she followed the circle of the tower from the back of the house around toward the front. There were no streetlights in this tiny village, but friendly lamps burned in several of the old Victorian houses that lined the country road. In a strange way she felt less alone up here in their company than she'd felt downstairs with the woman who was her grandmother.

In the darkness, her hand came to a break in the rail and she stopped. She knew she had reached the part of the balcony where the stairs Hallie Townsend had climbed descended to the ground. Opposite the top of the stairs was a closed door that must lead into the partitioned section of her larger room. She tried the door and found it locked.

She felt mildly curious, but went on to explore further, crossing the gap where the stairs began. Rounding the tower, she could make out the back lawn sloping toward the water with the creek shining beyond, and an intermittent moon painting its surface. Up here everything seemed hushed except for the lapping of gentle waves against dock pilings, and frog sounds from the nearby marsh. The night smelled salty-fresh. A mere whisper of wind blew through treetops that grew only a little higher than the roofs of this house.

Down near the water she saw a stretch of shadowy building that must be a boathouse. Light shone in a window at the land end of the building and, as she wondered who was there, a door opened—revealing an oblong light that briefly silhouetted a dark shape. An invisible hand reached inside to touch a switch and the doorway vanished. Someone crossed the lawn toward the house, and Susan recognized her grandmother's lonely, rather mysterious presence as she turned to look for a moment toward the creek. An unexpected feeling of compassion touched Susan—something sad that she could not name.

The woman on the lawn went into the house, and Susan walked on around the tower to her room. Now she felt she could indulge in a lovely luxurious soaking in water scented with the lavender salts provided in the great glass apothecary jar on the bathroom shelf. When she finally got into bed she felt relaxed and ready to sleep. Only

96 a momentary uneasiness concerning those outside stairs disturbed her. There was no bolt on the balcony door to her room—though what did it matter? This house was as safe a haven for her as any place could be. Only talk at dinner about the murder of Peter's wife left a twinge of uneasiness. And a deep sadness for her childhood friend.

Thoughts slipped into dreams, and she slept deeply. Anyone could have climbed the outside stairs and gone into the locked room, or into Susan's room, for that matter, and she would never have been aware of an intruder.

Sunlight pouring through the tower windows awakened her early, and Susan found herself rested and ready to face the day. Whatever her dreams had been, she didn't remember them. Now she was eager to see her grandmother again and learn more about her and, above all, about her own mother. A trace of the feeling she'd experienced last night, when she'd looked down upon that solitary figure coming out of the boathouse, remained, and she made no effort to dismiss it. How sad it must be to be old and have all your life behind you. Her own life still lay ahead, even though she wasn't happy about the part she had lived. It was up to her to see that the future was better.

When she went downstairs she found Theresa breakfasting alone in the red dining room.
For a moment Susan stood quietly in the doorway, observing this Montoro cousin. Theresa's
Spanish heritage had left its mark in her beauty.

When Theresa looked around, Susan was
again aware of her huge dark eyes, with an unsettling rim of white showing beneath the pupils.
Strangely haunting eyes.

"Good morning." The tilt of Theresa's chin
seemed almost regal, and there was no warmth in
her greeting. "We all take care of ourselves at
breakfast. George and Gracie have their own
house, and we don't expect them early. If you
want anything special, you'll need to fix it yourself."

"Toast and coffee and orange juice will be
fine." Susan went to the long buffet set beneath
the painting of a crab apple tree in bloom.

"No orange juice," Theresa said. "There's too
much sugar in fruit juice, and sugar is an enemy
for Alex—hypoglycemia. Peter allows her half a
banana. I go along with Alex's diet—it's better
for me too."

An American breakfast without orange juice
seemed a bit strange, and Susan's growing impatience with doctors surfaced again, though she
didn't comment. When she'd dropped whole
wheat bread into the toaster on the buffet, she
poured hot coffee from the percolator into a blue

98 glazed cup. Then she leaned closer to read the name of the artist who had painted the crabapple tree.

"You painted this?" she asked Theresa with surprise.

"I was younger then," Theresa said indifferently. "I had more time."

Susan joined her across the table. "You don't paint anymore?"

The beautiful mouth twisted in self-derision. "I paint eggs." And then, as Susan stared blankly, she said, "Oh, they are very handsome eggs! In the Ukrainian style, though with intricate designs that are my own. They sell rather well during the holidays, but they're only a hobby. These days my work is to look after Alex's affairs, as well as to look after Alex."

There seemed a challenge underlying Theresa's words, and Susan spoke mildly. "I'm sure you must be a great help to her."

Theresa was scornfully silent. Outside the open windows bees hummed industriously, and the smell of flowers drifted into the room on a warm early morning breeze. It was all wonderfully peaceful and relaxing, except for Theresa's scarcely hidden resentment. Susan made an effort to counter her hostility by speaking directly.

"I'm not moving into your territory, Theresa. I already realize that I don't belong here, and I don't expect to stay long. I will leave my grandmother and her affairs to you. I just wanted to see this place for myself, and meet my Virginia family. I want to know much more about my mother, and when the blanks have been filled in, I'll go."

"What if it's better not to fill in those blanks? I have a bad feeling about your coming."

"Why?" Susan asked, barely controlling her annoyance. "Please tell me why."

"How can one know about such things? Juan Gabriel used to say I had a special sixth sense. I have a feeling that you will bring trouble to your grandmother—and to yourself."

One didn't argue with crystal balls—however imaginary.

"That's the last thing I want, Theresa. I would never willingly upset my grandmother." Susan took a sip of coffee and said, "When I was little you used to tell me stories about when you were an Incan princess. Do you remember that?"

"So you do have memories of the time you lived here."

"Bits float to the surface now and then—but they are only bits. I remember you quite clearly. *Did* you tell me those stories?"

Theresa's manner softened a little. "I exaggerated, I'm sure. I was always an imaginative, dramatic child. Though your grandfather told me once that there was a trace of Incan blood in my heritage from my mother. He felt that I should be proud of it. Once he even put me into one of his books, though I didn't feel flattered because he portrayed me as an Indian peasant woman—hardly the princess that I wanted to be. I forgave him, of course—he was such a remarkable man. He deserved much more from life than he ever got."

Criticism of her grandmother seemed implied, and Susan spoke up quickly. "It seems to me that he must have gotten a great deal from life: fame, wealth, satisfaction in the writing of books that were widely acclaimed. I want to know more about him too."

"What can I tell you? You've probably seen the photographs on his book jackets. Even in his older years he was strikingly handsome, with thick white hair and those unexpectedly blue eyes —perhaps from that Highland ancestor who dropped in on the family centuries ago. He was tall and rather thin, and I remember the strong, aristocratic beak of his nose. His voice was beautiful—it could make the back of my neck prickle."

"How do you mean?" Susan retrieved her toast and sat down to butter it, while Theresa thought about her answer.

"Sometimes Juan Gabriel could be coaxed into reading aloud from his books. He would change his voice level to make it run up and down the scale, so he sounded almost spooky when he wanted to. He could also throw in silly words in a lighter voice that made us laugh."

"You were very fond of him, weren't you?"

For once Theresa sounded entirely sincere. "After my parents died, he was like a father to me—much more than Alex was ever like a mother."

Theresa's devotion to Juan Gabriel was clear, and so was a hint of resentment against Alex. Yet most of her time seemed to be spent serving Juan Gabriel's wife.

"Last night," Susan said, "when I stepped outside on the tower balcony, I saw a light burning at the near end of the boathouse. My grandmother came out the door. What is down there?"

Theresa seemed suddenly attentive. "That's where Juan Gabriel used to work. His study was in this end of the boathouse. All his last books were written there. I can't think why Alex would have been there at night, or any time. She's avoided that place for years."

Susan let that go and asked another question. "Yesterday, when I met Dr. Macklin at the library, he warned me that my grandmother hadn't been well. Can you tell me what's the matter?"

"Sometimes she has an irregular heartbeat, and her blood pressure can rise. Nothing serious, Peter feels. We all try to shield her, but her own

102 independence makes that difficult. Also your coming has been hard for her."

"Why should that be? I don't think she feels very much about me, one way or another."

Theresa seemed to ignore her. "Of course Marilyn Macklin's death devastated her. They'd grown to be good friends while Marilyn was working on her biography of Juan Gabriel Montoro. Alex seemed to feel responsible in some way for her death—though of course that's absurd. Alex was quite ill for a time, but Peter pulled her through. Perhaps his own troubles made her get out of bed to fight for him."

"How do you mean?"

"She appeared before the grand jury to vouch for him, and of course everyone knows and respects her. But it was a difficult experience and it sapped both her physical and spiritual energy."

As she finished, Theresa glanced toward the hall door, smiling. "Here's your grandmother now. Good morning, Alex. You're early. What can I fix for your breakfast?"

Susan turned in her chair, startled by Alex's appearance. She had discarded her long white pants for a full skirt of warm saffron, with a tiny blue print woven into the silk. An embroidered jacket of pale azure topped the skirt. Her hair had been wound on top of her head in a thick coil, with an amber Spanish comb thrust into its pile.

On anyone else this might have seemed an odd way to dress for breakfast, but obviously Alex Montoro knew what suited her, and she set her own style. This morning she'd chosen to be a bit exotic, and the hint of a lovely scent floated around her.

"Hmm—you smell good!" Susan said.

Alex's laughter was warm, natural. "You used to tell me that when you were small."

"It's a perfume called Drina that Worth made up for her," Theresa explained proudly.

"About a hundred years ago!" Alex smiled. "When it was no longer on the market, Juan Gabriel bought up all the leftover stock, so it will last me another hundred years." She nodded to Theresa. "Thank you—I'll have my usual breakfast this morning."

Theresa went out to the kitchen, and Alex sat down in her place at the head of the table. "Did you sleep well, Susan?"

"Very well, thank you."

They were being formal and courteous now, and Alex said nothing more until Theresa returned with a bowl of hot oatmeal and a sliced banana. Whole grain toast and an herbal tea completed her menu, and she ate with good appetite. When Theresa rejoined them at the table, Alex continued.

"You're going to be good for me, Susan. This morning I feel more purposeful than I have for a

104 long time, and I have a plan. There's a place I want you to see. Perhaps if we go there together I'll be able to make a decision about something that faces me."

Theresa looked upset. "Not that church again!"

Alex's smile was kind but firm. "I know you dislike my going there, but you have a mistaken idea about what that historic place means to me."

Susan caught the flash of resentment in Theresa's dark eyes. The relationship between the two women was hardly affectionate.

"Do you like your tower room, Susan?" Alex asked. "Do you remember it at all?"

"Sometimes I have a feeling that I do. It's a feeling that leaves me a little uneasy—though I haven't any idea why. Last night when I went outside on the balcony and walked around, I found a door that seemed to lead to another part of the tower room."

"That door is kept locked," Theresa said with a sharpness that seemed unwarranted.

"I know. I was curious, so I tried the door." She didn't ask why it was kept locked, but the question seemed to hang in the air.

Alex explained quietly. "Juan Gabriel didn't build this house. The man who built it was an inventor who liked to shut himself off from his family so he could work without interruption. The tower rooms were where he escaped to be alone. He used the smaller room as his workshop, and the outside stairs gave him access to it without disturbing the rest of the family. His grandson, from whom we bought the house, told us about him." Alex set down her cup and looked directly at Susan. "We use it now as a storeroom and keep it locked."

"As it should be," Theresa said tartly. "Please excuse me—there's something I need to do."

She was leaving to show her annoyance, Susan thought, but Alex let her go without comment.

"Perhaps we can start off right away?" she suggested to Susan. "I'll fetch my car keys, while you get ready for a short trip."

As her grandmother left the room, Susan started for the door and ran upstairs for her purse. In the doorway of the tower room she stopped in surprise. Theresa stood near the head of the bed, having apparently just hung a picture in the empty space Susan had noticed the night before. She looked faintly amused at Susan's surprise in finding her there.

"Your grandmother asked me to find a picture for this spot, and I thought this one might be appropriate."

Appropriate in what way? Susan wondered. She recognized the stone ruins atop a mountain, having seen pictures of Machu Picchu before. This black and white photograph of the famous

106 Incan temple had been taken from the air so that the view of walls and terraces, walks and wide steps—all built some two thousand years before Christ—were spread across several levels of the mountaintop. Two tiny human figures at the foot of crumbling steps gave a sense of vast spaces and massive structures that dwarfed them completely.

Theresa mused aloud. "How I would love to go there! I can almost feel the wonder of it just looking at that picture."

Susan's focus was elsewhere. "What hung there originally, Theresa?"

There was a slight hesitation before she answered. "A picture of Juan Gabriel. I never understood why Alex wanted it removed, but it's not my place to question what she chooses to do."

This was probably false humility, but Susan had no time for Theresa now. She picked up her purse and left, leaving Theresa still studying the photograph of the temple ruins.

When she had joined Alex in her car and they were on their way, her grandmother explained about the place they would visit. Susan listened with interest as she related the story of "King Carter" and the rule he had held over Virginia.

"Robert Carter built his church on the same spot where an earlier one had been built by his father—a building that had become too small for the growing congregation of family and friends.

It's a remarkable building, Susan. I hope you'll be
interested."

This seemed more than a visit to a historical
site, Susan thought, and wondered what lay behind it. If a few mysteries could unfold their answers during this visit, that would be fine. Her
own father had been indifferent to religion and
had sometimes spoken scornfully of his first
wife's faith. Only the intervention of Susan's
stepmother had caused her to be sent to Sunday
school, so she wouldn't grow up a "heathen."

The drive from Kilmarnock ran through
wooded countryside, with occasional houses visible. When they reached a great tree-shaded area
at the side of the road, Alex parked her car, and
they got out to walk past a small cemetery.

"I'll show you Carter's tomb and those of his
two wives later," Alex said, and Susan continued
to feel that they were not really here for sight-
seeing.

At an open gate Alex paused, musing aloud.
"In Peru, when I was very young, I was taught
by nuns. I was a devout little girl, but when I
grew up God seemed to fail me, and since Juan
Gabriel disliked all formal, 'limiting religions,' as
he called them, we weren't churchgoers."

Looking up at the great red bricks glowing in
the sun, Susan felt more confused than ever.
"Then why are we here?"

Alex's answer continued to be evasive. "This

108 is part of Virginia's history, Susan. You were born in Virginia, though you remember very little."

So far, she'd felt no particular connection with Virginia. Though all she had seen was beautiful, her eyes were more accustomed to the colors of parched desert and earth-colored adobe, and to the marvelous red rocks that cropped up dramatically in unexpected places. All this greenery seemed monotonous.

Alex went up the steps and through the open door of the church, and Susan followed, feeling oddly hesitant and uncertain. Her grandmother seemed to have some sort of obsession about this place that made Susan uneasy.

Out of the sun's heat, the air inside seemed several degrees cooler, and she shivered. At the foot of the main aisle, the high walls of wooden pews rose on either hand, and her apprehension increased. She suddenly felt as though she might open herself to some strange quality within these walls—something she might prefer to resist.

"Look up!" Alex directed.

Susan tilted her head back to encompass high spaces of floating light—light that poured in filtered beams through three oxeye windows set into deep eaves. For a reluctant moment a sense of awe held her—a feeling that she quickly dismissed, remembering her father's scornful laughter echoing out of the past.

"Why *are* we here?" she repeated.

Alex heard the note of rejection in her voice, and she placed a quieting hand on Susan's arm. "Don't try to ask reasonable questions. Just give it a chance; let yourself feel whatever is here. Sometimes this place restores me, works a special spell. I thought it might do the same for you. You are my daughter's daughter—but we seem so very far away. I'd like to bridge the distance between us."

Touched, though still resistant, Susan followed as Alex moved toward the transept aisle.

"I wish I could have seen you dance," she said softly.

"I know no one anymore who has ever seen me dance."

"I suppose my grandfather saw you on the stage? Was it your dancing that drew him to you?"

Her grandmother's sudden vehemence of denial took her by surprise.

"No! Your grandfather never saw me dance!" Then confusion seemed to possess her and Alex immediately corrected herself. "What am I saying? You were asking about Juan Gabriel, and of course he saw me dance many times, before Rudy Folkes died. He would even travel to other countries where the Folkes Ballet was appearing."

"Did he ever write about you as a dancer?"

Alex seemed to find the question disconcerting, and for a moment Susan thought she wouldn't answer. Then she said, "Only once—in his book *The Black Swan*. He wrote that book during our early years here, when he could still describe me perfectly as I danced the role of the white swan in his story."

Pain had touched Alex's voice—some deep pain out of what was long past. Hearing it, Susan spoke more gently.

"At least I'd like to read a description of your dancing. That book isn't one my father had in his collection, so I've never seen it."

"Let's get out to where it's warm," Alex said abruptly. "There's nothing here for us today, after all."

In spite of Susan's reluctance to surrender anything of herself to this place, it was as though something held her here—as though she could sense that something was about to happen.

What happened was a sudden small explosion of sound in the form of a human sneeze.

"There's someone here!" Alex went quickly to pull open the door of a nearby pew.

On a high-backed bench that ran around the pew's interior sat an elderly man. His graying hair, swept back from a wide forehead, indicated his years, though his striking face was scarcely lined. He had been writing in a notebook that was balanced on his crossed knees, and he set it and his pen down on the bench and stood up, his smile forced.

"I was wondering if you'd discover me, Alex," he said. "I've enjoyed this bit of eavesdropping. The spell this church appears to exert over you fascinates me. And this must be Susan Prentice whom you're trying to convert?"

The hand he held out to Susan was large and summer-browned, its size matching the rest of him. Susan put her own hand into an enveloping clasp that somehow seemed unwelcoming.

"I'm Gilbert Townsend," he said, without waiting for an introduction from Alex. "I was very good friends with your father, whom I respected a great deal."

Alex broke in. "Do you live in this church, Gilbert? This is the second time in two days that we've met here."

"The book I'm writing is about Christ Church—have you forgotten? I come here often." His voice was tinged with annoyance as he answered Alex, but it softened deliberately when he addressed Susan. "How long are you staying with your grandmother, my dear?"

The question seemed surprisingly direct. "Probably a few days," Susan told him, retrieving her hand from his smothering clasp. "I'm glad to meet friends of my parents. Your sister Hallie came to see me yesterday soon after I arrived."

"Hallie could never contain her curiosity," he

112 said lightly. "I hope she didn't disturb you too much. She can be pretty unexpected at times. Don't believe everything she tells you—she could have made a great fiction writer, with her imagination." In spite of his mocking tone, he seemed disturbed that Hallie had visited her.

"I liked her," Susan told him. "She said she was my mother's friend, and brought me a picture my mother had given her."

Gilbert Townsend looked doubtful. "I don't think that she and Dolores were close, Susan. But never mind that. It's just as well that you're not staying too long. I think your father would not have wanted you to come here."

"Oh? Perhaps you can tell me why, Mr. Townsend?"

Apparently he found her question discomfiting, and while he hesitated, Alex drew Susan away.

"Let Gilbert get back to his work. I want to show you the Carter tombs, Susan."

Gilbert Townsend made them a derisive bow, and when Susan glanced back as they left the open door of the pew, she saw that he'd picked up his notebook and pen, but was looking after them. He certainly hadn't been pleased to see her —that was evident. There were undercurrents here she didn't understand.

"He doesn't approve of you, does he?" she asked as they went outside.

"That's all right—I don't approve of him." Alex dismissed Gilbert with a flick of her fingers.

"If he was my father's friend—" Susan began, but her grandmother spoke sharply.

"All the more reason to stay away from him. No one needs a friend like Gilbert. Come, we'll walk around the back of the church to the tombs. The Visitors Center is over there, and perhaps we'll look in on Hallie before we leave."

The subject of Gilbert Townsend had been put aside, but Susan's stubborn streak could be as strong as her grandmother's and she meant to return to her questions about him soon.

Robert Carter's large stone tomb was a monument in itself. It stood intentionally higher than those of his two wives, its decorations ornate. On one side a great coat-of-arms had been carved into the stone, and there were other carvings and inscriptions.

"The slabs that covered the tombs were so worn," Alex explained, "that they've been replaced and duplicated, even to the Latin inscription that tells us that Robert Carter was 'possessed of ample wealth, blamelessly acquired.' Perhaps not everyone in his time would have agreed to the word 'blamelessly.'"

In a sense Susan felt even more uneasy standing before these three tombs than she had inside the church. There seemed an all-enveloping loneliness here—perhaps the loneliness of death.

114   These tombs held all that remained of so much human loving and loss; so much grief and anguish and physical pain. Here in the shadow of the church she continued to feel cold, though it was so much warmer than it had been inside.

"Let's go find some more cheerful shade," Alex said briskly. "I can sit on the grass if you'll help me to get up."

She still seemed strangely insistent, and Susan knew there was more to come from their visit to this place.

"I wanted all this to touch you, as it has touched me." Alex spoke almost wistfully as they walked past the tombs together.

Susan wished she could please her. "What I feel right now is unsettled, isolated—not connected to anything."

"Uprooted," Alex said. "I can understand that. You need to find something to take hold of, so that new rooting can begin. Even though you may be here only a short time, I would like you to find a connection with us, Susan. This land, these people are in your blood."

They'd reached a great oak tree, where morning shade offered a resting place. Susan helped Alex lower herself to the grassy earth, where she could lean back against the trunk of the tree. Then she dropped down near her grandmother.

Overhead, leaves rustled their summery

sound. Closing her eyes, Susan let pictures drift idly through her mind. She could see the tower room where she'd spent the night, see Theresa hanging a picture—that photograph of Machu Picchu that she'd placed in the empty space over the bed. When Susan told Alex about this, her grandmother's smile was uncertain.

"I wondered what picture Theresa would choose. She must have taken that one out of her own room. You can feel flattered that she's loaned it to you. Theresa has what comes close to an obsession with Incan history in Peru."

"I'm not sure she meant to flatter me. Perhaps she only wanted to disturb my dreams. I can still remember the scary stories she used to tell me when I was little."

"Do you remember anything else, Susan— anything that was frightening?"

The question troubled her. There *was* something—but it always slipped away. Perhaps because the terror was too great to be faced?

"So far I haven't remembered very much. Why did you remove the picture of my grandfather that hung on that wall originally? Theresa said you had it taken down."

"It was the wrong picture of Juan Gabriel," Alex said shortly.

A strange answer. They both remained silent for a few moments, then Susan said, "What *do* you want of me? I keep feeling that you are asking me for something, but I don't know what it is."

"I'm not sure I know either," Alex said, and Susan heard sadness in her voice.

Somewhere nearby a bee went about its summer duties, and a yellow butterfly lighted on the same bush. When a twig dropped beside her, Susan picked it up, twirling the leaves in her fingers until they seemed to pirouette like a dancer. She asked the question that came most naturally to her mind.

"How did you come to be a dancer, Drina?"

Perhaps hearing the name spoken again sent Alex's thoughts back in time, for she began to reminisce.

"I had always loved to dance. I could do a good flamenco when I was ten, and I mastered the castanets on my own. I knew nothing at all about ballet until one year that I will never forget. Our family used to visit a village up in the mountains every summer, when the weather grew hot down by the coast."

She was quiet for a moment, lost in the past. Then she went on, drawing scenes from her memory.

"What I remember best about that high place was the volcano—a great red mountain with steep sides that rose straight up behind the walls of the convent. Sometimes red dust would streak the habits of the nuns, and I thought it made the white cloth even more beautiful. The nuns didn't like it, of course, and they spent too much time dusting it off and washing their garments.

"I remember the volcano especially because I was afraid of it. A hundred years before, it had erupted and killed a great many people. The damage could still be seen in the village. The volcano had remained active, and there was always a drifting of smoke from the crater. At night the glow of that inner fire frightened me." Alex was quiet for a moment, lost in her remembrance. Suddenly she shook her head, as though emerging from a dream. "But I wasn't afraid for long because Madame Magdalena came into my life and took my attention away from everything else."

Susan relaxed against the rough bark of the tree, her eyes closed as she visualized the pictures her grandmother painted so brightly of a country on a faraway continent. Perhaps she could find the connection she longed for in Alex Montoro's words.

"Madame Magdalena had been a dancer when she was young," Alex explained. "Even though her knees would no longer bend in more than the shallowest of *pliés,* Magda was a magnificent teacher. Wherever she happened to be, she would look around among the young girls and single out those she wanted to teach. She would charge the rich families handsomely. Poor ones

118 she would teach for nothing. Everyone knew her, and it was an honor to be chosen.

"I can still remember the rap of her stick on my ankles when a step was wrong!" Alex twisted her mouth expressively.

Magda had told Alex's parents that their child had been created for dancing. Her slender body and small, strong ankles were formed for power. She possessed arms and hands that never made an awkward movement. Her small, graceful head, with its long neck, possessed a natural balance, even before Madame began to train her.

Alex spoke affectionately of the young girl she had been, as though of someone distant from herself. Susan warmed to the picture her grandmother was creating. She would like to have known that young girl.

"Of course it was only during the summer that I could take lessons, but I worked fervently the rest of the year—making mistakes and falling into bad habits that had to be painfully corrected when I was with Madame again.

"When I was fifteen and proficient on my toes, and perhaps even a little better than she had expected in my technique, Madame came down to the coast to visit my parents' old Spanish house in Lima. She brought a guest with her because she wanted him to see me dance. She told me I had the passion, the spark, to make a great dancer, but I needed to believe in myself. When

it came to a public performance, I was still frightened and unready.

"His name was Rudolf Folkes, and he must
have been impressed by something he saw in me,
even though I needed intensive training. He told
me that he wasn't sure whether I would be willing to work hard enough to please him, but I
convinced him that I *would* work. I would do
anything for this chance. Of course I worshiped
him. He gave me the name Drina, and when he
touched me I knew I could do anything. He was
my first love."

Susan glanced at her grandmother, seeing her
with new eyes. Alex might wear the guise of an
old woman, but all these wonderful experiences
lay beneath the surface, keeping the younger
woman in her alive.

"My parents were doubtful in the beginning,
but they would never have opposed something
that I wanted so passionately. I danced in Rudy's
corps de ballet for a year, becoming accustomed to
the life, and to dancing on a stage.

"For a little while—such a little while!—my
life was filled with work and magic. And love.
He made me a prima ballerina. Have you any
idea, Susan, what such a life could be like? The
adulation, the applause that sent waves of love
and approval to a dancer, the tremendous baskets
of flowers that could fill a dressing room! What
pampering! And the grueling effort that never

stopped, even when my toes bled. Even when I danced on a broken ankle.

"Of course my dancing had an aura of unreality about it. When a spotlight followed me, I felt only the passion of the dance, never the physical pain. It was worth anything to be so loved by all those people out there in the darkness of a theater. When Rudy died, I went home to Lima. I knew that my dancing was over, but I thought my life was over as well. The young are like that, never dreaming that what lies ahead may be more remarkable than anything yet experienced. And sometimes far worse, in terms of pain."

Alex was silent for so long that Susan dared to ask a question. "How did Rudy die?"

"In a senseless accident. He was swimming off an island in Greece and got caught in an undertow that carried him away."

"Why didn't you go on dancing anyway? You must have been famous by that time, and wanted everywhere."

"What I lacked was not the talent and passion to be a dancer, but the confidence. Without that, one is nothing. Rudy could touch me, and I knew I could achieve anything, no matter how difficult. His belief in me was absolute but it nevertheless challenged me. He created four ballets for me. Ballets that no one else has danced as well. When he died, the magic died with him, and I could do nothing."

This seemed unbearably sad. "How is that 121 possible? I knew the moment I met you how strong you are, how enormously confident. I felt in awe of you—I still do—and I expect you know very well that you have that effect on people."

Alex smiled slightly, pleased perhaps. "If only we could understand our potential while we're still young—then anything would be possible. But I suppose the young would be even more impossible if that were the case. What you think you see in me now is partly façade and partly a lot of hard-won effort."

Slowly the world around them became real again, and Susan looked up at the great edifice of the church, overpowering in its bulk beyond the low brick wall. Alex's red volcano in the Andes seemed lifetimes away from this sheltered spot, yet somehow Susan felt closer to the past that existed in her grandmother's memory than she felt toward her own uncertain present.

"I'm not as young as you were then," Susan said, "but I still have more doubts than I can deal with. Perhaps that's why I've come—to find some sort of balance by discovering the past."

"I'm not sure you'll find balance here," Alex said, and made a movement to rise.

"Wait!" Susan put a hand on her arm. "What happened next? I want to hear the rest of the story."

"I met Juan Gabriel Montoro, who appar-

122 ently found me fascinating, not only as a dancer, but as a woman after he met me through my parents. He was already a distinguished writer, and he rescued me from my fears and my grief. My desire to dance was gone—it would never return—but that didn't matter to him. Now, when I look at the old photographs I showed you yesterday, it's as if they were pictures of someone I knew long ago. The only time anything touches me from those years is when I hear some phrase of music I once danced to. The music from *Swan Lake* can carry me back in an instant."

"You must have been truly wonderful for Rudy Folkes to believe in you as he did."

"It wasn't all mystical and magical. There was a lot of hard work and physical pain. But I had the long legs, the stamina, and I had the necessary concentration. In *Swan Lake* there are all those little swans fluttering around, and one must never allow oneself to become distracted. It's a very technical ballet. Rudy did his own version, and he wanted more buoyancy than the Russians gave it. He knew I could float in the air when he wanted me to. The white swan almost flew at the end. Her part was easy for me to dance, and I loved the very feeling of being Odette."

Alex's eyes closed, and Susan knew that some part of her was experiencing the movements of the dance. "What about the black swan?" she asked.

"That was more difficult. Rudy wanted Odile to be especially evil. My arms had to entice and the movement required a great deal of flexibility. I had trouble with my arms. But when I danced on a stage, it all came together and I only thought of *being* Odile—the black swan, who would take away the white swan's innocent prince. Now, when I hear a snatch of Tchaikovsky something in me breaks into bits, like a shattering crystal."

Tears came into Susan's eyes. "You gave it up too soon!"

"Perhaps. But at least I stopped while I was one of the best. Do you know that even today I can dance every one of Rudy's ballets in my mind, though I could hardly manage a step physically. But never mind all that—it was so many lifetimes ago. I've no regrets about not dancing. There's been too much else in my life that I never expected. It's difficult for a ballet dancer to have any sort of life outside of her dancing, so I've been lucky. Enough about me. I want to know more about you, Susan."

"There isn't much to tell."

"I'm sure that's not true. What are the first experiences that come to mind when you think back?"

Susan sensed a longing in her grandmother, and an alertness—something she couldn't satisfy.

"I can't think back. What comes to my mind is recent and not very happy."

"Then go back further. What scenes do you remember?"

Susan closed her eyes. "There were mountains for me too. Always the Sangre de Cristo behind Santa Fe. Adobe colors that I love—earth colors. The desert, of course. It's beautiful when it's dry, and of course riotous with color when it blooms. Everything is different from all this lush greenery."

"Who were your friends?"

"My best friend for a long while was a Mexican-American girl, so I speak a little Mexican Spanish. My first work as a nurse was on the Navajo reservation in Arizona. I drove a Jeep and went where they needed me. Is this what you want to hear?"

"Yes—it tells me a little about who you are and what you care about. Go further back. Who was the first boy you fell in love with?"

Laughter bubbled from her throat, though she wasn't far from tears. "There was a boy in high school I was crazy about, though he didn't notice me at all." Suddenly, without warning, she knew why she'd been crazy about that particular schoolmate. He had reminded her of a young boy she remembered only as "Petey." That was both funny and sad. Especially since she'd never recognized this before.

Alex must have heard the full stop that Susan had placed on her memories. She reached for her cane, but before Susan could help her up, she sank back again.

"There goes Gilbert—over to the Reception Center. Now is your chance, Susan!"

"For what?"

"I brought you here to see if the church might have something to give you. I don't mean something connected with any special religion. No—don't refuse. Let the place decide what you might feel when you are inside those walls and totally alone. Look up into that vaulted light. Wait and be quiet. Close your eyes and let whatever needs to happen, happen. Go now."

Earlier, Susan might have held back. But she felt closer to Alex Montoro, who was her grandmother, but who was also a remarkable woman who had won her way to a certain wisdom. Perhaps that was what she could use now—Alex's wisdom.

"All right—I'll try. But don't count on anything."

Alex smiled again—her wonderfully warming smile which still held a hint of mystery about it. This old woman could charm anyone, Susan thought as she hurried off toward the door of the church. She was still a little on guard and wanted to get this over with as quickly as possible.

"You can't rush it," Alex called after her.

Again, when she stepped through the door, Susan felt how cool it was in contrast to the heat outdoors. But the quality of the air seemed different somehow, now that she stood here alone. She touched nothing, but walked up the main aisle to the point where it met the transept aisle. The light that filtered in from high windows in the tunneled eaves had a tranquilizing effect. In spite of herself, she felt her tension flow away, tight muscles seemed to untie. Even the tension she held in her jaw lessened. The skeptical part of her mind whispered, "So what?"

She didn't listen. Some ancient power existed in this place—something she didn't understand —didn't want to accept. Superstitious nonsense! She closed her eyes and waited for the twinkling light that danced under her lids to subside so that she could look into velvety blackness. She swayed a little, and steadied herself by putting one hand on a tall pew.

The darkness she looked into was an empty screen, upon which images began to appear. Without any conscious devising of her own, pictures appeared in full color. Pictures that were strange and far from reassuring. All around her were tombstones—old graves set aboveground, with dates from years past. Yet this was not a cemetery. On each side of the spaces of crowded tombstones were houses where people lived. She could see a swing in a yard where children played, with more graves visible beyond.

For a moment she felt afraid—as if of some horrifying portent. But the children seemed happy. One of them pushed another in a swing, and she could hear laughter. A sense filled her of life and death moving together, and she knew the vision was not to be entirely feared, even though she could not tell its meaning. There seemed a promise here—but of what?

The pictures vanished, and when she opened her eyes she felt strangely reassured, though she understood nothing of what had happened, or why she should have received so strange a vision. Anger that had been a constant companion for a long time seemed to have lessened, and she felt that perhaps now she could let it go.

She left the church and returned to Alex. Her grandmother knew at once that something had happened. "Tell me," she said.

Susan sat down on the grass and leaned against the trunk of the oak tree. "It was very strange. I saw a place where houses and graves seemed to exist closely together. Yet it was a happy place, with children playing and no sense of death or dying. I had the strong feeling that it was a dream about life."

As she spoke, Susan had closed her eyes again. When her grandmother uttered a choked

128 sound, she opened them to see something like terror in Alex's face.

"No!" the old woman whispered. "You can't have seen that!" She struggled to rise, shocked and denying, and Susan got up to help her to her feet. But before she could ask what was wrong, Hallie came out of the Reception Center and rushed toward them, her arms flung out awkwardly from her body as she ran.

Alex sighed and sank back against the tree, but at least this distraction had helped her to recover herself. "Hallie never restrains her slightest impulse. Something has happened that she thinks can't wait."

"Why did what I said upset you so badly?"

"Later, Susan. Not now."

"You looked frightened."

"I am frightened."

Even before she reached them, Hallie began to exclaim shrilly. "Thank goodness I found you! I've just had a phone call—with such strange news. Gilbert thought you might still be on the grounds, so I came looking right away."

She flopped down on the grass beside Alex, out of breath.

Susan and Alex both waited.

"It's about Marilyn Macklin's manuscript!" Hallie said, when she'd caught her breath. "Her biography of Juan Gabriel Montoro. Susan, did you know that it disappeared after Marilyn's

death? But today somebody left it at the library
in Kilmarnock, and Sheriff O'Donnell took it to
Dr. Mac."

"Eric has already told us about this," Alex
said calmly.

"Yes—I know that. But you haven't heard it
all. I stopped in to see Dr. Mac this morning
because my arthritis has flared up. He came to his
office especially for me. So I was there when Bill
O'Donnell came to talk to him. Dr. Mac looked
through the pages and found that the last chapters were missing. He hadn't read the manuscript
originally—Marilyn wouldn't let him—so he
didn't know what might be in those pages. Obviously the book was unfinished."

Disturbed by this outburst, Susan watched
her grandmother, but Alex's expression told her
only that she was being careful about what she
said.

"As far as I know," Alex said, "Marilyn never
completed her work."

Hallie was already shaking her head. "I saw
what Bill O'Donnell showed Dr. Mac. There was
a notation in Marilyn's own writing at the end of
the typed script. It said, 'Notes for last chapters
follow.' But there weren't any notes. So what
happened to them?"

"I really don't think it matters," Alex said.
"Please help me up, Susan. My legs are getting
stiff."

130   Susan helped her up and when Alex had limbered up a little, she gestured toward her car. "Let's go home."

Hallie came with them, still persistent. "You must have seen those notes, Alex. So what was in them?"

Alex managed to answer patiently. "Marilyn was undecided about how to handle the final year of Juan Gabriel's life. There was something left out earlier because I didn't want her to use it, and she still thought it should go in, if only at the end. Why does all this matter to you, Hallie?"

"Why wouldn't it? We've always been close to your family, Alex. Of course I'm interested."

Alex got into the driver's seat without further discussion, and when Susan joined her, she nodded to Hallie.

"Thanks for coming to tell me, but it really doesn't matter anymore. So relax."

As they drove away, Susan looked back to see Hallie staring after them—a tall, thin figure that reminded Susan a little of a scarecrow.

"What a strange woman," she said.

"Strange, yes. And much too meddlesome," Alex said shortly.

They hardly spoke on the drive home, and Susan knew better than to push on questions concerning the vision she'd experienced in the church. She wanted very much to know why what she had seen had seemed to shock her grandmother, but there was no use in asking her now.

Not until they were nearly back to the house did Alex seem to relax. "I've arranged an outing for you this afternoon, Susan. Peter Macklin is coming to take you to lunch. You need to get out with someone your own age."

Susan found that she felt ambivalent about such a high-handed arrangement, made without consulting her. Yet, the small child she had once been leaped with eagerness at the idea of being with Peter. Her grownup self was immediately on guard against falling into something she was totally unready for. Peter was deep in his own troubles and the sorrow over the loss of his wife. He didn't need to have her thrust upon him right now.

Alex went on calmly, as though certain of Susan's agreement. "We have an hour before you need to be ready, and there's something else I want to show you."

When they reached the house there was once more the ritual of George coming out to help Alex from the car, which he then took around to the garage.

"We'll go upstairs," Alex said. "I've decided

132 to satisfy your curiosity about the locked room in the tower. We'll look into it together. It's time."

Her strength seemed to have returned, and whatever had upset her earlier, had been neatly hidden away.

When they reached the third floor, Alex walked into the tower bedroom and stood for a moment regarding the photograph of Machu Picchu that Theresa had hung over the bed.

"I'm not sure that's a good choice," she said. "I wouldn't want that place to haunt your dreams the way it once did mine. My parents took me there when I was about eight, and I remember it clearly. All that grandeur—an entire people lost in the centuries, leaving a mystery behind. Do you see that black peak that towers over the ruins in the picture? That mountain used to haunt my dreams and frighten me. Before adolescence children are closer to whatever came before. What do we know about where we came from, or where we will go later on?"

Susan felt herself withdrawing. "Do you mean reincarnation? My father always dismissed that completely."

"Of course—Lawrence would!" She moved toward the balcony door. "But what about you? I have an idea that you think for yourself."

"I haven't thought about it at all," Susan said, not liking the mystical turn this conversation was taking.

"Never mind. You have years of change ahead of you. Right now you have no notion of the person you'll have become by the time you're my age. Some people manage to stay in one spot all their lives, but I don't think you're like that. Now let's go and find your mother."

Alex walked out onto the sunny balcony, but her words had stopped Susan in dismay. This was what she had come to Virginia for—yet confusion seized her, and a dread of what the locked room might hold.

Alex extended a reassuring hand. "It will be all right. This may hurt us both a little, but it may also help you to remember some of the things you've forgotten. Gilbert is worried about your remembering. He wanted me to send you away before anything came back to you. But I can't do that. You've just had a remarkable vision which can't be denied. No, Susan, I can't tell you about what you saw, but I have to consider it an omen. Whether it's good or bad, I have no idea, but I know we must go ahead." She held out her hand. "Come, please."

Like a child, Susan took her grandmother's hand, sensing her strength—even her protection. Alex's fingers were cool, but a sharing of courage came through to Susan. Now it was the older woman who supported the young one.

They rounded the tower and stood before the

134 locked door. Alex brought out a key and slipped it into place with a click.

"If you really want to turn back, I won't stop you. But perhaps there are truths one is better off facing. If we confront them together, we can put a great deal behind us. This look into the past is for me, as well as for you. I've never been able to do this until now. Dolores was your mother and my daughter. We both loved her. So if we can deal with what's in this room, perhaps we can get on with our lives."

Tiny sparks of memory had been flashing through Susan's mind ever since she had come to Virginia, but they were seldom clear enough to be grasped. Nevertheless, she was deeply afraid of what she might learn.

"Was I alone with my mother on the day she died? Please tell me."

Alex paused with her hand on the knob. "Not exactly alone. Your father was down near the water in his workshop shed, making something or other. He liked to work with his hands. I believe that Gilbert was with him."

Susan waited.

"Juan Gabriel was in his wheelchair in his bedroom on the second floor. We believe that you and Dolores were together in your playroom on the same floor. You were the only person who might have seen Dolores fall. You are the one

who really knows what happened. Though afterward you could remember nothing."

Some warning gripped Susan: *Stop while
there's time. You don't want to know what happened.* She held back, ready to resist.

Five

The key had been turned, unlocking the door, but Susan's hand tightened on Alex's arm.

"Wait, please. Give me a minute to get ready. Let me walk around the tower first."

Alex watched her go. Susan moved slowly, delaying, postponing, and Alex wondered if *she* dared to open this door. Her own memories held her in an unwelcome grip, bringing back vivid pictures she'd suppressed for too many years.

She had come home that day to find Dolores lying at the foot of the stairs, her head crushed against the brass jardiniere that had belonged to the Montoro family for generations. If that pot had not been there, perhaps Dolores would have lived. It was the huge brass pot that had killed her. Why had she fallen, when she was young and surefooted? It was the unanswered question that had haunted them all.

Theresa was still convinced that Dolores's small, angry daughter had pushed her mother at a moment when she was off balance at the top of the stairs. The child had often shown a temper when she was crossed, and Theresa claimed that when she'd gone out that morning, Susan had been throwing a tantrum. All children threw tantrums, and Alex had told herself a thousand times that no small child could be blamed for consequences of an action she couldn't understand. *If* it had really happened like that in the first place. Theresa, at twelve, had been a jealous girl. Until Susan was born she had been close to Dolores, like a younger sister.

In any case, Alex didn't believe Theresa's theory and had frightened her into silence. There had been one other person who might have seen what happened. Juan Gabriel had somehow struggled from his wheelchair—where he'd been

138 confined since his stroke—as though he'd tried to reach Dolores. When they found him, he was unconscious, in a coma that lifted only in the few moments before his death. He'd uttered strange words in those moments, words she had never been able to understand.

When Theresa learned that the grownup Susan was coming home, she'd said, "Perhaps she will remember. Perhaps then you will believe me."

Alex had told her sharply that she didn't want Susan to hear this story Theresa had concocted. Even if the story were true, so young a child could only be held blameless—unless Susan began to blame herself. That was the risk in what Alex was now doing—the tower room might rouse a slumbering past from which Susan might never be free. But was one ever free of suppressed memories?

Of course, there was also the possibility that what Susan remembered might prove her own innocence. Alex longed for this to be true, although if it were true, a great, unanswered darkness remained, since Alex had never believed that Dolores's fall was an accident.

Susan completed her walk around the tower, and Alex saw new purpose in her eyes and courage in the way she moved. She had made up her mind.

"Before we go in," Susan said, "tell me what to expect. I don't like shocks."

"There'll be no great shocks, I think. Only dusty memories. Some of your toys and clothes are in there. Some of your mother's dresses. I gave a great many away, but there were a few I didn't want others to have, so I stored them up here. Then I locked the door and never set foot in this room again. I no longer remember what I kept, so if there are any surprises, they will be for me as well. If you'd rather not do this—"

"Let's go in," Susan said, and reached past Alex to push open the door.

The room was formed in the shape of a half moon, rounded on the balcony side, flat on the wall it shared with the bedroom beyond. Dust rose gently as the air stirred, and Susan sneezed.

Suddenly nervous, Alex snatched at an excuse to postpone what no longer seemed a good idea. "We can never do this until the room has been cleaned. Let's close the door and leave it for now."

Susan shook her head. "We'd better do it while we're feeling brave. It's not dust and cobwebs I'm afraid of."

Nor were dust and cobwebs what Alex feared, but she gave in reluctantly, wishing she had never suggested this.

The room contained piles of cartons, an old trunk, and various odds and ends of discarded

140 furniture, including a faded blue armchair that stood against the flat stretch of wall. Alex lowered herself into it.

"My mother used to sit in that very chair and hold me!" Susan said with amazement. "She used to read me stories while I sat on her lap. Wonderful stories!"

Alex closed her eyes, unwilling to watch Susan's bright face—so beautiful at times, so terribly young. Her eagerness broke her grandmother's heart. How could such innocence survive the truth—whatever it was. The last thing Alex wanted to talk about was the stories Dolores had read to her small daughter. She had written them herself and it was best if they were lost forever.

Stiffening her own resolve, Alex gestured. They had to get this over. "You might as well start with that clothes rack over there. You'll find a few of Dolores's favorite dresses—I had them stored in bags."

Susan slid down a zipper on the first bag and drew out a long frock of filmy golden chiffon, with trailing velvet ribbons to match. Alex closed her eyes. "Your mother wore that for her birthday party when she was twenty-eight. Your father didn't care for parties, but he could hardly forbid one, when this was my house. Your mother always resisted Lawrence when he brought up the subject of moving away. She wanted to stay near Juan Gabriel, who was grow-ing old."

"She was three years younger than I am now," Susan marveled as she tucked the material back into the bag. "I wish I could really remember."

A child who had never known her mother had probably built fantasies around an imaginary figure. Fantasies that a real woman might never live up to.

"Perhaps you can look into the trunk," Alex suggested. "I think some of your things are there." At least toys might bring more joy than hurt.

The brass latches were open, and dust and cobwebs stirred as Susan lifted the lid, along with a spider that scurried off. Susan uttered a cry of pleasure as she reached into the trunk to pull out a stuffed toy—a dirty, dilapidated white rabbit.

"Petey! That was his name, wasn't it? I must have named him after Peter Macklin." She nuzzled her nose delightedly into the limp body of the rabbit, and then sneezed again at the smell of camphor. "I didn't want to leave him behind, but my father was so angry that I didn't dare ask to take him with me."

Alex winced. Dolores's death had given Lawrence an excuse to get back at his wife's mother in the cruelest way he knew. If Juan Gabriel hadn't been so ill, Alex might have fought for

142 Susan with any weapons she could use. Lawrence was far from being a loving father, but at the time there'd seemed nothing she could do.

Susan went on with her exploration, delighting in new discoveries, reacquainting herself with her earliest years. Alex watched her dark head bent over the trunk, the look of that long-ago child shining in her face. Susan was recalling only happy times with each new discovery, yet Alex had a sense of foreboding. There was the vision Susan had seen in the church, which had frightened Alex badly, and now she didn't know *what* might turn up in the trunk.

As Susan pounced and pulled out the shabby notebook with a cry of pleasure, she knew what it would be.

"I remember this!" Susan's delight broke her heart.

Of course it would turn up here—that collection of stories Dolores had set down for her small daughter. Disturbing stories, somehow dredged out of Dolores's own subconscious.

Juan Gabriel, unfortunately, had praised them—they were kin to his own dark side.

As Susan flipped the pages, Alex glimpsed her daughter's distinctive writing.

"These are stories my mother made up, aren't they?"

Alex nodded silently. There was no way to stop Susan, any more than she'd been able to stop

Dolores from reading these stories aloud to her child.

"I always thought they were unpleasant stories, Susan. Too Grimm! Should you bother with them?"

"I want to read them again. I remember they could be scary, but then she would hold me and keep all the bad things away. When my father took me to Arizona there was no one to keep the bad dreams from coming. He spanked me a few times for screaming at night. Things were a lot better after he married Connie. She was good to me, and we do love each other. Perhaps I can get a little closer to my mother through her stories. Did she write anything else?"

"Nothing. She stopped writing a little while before she died."

"The way you stopped dancing?"

Pain struck fiercely, deeply. She hadn't believed she could feel the old wounds all over again like this. That terrible mistake she'd made! No inner voice had warned her to avoid the impulsive step she had taken with Dolores. Her own longing for her daughter to know about her true father had been so strong that she wouldn't have listened to inner warnings anyway. She had told Dolores about her love for John Gower and something of what had transpired. She'd confessed that Juan Gabriel was not Dolores's real father. Now that he was so ill, she'd felt it safe to

144 tell John's daughter, since Juan Gabriel would never know.

Not in her wildest imaginings had she expected what would happen. Or had she merely been stupid and insensitive, blinded by her own emotions? Dolores's devastation seemed shattering. She had never wanted any father except Juan Gabriel—no matter how austere, remote, and sometimes irascible he could be. He was forever exciting in her eyes—a famous, distinguished writer. She had believed that her own writing talent came from Juan Gabriel. He'd appreciated her stories and praised them as no one else ever did.

Given a little time, Dolores might have come to her senses. Though this was seldom a characteristic of the young—as Alex herself knew very well. Perhaps Dolores had stopped writing as a way of punishing her mother for the terrible thing she had done, but Dolores's love for Juan Gabriel had only deepened. She had written one last terrible, devastating story that Alex could only hope Susan would never read, and then she had stopped writing altogether.

She told her mother how angry she was. How hurt. John Gower was no one she could ever accept as a father. He was nobody—a fisherman! How could her mother, with all her own fame, and her marriage to so remarkable a man as Juan Gabriel, have been so foolish, so depraved? The fact that Dolores would not have existed if it hadn't been for John Gower, meant nothing.

Alex, listening to her daughter in pained astonishment, had realized that Dolores had begun to sound more like Lawrence than like herself. And then she had understood the bleak truth —Dolores had told Lawrence and she was taking her lead from him.

Slowly Alex returned to the present in this quiet tower room. The only sound was her own harsh breathing.

Susan looked up from the trunk, concerned. "Are you all right, Grandmother?"

This was the first time Susan had called her by that name, and she was surprised by her own pleased emotion.

"I'm sorry about what I said," Susan added. "You had every right to stop dancing, if that was the way you felt. I didn't mean to upset or hurt you."

Susan wasn't Dolores, Alex told herself. Susan was different, kinder, and more courageous and independent. She had never really known Juan Gabriel. He'd been too old then to pay much attention to Dolores's little girl.

"Of course you haven't hurt me. It was just that I was remembering—too much. I've often wondered what my life would have been like if

146 I'd been stronger and gone on dancing. Sometimes I have very little sympathy for Drina."

The flash of Susan's smile flung gloom away. "I'm glad you gave up being Drina! I wouldn't be here if you hadn't."

At least Dolores's daughter saw what her mother had chosen to ignore.

Susan dropped the notebook on the floor and came to where Alex sat. She put both arms around her grandmother and kissed her cheek warmly. Perhaps the gesture surprised them both, for at once Susan moved away and went to sit on a carton, looking uncertain.

"Thank you, my dear," Alex said. "I've wanted that to happen." And she really had, though she hadn't known it until this moment. "I used to teach you dancing, you know. Do you remember that?"

"I'm not sure. Perhaps."

"You were such a delight. You had so much natural grace—the way you used your arms, your hands. The quick way you learned the simple steps I showed you."

A dreamy look crossed Susan's face. As though she moved without volition, she stood up and held her arms curved over her head in a remembered fifth position. Her feet moved rapidly, leaving streaks in the dust as she crossed the floor in a creditable *pas de bourrée,* one foot before, then behind, over and over, clear to the balcony windows. So lightly and gracefully she moved!

"That was a *pas de bourrée,*" Susan said, marveling aloud as the name of the step came easily to her tongue.

Once more Alex realized how much she hated Lawrence Prentice for taking that little girl away from her. But she could no longer allow herself the luxury of anger. Such feelings would alarm Susan, and they were not good for her own health, as Peter Macklin often warned her. She must appreciate Susan for what she had become, in spite of Lawrence. Susan had been much loved when she lived in Virginia and at least that good early start must have served her well. Alex wanted to learn all the ways in which Susan differed from her mother and father. Perhaps John Gower's traits—something of his basic goodness and natural wisdom—had skipped a generation to turn up in his granddaughter. Though she hoped his darker side, his heritage from Tangier Island, had been lost, or at least diluted.

As Susan picked up Dolores's notebook, something fell from between the pages. From where she sat, Alex could see the Santa Fe postmark on the envelope.

Susan was already examining it. "This is from my father! It's addressed to you, and the date is soon after we reached Santa Fe. But it's never been opened—so you didn't read it?"

Alex held out her hand. "May I have it, please?"

Susan hesitated, but then surrendered the letter. "Perhaps it will answer some of the questions I've wondered about. Will you read it now?"

"I'm sure it answers nothing," Alex said. She remembered when the letter came; she had debated with herself about opening it. In the end she had slipped the envelope into Dolores's notebook and packed it away with the stories. Reading it would only have upset her further, as she'd known very well. But now it must be read. Only then could she decide whether to share it with Susan.

Even as Susan handed her the envelope, a look came into her face that Alex recognized. It was stubborn determination—a look she'd seen often enough in her own mirror.

A sudden, silent tension held them both— Alex, however, was older and her will even stronger. After a moment Susan threw up her hands in surrender, a gesture that was as graceful as Alex remembered in the small girl she'd been.

"I can't be angry with you," Susan said. "It's *your* letter and your right to do what you like with it. I just hope you'll answer my questions sometime."

"I'll try to," Alex promised. Susan was *not* like Dolores. Still, she must never again make the mistake she'd made with her daughter. First, they must go to Tangier Island. She must face that ordeal, though she'd been unwilling to until now. While the trip could no longer be avoided, nothing must be done impulsively. She needed to see John Gower and Susan together. Only then could she decide. Somehow this must be arranged soon.

She nodded toward the trunk. "Are you going to empty that?"

Susan took out more toys, and several little dresses, a few of them exquisitely handsewn by Alex herself, even to the touches of embroidery. A neglected art taught to her as a little girl by Peruvian nuns. Susan held each one up in turn, admiring the work, a little tearful—perhaps as she recognized and remembered.

The next article she lifted from the trunk was a carved black box, perhaps eight inches square. But before she could open it, Alex stopped her sharply.

"No! Put that back. It's something I never want to see again!" Alex could almost hear the thumping of her own heart at the sight of that box whose contents she could hardly bear to think about.

Her tone allowed for no argument, and Susan pushed the box into a corner of the trunk and asked no questions. She reached instead for something large wrapped in an old dressing gown. When Alex saw what she'd lifted out, she

150 sat very still, waiting, her hands clasped tightly in her lap. *This* she dared not stop. It was better for Susan to face what had happened than to be forever shielded.

Susan lifted the heavy object from the trunk and unwrapped it, to reveal a huge brass jardiniere tarnished with age, but still a handsome piece. Perhaps she wouldn't remember, Alex thought. She could only leave the matter to fate.

But Susan remembered. The horror with which she regarded the object showed in her face.

"This is what killed my mother! This is what she fell against when she went down the stairs."

Alex controlled her voice carefully. "You were there, Susan. You *saw* what happened."

Susan sat back on her heels and covered her face with her hands. "No—I don't really remember. Sometimes bits come to me about something frightening and terrible, but never anything really clear. I never see her fall."

"Then how can you recognize that brass pot?" Alex asked.

"I just *know*. Grandmother, tell me what happened. Please tell me."

"How can I? We never knew exactly what happened. I came home to find Dolores lying at the foot of the stairs. You were sitting beside her, and her blood was on your hands and your dress. You were crying hysterically."

It was inevitable that this brass "weapon" would reappear now—with all its ramifications and questions. Alex had forgotten that it was here. Why had she saved it?

Susan covered her face with her hands, and Alex left her chair and touched her granddaughter's shoulder gently. She could hardly endure what was happening, but she managed to speak firmly. "We must let this go for now. You can come up here another time, Susan, if you like." By which time Alex would have the brass pot given away, disposed of—buried!

Susan made an effort to wipe away her tears, and Alex went on, her voice well under control. "Until all these dusty memories are swept away, we can never get on with our lives."

"But how do we *do* that?" Susan asked miserably.

How indeed? "I'm not sure. By standing up to them, I suppose. Once we know they are there, we pull them out of our own dark corners so that floods of daylight can expose and cleanse them. But we must approach this slowly and do nothing reckless."

Susan looked up at her grandmother, and Alex saw in her eyes something that was no longer as young as she'd thought.

"Because there may be monsters hiding in the dark?" Susan asked. "Will we be able to deal with monsters?"

"We *must* deal with them. We can deal with them together."

Why had she said that? She had always dealt capably with her problems alone. The sudden flash of Susan's smile rewarded her.

"You've been fighting dragons all your life, haven't you, Grandmother? I only hope I can be as brave as you are."

"Brave" was not the word she would have chosen for herself, and Alex drew back from dangerous emotion. She could not lose control now, when so much was at stake. There were so many more dragons than Susan ever dreamed existed.

She spoke briskly. "Peter will be here soon to take you to lunch. Do you want to get ready now?"

"I've been thinking about that." Susan looked doubtful. "I'm not sure I want to go to lunch with Dr. Macklin. You should have asked me first."

"You might have refused, though I don't know why. You do need to get away from this house for awhile. And there's another reason why I've suggested this. Peter has been terribly depressed since his wife's death, as you can imagine. Perhaps you can cheer him up a bit, or at least furnish something outside his own troubles for him to think about."

Susan gave in, as Alex knew she would. She

left her granddaughter in the tower bedroom and went down to the second floor, where she stopped at the open door of Theresa's workroom.

Theresa had turned the big, unused room that had once been Susan's playroom into her studio. Though she had shown promise as an artist, Dolores, who was so much older, had been more gifted, and Theresa had finally given up, not wanting to compete with the dead. Now she kept busy painting her "Russian" eggs. Each egg took great care, time, and creative talent. Her decorations were bright and original in their intricacies, and they had been selling well, both to local people and to visitors who came to the Northern Neck. Though when Alex tried to praise her work, Theresa shrugged off her words.

At the moment she sat before a long table covered with rows of egg cartons, some filled with painted eggs, some with white ones from which the contents had been removed. Her pink smock brought a touch of color to her dark, brooding face.

"May I interrupt?" Alex asked.

"Of course." Theresa set down her brush.

"I wonder if you will do something for me? It won't take long."

"How did your morning go with Susan?" Theresa countered.

"I think it went well." Alex could hardly repeat all that had happened.

"What would you like me to do?"

"Make a phone call for me, please. To Emily and John Gower on Tangier Island. Just ask if I may bring my granddaughter over for a visit tomorrow."

Theresa raised expressive black eyebrows. "Why don't you make the call yourself?"

Alex drew herself to her full, impressive height, and Theresa, who had seen that look before, let the question go.

"Of course I'll phone the island for you."

They went downstairs to the living room together, and Alex waited while she made the call. Sitting nearby, she could hear a woman's voice answer. If she had been sure of reaching Emily, she would have phoned herself. But since John no longer went out crabbing all day, he might easily have answered the phone. When she spoke to him again, she didn't want it to be on a telephone.

Theresa turned to Alex. "Mrs. Gower wants you to come to lunch."

Alex held out her hand for the phone, and Theresa passed it to her. Emily wouldn't think it strange that Theresa had called. She would expect Alex Montoro to have a secretary, and that was one of Theresa's roles.

"Hello, Emily. I'm glad I caught you. We'd enjoy coming for lunch, if it's all right with you and John. Though I'm not sure how we'll get there. Perhaps the tourist boat—"

"We can send over a plane, I'm sure. I'll let you know." Emily's response seemed careful and not altogether welcoming, which was natural enough after the years of silence that had been mostly Alex's fault. Their coming over was John's idea, not Emily's, Alex was sure.

When she hung up she found Theresa watching, her eyes bright with curiosity. "Thank you," Alex said and walked out of the room, her dignity intact. Theresa didn't follow.

In the kitchen Alex sat down at the table and asked Gracie to fix her a sandwich. As she waited, she began to muse aloud.

"Since my granddaughter came, I've been thinking back over the years, Gracie. A long way back. How old were you when you came to work for us?"

"Seventeen, Miss Alex. I didn't marry George till I was nineteen."

"We could never have gotten along without you and George."

Gracie was only a few years younger than Alex, and she was a closer friend than Theresa had ever been. She probably knew more about this family than anyone else, and Alex wondered whimsically what secrets Gracie might be keeping.

These days younger help came in part-time to

156 take care of the heavy work, and someone as-
sisted George in his yard chores. They were all
growing older together and comfortably depen-
dent on one another. That was good in some
ways, difficult in others, since Theresa seemed to
be putting herself more and more in charge, and
Gracie and George weren't happy about that.
Lately, Alex hadn't felt strong enough to oppose
this less-than-subtle takeover.

Theresa didn't need the money she made
from her painted eggs. Juan Gabriel had left her
a good income. And Alex's will put almost everything in Theresa's hands. Though that might
change, now that her granddaughter had come
home. She would wait and see.

"Gracie, your mother worked for Marilyn
Macklin's parents, didn't she? Did you know
Marilyn well when she was a little girl?"

Slicing a garden tomato, Gracie nodded.
"Guess I was kind of a mama to Miss Marilyn
after her mama died. What happened to her still
makes me cry—like I lost one of my own."

Gracie and George had two grown children
and were grandparents to three. All had moved
north and seldom came home to visit. Alex recalled how often Marilyn had dropped in just to
see Gracie. Yet no one had thought to ask Gracie
questions after Marilyn died.

"Gracie," Alex said, "did Marilyn ever talk to

you about the book she was working on? The one about Juan Gabriel?"

Gracie added cucumber and lettuce and too much mayonnaise—a sign that she was thinking of something else.

"Take some of that off, please," Alex said.

"Sorry, Miss Alex. I forgot." Her eyes met Alex's across the table. "Miss Marilyn was upset about something for awhile before she died. She said once that what she was writing was important—things that ought to be told."

"Did she tell you what she meant?"

The sandwich took on a less juicy appearance and was cut into neat triangles, then placed on a blue plate. For a moment she stood, plate in hand, before giving it to Alex.

"All I know is she was scared to tell you about what she was going to write. She said maybe she'd figured something out, but she never said what it was. I just had a feeling that it was something Mr. J.G. said or did before he died."

Alex was unhappy to find that her hand trembled slightly when she took the plate from Gracie. *She* had never understood Juan Gabriel's last words before he died. Perhaps hadn't wanted to understand. There were some things it was better not to know.

"Thank you, Gracie. I'll take this outside." She glanced at her watch as she went down the back steps. There was time to get something for

158 Susan and still catch Peter before they left. She wanted to tell him what Gracie had told her. Perhaps Peter knew some piece of the puzzle that he hadn't recognized as such.

A certain excitement began to build in her as she crossed the lawn to Juan Gabriel's study. It grew from her decision to take Susan to Tangier Island. Of course it was difficult to remember that John was old now, as she was old. The picture in her mind still belonged to a vigorous young man who no longer existed. She was not yet sure whether she could ever admit the truth to him. She could only decide when she saw John and Susan face to face.

Right now she must concentrate on what she had come here for. She wanted to find a copy of *The Black Swan,* the novel Juan Gabriel had written during his early years in Virginia. When his main character of Tamara, a famous ballerina, had danced in *Swan Lake,* he had used Drina for his model and he had described her dancing so beautifully that the scene might give Susan a glimpse of what her own dancing had been like. However, it might be better if Susan didn't go on to read Juan Gabriel's description of the black swan's dancing.

Inside the boathouse study, Alex set the sandwich down on Juan Gabriel's desk—never dreaming that it was something she might regret in the hungry hours ahead.

Standing back from the wall of bookshelves, she studied the long rows, reading titles as she had not done for so many years. They were all here, the collection complete. Many posthumous editions had appeared—new reprints that were still read widely. As each new edition was published, she sent Gracie here to add to the collection, not always wanting the hurt of coming here herself.

Of course the fiercest pain of Juan Gabriel's death lay far in the past, but pangs of guilt over her betrayal could still rise to cut at her unexpectedly. Nevertheless, she could not regret those brief, glorious hours with John Gower. So there was still at times a disturbing ambivalence about the past.

It was time, she knew very well, for her to forgive herself, and she longed for Juan Gabriel's wisdom to guide her. Wherever he was now, he would be beyond anger or blame, and would harbor no ill will about the past.

"Help me to know what to do," she said softly as she moved on.

The Black Swan was the one novel Alex had never been able to finish reading. Not after she realized how cruelly Juan Gabriel had treated his ballet dancer. He had written about the white swan so beautifully, but the rest carried an undercurrent that frightened her, even though she knew this was fiction.

In the past Juan Gabriel Montoro's novels had often released anger, moral indignation—a desire to right what was wrong in society. Only in this book had he seemed to express a private anger. When she'd read it—that part of it she could stomach—she had been terrified that he had guessed about John Gower. But when it was published and he had seen how wounded she had been by his words, he had tried to reassure her.

It was then he had confessed to his long-hidden jealousy of Rudy Folkes. He had fallen in love with Drina, the dancer, while Rudy was still alive. Not until he had met her and then married her had he begun to know Alex, the woman, but even then his jealousy had lingered. He had not been able to reconcile himself with the past until he had poured his angry feelings into the novel.

He had made her understand, but Alex was still hurt that he had set down his feelings for the world to see. Not that many of his readers had known what he was saying. And none of this mattered anymore, except that it was not yet released from her own consciousness.

Now only one memory still tugged at old pain—that carving Juan Gabriel had done of the ebony swan. A carving which he had shown her only once, but which she had found in his hand after Dolores's fall. In a way, she had understood why he had done the carving. It had been another medium for releasing the same feelings that

had driven him when he wrote the novel. His use
of woodworking was not unusual. Working with
his hands seemed to help the creative process, and
there were examples of such carvings that she'd
placed in a glass case in the dining room. Each
one had been connected with some novel he'd
been writing at the time.

Nevertheless, he must have known how
wounding that particular carving would be to his
wife, and he had hidden it from her in his safe.
Had he *meant* for her to find it after his death?
Or had he simply waited too long to destroy it?

Today in the tower, when Susan had brought
out the box that contained the ebony swan, Alex
had prevented her from opening it, but now she
wondered if she should challenge Susan by showing her the carving. She had a deep wish to know
how her granddaughter would react. But she
could decide about that later.

Once more she turned her attention to the
titles on the shelves beside her. Titles that were as
familiar to her as members of her own family.
Perhaps she would sit in Juan Gabriel's great
armchair for a little while and open herself to
whatever might come through to strengthen and
guide her. She would need this before she returned to Tangier Island.

She put out her hand, touching the spines of
the books as she went past. The titles were arranged according to the year of publication, with

162 all of one edition placed together—book clubs, paperbacks, foreign translations. The American edition of *The Black Swan* would be with those books written after their move to Virginia.

She read a few titles aloud in Spanish, and when she came to the right place, she took the book down, and found that it felt thick and solid in her hand—dense with Juan Gabriel's words and thoughts. She had always marveled at her husband's ability to pour out more and more stories—all those millions of words, telling his tales to the very end of his life.

The heaviness of the book seemed to add immeasurably to her own weight. An illusion, of course. With full assurance she set her foot on the next floorboard, and heard an ominous cracking sound. She clung to the book as though it might save her as the wood splintered beneath her weight. There was no way to prevent herself from falling, however, and searing pain ripped through her leg as the broken floorboard slashed her flesh.

There was a crawl space underneath the floor, so she didn't break through completely. Only one leg dangled into empty space, caught by sharp daggers of wood. After a first effort to pull her leg free, she found the pain too great to struggle against.

When she reached out with her arms, she found she could lean upon solid floorboards and

gain some sort of purchase that would help her to
pull free of the trap more gently. But again in-
tense pain forced her to lie still, her body
stretched out upon the floor, her head resting on
her arms. *The Black Swan* lay under one hand.

Her only chance was to scream for help—
make someone hear. However, the cries she uttered sounded faint even to her own ears. Not
nearly as loud as the thumping of her heart and
the roaring in her blood.

The boathouse was too far from the main
house for anyone to hear. No one was likely to
look for her in this place—at least not right away,
since she came here so seldom. This would be the
last place Gracie and George would look.

In order to ease the pain, she made herself lie
quietly. She must *think*, find a way out of her
predicament. But her mind seemed to wander
unprofitably. Beyond the partition that separated
this higher section, she could hear the creek lapping, murmuring its song that had been part of
her life for so many years. Ordinarily it was a
peaceful sound but now there seemed nothing
peaceful about it.

Unwanted, unasked for—much too disturbing—the vision Susan had experienced in the
church returned to her mind. How could she
have seen those tombstones aboveground? How
could she have known that place existed? This
was not what Alex had hoped for when she'd

164 sent Susan back to the church. She had hoped that if anything came to Susan, it would be uplifting, inspirational. What had happened was mysterious and frightening, yet it increased her own belief in some powerful spirit that came into focus in that place. Perhaps under that vaulted ceiling, with its ancient walls and windows, the beholder was brought to respect, to revere whatever was there.

Never mind all that. For the moment only her own physical predicament was important. Once, long ago, she'd told Juan Gabriel that she didn't like him to work here alone. If an accident occurred or he became ill, he would never be able to call for help. He had solved this by having a bell installed near his desk—an alarm that would sound in the house if he needed assistance. The bell was undoubtedly still there, but too far away from where she had fallen, just as the food she hadn't eaten was too far away. What she had feared for her husband had happened to her.

It was difficult to breathe, and she began to feel light-headed and dizzy as her brain filled with drifting, cloudy pictures. *She must not faint.* In order to bring help she must remain fully conscious.

Once she felt sure that a bright light shone upon her—a spotlight. No, of course that wasn't applause she seemed to hear, but only the sound of water beyond the partition.

When the door opened, she didn't really *hear* 165
it. She only knew that John was there. A young,
strong, beautiful John, who had come to rescue
her. She needn't worry now.

She closed her eyes and gave herself joyfully
into his arms.

Six

*A*s Susan sat on the porch waiting for Peter, she found herself replaying what had happened in the tower room. When she'd knelt before the old trunk, a wonderful warmth had filled her, as though for the first time since she'd been a small child she could recover something of her mother. Touching Dolores's dresses, pulling out her own old toys that her mother too must have handled,

Susan had felt a tie with the past that had always eluded her.

Perhaps if she could release these inner feelings that had been unreachable for so long, she might dare to know more about herself. A lingering sadness concerning the present had surfaced in her. More for her grandmother than for herself. What were Alex's "dusty memories" that she had not been able to sweep away? The young woman Alex had once been had emerged in glimpses now and then—not nearly so remote as Susan had thought.

Haunting her thoughts most of all was that strange vision she had received in the church—and which had seemed to shock Alex. The impression of a place where tombstones had been crowded into yards, side by side, was still imprinted vividly in her mind. The images had seemed so sharp and clear that they must have meaning. Even the presence of that great, mysterious church haunted her. It had known centuries of existence—families who had come and gone, leaving their stamp upon history.

For just those few moments when she stood in the church, something had seemed to center around her, offering revelations she lacked the wisdom to understand.

So lost was Susan in these mysteries that she didn't notice Peter Macklin's car at the front of the house, or see him until he was halfway up the

168 walk. Until now she had refused to think very much about the reaction she'd had to seeing Peter again when she arrived, but now, discovering him suddenly before her, the Susan who had known Peter as a child seemed to take possession of her without warning. Perhaps love as strong as that which she'd felt for Peter as a little girl could never be entirely erased. All the more reason for her to be careful. She was not about to go down some road that could only lead to more hurt and disillusionment.

Peter walked with his head down, as though lost in his own troubled thoughts. When he looked up and saw her, he smiled, though the lines between his eyes remained. Instinctively, she wanted to touch and smooth them away. Of course that was just her nurturing nature. It meant nothing more.

But she was much too aware of emotions she wanted to dismiss, and her smile was awkward and self-conscious. "Hello, Peter. I'm sorry my grandmother has given you this chore. If you need to cancel for any reason, I'll certainly understand."

Inwardly she told the foolish child who was prattling on to be still—or at least to grow up.

He studied her for a moment, as though uncertain about what he wanted to say.

"Don't worry, this isn't a chore. Suppose we get started now, if you're ready."

As they walked to his car, he explained where they were going. "Since you've met some of the Townsends, I thought you might like to have lunch at The Mulberry Tree, the restaurant Gilbert Townsend has created out of an old mansion."

Thinking of the uncomfortable meeting with Gilbert at the church, Susan wasn't sure she wanted to see him again, but she couldn't say this to Peter, so she agreed.

"What did you do this morning?" he asked when he had turned the car north through stands of loblolly pine.

She avoided mention of the church and the strange meetings with Gilbert and Hallie Townsend. Instead, she told him about going with Alex to the tower room and finding the old trunk that held all the treasures of her early childhood.

"You know, Peter, every time I'm with my grandmother I have a sense that she's holding something back. She's not sure of me yet, and I have no way to get past her guard."

"Give her time. She needs you in her life, Susan. Ever since I've known Alex Montoro, she's seemed a lonely woman. Yet she doesn't allow anyone to come too close to her. Perhaps you'll be the one who breaks through finally. Sometimes I have a sense that she's onstage, playing a role, and that none of us knows who she really is. Or even what play she's acting in."

"All that wasted talent!" Susan spoke regretfully. "She told me a little this morning about how she came to be a dancer. I don't understand how she could give up a successful career and never dance again."

"Sometimes I've wondered if dancing could really have been that important to her, if she only believed in herself while Rudy Folkes was alive. She gave it all up too easily."

"Is there something else that's more important to her?"

"Perhaps, but, if there is, she hasn't discovered it yet."

She glanced at the man in the seat beside her, and saw once more the lingering sadness that lay close to the surface in Peter Macklin.

"Isn't it a bit late for such a discovery?" she asked.

"I'd like to think it's never too late. Not as long as we can breathe and find the courage to stay alive."

Was he thinking of his own changed life since his wife's death—his closed office and the patients he no longer treated? She had a strong feeling that he would survive what had happened and find a new life for himself.

"I think you must be a very good doctor, Peter."

That seemed to startle him. "What do you know about me as a doctor?"

"You listen. Not all doctors know how to listen. They're too busy pontificating."

He didn't say anything, but the sadness remained. She went on more matter-of-factly.

"You mentioned that my grandmother hasn't been well. Can you tell me about that?"

"It's nothing that can't be managed successfully. Her heart shows an irregular beat at times, and her blood pressure can go too high. Though mostly these things are under control—when she behaves herself."

"What medications are you giving her?"

"That's right—you're a nurse, aren't you, Susy? She's not on any drugs. I use drugs only for emergencies, or when nothing else works. Blood pressure is one of the simplest things to bring down with natural therapies. Even her benign heart arrhythmia can be controlled without drugs."

He had caught her interest. "How do you manage that?"

"A good high-fiber diet with no sugar. Sugar's the first thing to eliminate. Garlic is an old remedy, and since it comes in capsules these days, one doesn't have to become antisocial to take it in large doses. Potassium is important. Calcium and magnesium are good for both blood pressure and the heart. I hope you know about the fish oils, and the omega-3 oils? The Japanese —who are often way ahead of us—have done a

172 lot of research on Co-Q10, which we all need to take. Alex has been doing fine on these supplements for a long time. Of course emotional upsets need to be avoided."

"Which is where I come in?" His list of natural remedies had left her hopeful, but she knew what Colin would have asked. "Has this approach been proven with double-blind tests, Peter?"

He snorted rudely. "They've been tested thousands of times by recovering patients. Only drug companies have the millions of dollars it takes to do double-blind tests. Double-blind doesn't succeed in this field anyway, because all these nutrients work together. It's almost pointless to pick out one and test it alone. Since nobody can own a vitamin or any other nutrient, the money for testing is just not there, even if it would work. The most important thing about what I'm doing is that none of these things has side effects. Most drugs can do a lot of damage, as you undoubtedly know. That's why this is the future, Susan. Something that works can't be stopped. The propaganda against what we're doing is just another sign of panic. All patients need the freedom of choice to decide on their own treatment and doctor."

Susan nodded. A new medical world was opening for her.

Peter went on. *"Not proven* doesn't mean *un-*

proven. About three hundred years ago it was discovered that blood circulates. This was *proven.* Does that mean that blood didn't circulate until somebody was able to prove it?"

She laughed delightedly. "I think I've been waiting to meet you all my life, Dr. Macklin."

They had both relaxed, and Peter seemed pleased by her interest. "I like to think of myself as a doctor who calls on all available therapies for help. There's so much that the medical profession hasn't paid enough attention to—herbal remedies, homeopathy, acupuncture. And, of course, there are all the ways the mind can be taught to assist the body. We're only beginning to tap into that. It's not a matter any longer of curing a disease."

"What do you mean? Diseases are real enough, and they have to be dealt with."

"That's true, but we need to look at the whole man and treat the patient instead of being concerned about something to which we've given a fancy name. Cause is important, and prevention is the key for me. All the mechanisms to achieve good health are given us at birth, yet we spend a good part of our lives destroying them. What I want to do with every patient, when it's still possible, is to strengthen the immune system."

Listening, Susan remembered the excited young boy she had known. Now that his interest was aroused, the man was coming to life in the

174 same way. Her own warm response startled her. It was not only his words, but the man, to whom she was responding so readily, and she wasn't ready for this. She knew she must be very careful.

"How else are you treating my grandmother's heart problem?" she asked, glad to find that her voice betrayed nothing of the inner leap she had taken.

"I'm giving her L-Carnitine and taurine, to begin with."

"Amino acids?"

"Yes. They help the heart to regain its normal rhythm. And we've found the herb hawthorn to be especially helpful. All the other nutrients I've mentioned work together with these, and the result is gratifying."

"Perhaps you're dealing with an enlightened group, but the patients I've been seeing are too much in awe of their doctors to object to anything they recommend."

"That's changing too. The public is beginning to demand treatments that work. You'll see, something will happen. It has already begun."

"With your approach are there always cures?"

"I wish I could promise that, but we're still learning as we go, and there are too many variables. Alex can indulge in some tempting sugar dessert and stir up her heart, even though she knows better."

"How can I learn about these things? Did you take a course, or is it self-taught?"

"No courses yet, but there are hundreds of books and papers, if you want to learn. I can loan you all you care to read."

"I'd like that." She knew Colin Cheney would dismiss what Peter was telling her. But then, Colin was an expert when it came to a closed mind.

"There must be a good deal of opposition to what you're doing."

"There is. Most medical journals won't print our papers—even when the findings might change the status quo. But the grapevine *is* working, and young doctors are beginning to look past the blockade of orthodox opinion."

Susan became increasingly aware of the contrast between this vital, interested man and the one who had picked her up at the house. The very contrast troubled her, and she tried to put her feelings into words.

"What about you, Peter? I hear you've closed your office and are turning away your patients. How can you bear to do that when you have so much to offer?"

For a time he drove in silence. When he spoke again, the vitality had gone from his voice.

"I hope this is a temporary hiatus, though I'm not too hopeful right now. In spite of the grand jury's dismissal for lack of evidence, there's a

176 cloud over me. Either I had a hand in Marilyn's death—or someone else did. The police don't have a clue as to what happened, and neither do I. I'm still their best suspect. So until Marilyn's death is cleared up, I won't force my patients to make a choice."

Again she heard a deep sadness in his voice. There was so much more to consider here than the loss of his practice as a doctor.

"I've been hearing about the return of the manuscript your wife was working on. Does that have any helpful significance?"

"No one seems to know who left it at the library or why. Nor do we know why it was taken in the first place."

There were no answers, and they were both silent for a time.

Then Peter said, "We'll be at the inn soon, so I'd better warn you that we're meeting someone there. Priscilla Bates was Marilyn's good friend. In fact, when Marilyn and I decided to separate, she was going to move in with Priscilla temporarily in Richmond. This morning Priscilla phoned to say she wanted to see me—something to do with Marilyn. So I suggested she meet us at the inn, since I'd already planned to have lunch with you. I hope you don't mind."

Susan murmured that of course it was fine, but her attention was elsewhere. That Peter and Marilyn had intended to separate left her curious.

Peter reached out to pat her arm. "We're nearly there. I'm glad you're along, Susan."

He turned the car off onto a straight, paved drive that led between a long row of mulberry trees. The trees cast thick black pools of noon-time shade along each side of the way.

"The early idea," Peter said, "was to obtain silkworms and mulberry trees from Japan, as an adjunct product to tobacco. However, the silk-worms wouldn't produce and died in our climate, so a silk industry never developed in Virginia. These trees were left from that project."

A wide Victorian house stood across the end of the drive—white clapboard, with a slanting red roof of recent vintage, and decorative dark green shutters. Except for a touch of carpenter's gothic on the edging of peaked roofs, none of the fanciful touches of the Montoro house existed here. The Mulberry Tree, for all its new life, was a dignified dowager, handsomely conservative. They left the car in a parking space and went up a red brick step to a roofed portico. The door stood open, and they entered a hall that was graciously wide. Stairs, carpeted in dark maroon, curved up along the wall on one side, and parlor and dining room doors opened on either hand. This was a bed-and-breakfast inn, as well as a restaurant open to the public.

Eric Townsend came to welcome them, tall and blond and assured to the point of arrogance.

178 He gave them a wide, false smile, and she couldn't help but wonder if he'd ever make it as an actor. "Hello, Susan. Hi, Peter. I have a perfect table for you."

He led the way to an open gallery that was clearly a recent addition, and which overlooked the Rappahannock River. Iron frontwork patterned in a leaf design protected the outer rim of the gallery. Overhead, a slanted roof and awnings kept the sun away from diners. Only two other tables were occupied at the moment, and theirs was in a secluded corner.

Eric presented large menu cards with a flourish. Aware of Susan's attention, he grinned cockily. "Don't mind me. I might as well make a performance of waiting on a table, since this is the classic job for an out-of-work actor."

How much like his father he seemed—both in appearance and slightly flamboyant manner. But while Gilbert exuded confidence, Susan suspected that Eric's manner was something he clearly put on for protection.

She gave her attention to the generous array of foods on the menu, conscious of the pleasure of being here with Peter Macklin. No matter what questions threatened the future, she wanted to enjoy this moment.

A waiter filled their water glasses and brought a warm loaf of bread in a covered basket.

When they'd both ordered crab cakes, along

with salads, Eric's pencil halted, and Susan looked up to see that his attention had been caught by a white cruiser cutting its way through Rappahannock waters below their gallery.

"Someday I'm going to own one of those babies," Eric said dreamily.

"You're expecting an inheritance?" Peter asked.

"That—or a good role in a movie. There will be a way."

No one pursued that, and Peter told him that Priscilla Bates would be joining them. At once Eric looked interested.

"Is that the Bates who writes a column for a Richmond paper?"

"Do you know her?" Peter asked.

"Only by sight. I'll keep an eye out for her." Eric gave Susan a look that was somehow challenging and went off toward the kitchen.

When Susan lapsed into thoughtful silence, Peter asked, "You don't like Eric, do you?"

"Both Eric and his father make me uncomfortable, though I feel a little sorry for Hallie."

"As we all should," Peter said. "However, Eric's had a rough time growing up. His mother decided that she'd had enough of marriage to Gilbert while Eric was still a little boy, and she took off for parts unknown. His father's only interest in him then seemed to be to discipline him. Hallie was always on his side, and of course Eric learned how to twist his aunt around his finger. She's stood up to Gilbert for him many times. Always the little mother. Even though she's younger than her brother and sister, she used to mother them both. Of course Emily's out of reach now—having married John Gower and moved to Tangier Island long ago. And Gilbert doesn't pay much attention to anything Hallie says if it opposes what he wants."

As the cruiser glided past, Susan glimpsed passengers in deck chairs watching their gallery with lazy interest. A small boy waved, and Susan waved back.

"There was a time," Peter said, "when that might have been a gunboat out there. This house has a collection of musket balls from the War of 1812. There's even a place where a shot went clear through and embedded itself in a far wall."

Susan's thoughts were focused on more recent history. "What can you tell me about Juan Gabriel, Peter?"

"I was only a young boy when I knew Mr. Montoro, and I thought him a bit frightening. He seemed terribly old and distant and austere. I'm sure he loved Alex, but she was so much younger, and perhaps he worried about her. I still remember the way his eyes followed her when they were in the same room. Even though he must have quieted down a bit from those fiery years in Peru that he wrote about in his early books, there was still some residue of Spanish excitability. Though I saw him really angry only once."

"What happened?"

Peter hesitated. "I'm not sure I should have brought this up. I was too young to understand what was going on, and I may have gotten things wrong."

"That's okay—please tell me."

"It must have been some months before your mother died. Juan Gabriel had a fight with your father—a physical fight. The Montoros always fascinated me, so I watched and listened to more than I was supposed to."

"Did what happened have any bearing on my mother's death?"

Peter sliced bread for them both, postponing an answer. Susan waited, and after a moment he went on, sounding as though he needed to convince himself.

"Your mother's death was an accident, so of course the fight had nothing to do with that."

"I wonder. I wonder how much everything ties together. Something doesn't feel right to me. There's been concealment about so much that happened. Alex told me about my mother's fall in a flat sort of way—as though she held back her real feelings."

"I can understand that. She's never recovered from Dolores's death. Perhaps some sort of healing will come to her through you, Susan."

182   She thought of the unexpected moment of closeness with her grandmother in the tower room this morning. Susan had reached out to her, but she still wasn't sure what the reception to her gesture had really been.

"Tell me about the fight Juan Gabriel had with my father."

"It happened in that shed down near the water on the other side of the lawn from the boathouse. Your father liked to work with his hands when he wasn't teaching. He used to make fine articles of furniture. Benches, chairs, tables—really handsome pieces. Did your father continue that work when he moved to New Mexico?"

"No, he must have lost interest. He lost interest in a great deal, I'm afraid." One of the things he'd lost interest in was his daughter. "Go on," she said to Peter.

"That day Juan Gabriel went down to Lawrence's workshop. I was outside mowing the lawn with a riding mower I was learning to use. I stopped the machine so I could listen to those angry voices. I couldn't hear the words, so I don't know what the quarrel was about, but the door was open, and suddenly your father came flying through, hurled out by the old man. I never saw anyone so mad as your grandfather was that day. I think if he'd had a gun in his hand, he might have killed Lawrence Prentice. His anger made up for the difference in their ages and physical strength. But Lawrence had a temper too, and when he got up from the grass he turned on Mr. Montoro and knocked *him* down. He might have done worse, if George hadn't come running out of the house to pull Lawrence off. Your father went back to his workshop and slammed the door, while Mr. Montoro just lay there on the ground, not moving. I helped George carry him into the house, and Gracie ran upstairs to find Dolores and your grandmother. Juan Gabriel suffered a stroke the next day and was confined to his wheelchair for the months before he went into a coma."

"Then, when my mother died, my father took me away."

"Gracie really pulled your grandmother through. Alex had lost her daughter, and she lost you. A few months later she lost Juan Gabriel too. Though, at least, his death was expected, and he had lived a long, long life of distinguished achievement. Alex didn't want to see even her old friends, so my parents couldn't be as helpful to her as they'd have liked to be. I still did odd jobs for George, so I was around and saw how apathetic she was. I felt helpless because I was too young to be useful to her. For me, she'd always been—oh, I don't know—a magical sort of person. Then all the magic was gone, and she seemed older than she does now."

"Did you ever learn what the quarrel was about between my father and my grandfather?"

"The only person around who talked to me was Theresa, and I don't think she knew much of anything. She was only a little older than I was. I'm not sure she ever really loved your grandmother, but she had a strong sense of duty, and loyalty to Juan Gabriel. He was her only relative in this country. If Alex knew what happened between the two men, she never talked to me about it. Luckily, all her spirit and drive couldn't be held down forever, and she gradually came back to life. She's kept herself busy with various civic projects—especially the preservation of historic landmarks. But sometimes I get the feeling that there's something smoldering inside her, and it worries me. She's more fragile than she lets anyone see. Marilyn's death was especially hard for her—partly because she is fond of me. But then, everyone liked Marilyn." Peter stopped and looked around the room. "I wonder what's happened to Priscilla?"

A waitress brought their salads, while Eric hovered attentively, perfect in his role—though relaxing now and then when he caught Susan's eye. His message was clear: *We both know this isn't who I am.*

The movement of the sun-splashed surface of the Rappahannock was hypnotic. Susan watched as a log or a bit of flotsam drifted past, offering a focus for her eyes—though an absent focus, since a new heaviness of spirit had settled over her. When she had sat down at this table, she'd wanted only to enjoy being with Peter. A chance like this might not ever come again. But now all the unanswered questions had taken on a threatening cast. Too much that seemed alarming remained just out of sight, and certainly beyond comprehension. She hoped Priscilla Bates would come soon, so they could finish their meal and leave.

When Eric approached their table leading a tall, determined-looking woman, Susan suspected that something else disturbing was about to happen. Peter rose to greet Marilyn's friend, and introduced her to Susan.

Priscilla regarded her with an intent interest. An intelligent woman, Susan thought, though perhaps a little sharp. Her dark eyes possessed a searching quality, as though she questioned everything she saw. Graying hair had been wound into a severe knob on top of her head, somehow adding to her air of brisk efficiency. This woman, she suspected, wouldn't stand for much nonsense.

"How are you, Priscilla?" Peter said. "We've saved a place for you."

Priscilla dropped her carryall to the floor beside her chair and sat down. "Only coffee, please," she told Eric. "Peter, I'm sorry to be late. A last-minute crisis at the office in Richmond."

186 Then she gave her full attention to studying Susan. "So you're Alex Montoro's granddaughter?"

Peter said, "Susan's also an old friend. Tell me what has happened to make you want to see me in such a rush?"

"It's not all that sudden. I've been sitting on this problem and wondering what to do ever since Marilyn died. This morning I heard about her manuscript turning up at the library in Kilmarnock wrapped in brown paper and left at the door. It seems that the notes for the last chapters are missing. I have my spies, as you can tell."

"I suppose Hallie called you?" Peter asked wryly. "She's our private grapevine."

"Right! So I knew I'd better talk with you."

Priscilla began to search her bag. "Do you mind if I smoke?" She didn't wait for agreement, but took out a cigarette and lighted it quickly. After a few puffs she continued. "I've been losing sleep wondering what Marilyn would want me to do. I know there were questions when the manuscript of the biography Marilyn was writing disappeared. I have no idea why it was taken or why it's turned up now. I know that Marilyn was still trying to make up her mind about how to handle the closing chapters and was partly in disagreement with Alex. She needed to make a decision concerning which version to use. She made a number of notes about the ending and I found them among her things after she died. Since the manuscript had disappeared, they didn't seem to matter. But now I've begun to wonder. Did Marilyn talk to you about any of this, Peter?"

"I'm afraid she didn't talk to me about much of anything in the months before her death. You know we'd decided to separate."

"Marilyn always spoke affectionately of you, Peter. I suppose she needed to be on her own again. Even back in college, when we roomed together, she was an independent woman. She used to say she would never marry—until she fell in love with you."

"I understand," Peter said quietly. "We never meant to hurt each other, and we'd have stayed friends."

"I know. What happened to her is so terrible that it's still hard to believe. I have a strong feeling that I should give these pages to Alex and let her decide what to do. I hoped you might advise me on this, Peter."

"I don't know what to tell you," he said.

"Well, then I'll just have to make that decision myself." She discarded her half-smoked cigarette in the ashtray, which the attentive Eric had set beside her, and lit another.

"I keep thinking about that manuscript," Peter said, "and about what connection it might have had to Marilyn's death. Why were Marilyn and Alex in disagreement?"

Like Susan, Priscilla studied the river, look-

188 ing off toward the bridge by which she had come across from the direction of Richmond. When she answered, her own puzzlement was obvious.

"I don't understand why it should have mattered at this late date, but Marilyn told me that Mrs. Montoro was very sensitive when it came to her husband's reputation. Juan Gabriel killed a man before they left Peru—a political murder. The man was a thorough scoundrel, and it was done in a moment of high passion, of which Juan Gabriel was capable. His powerful friends got him and his wife out of the country quietly. As a noted author, he would have been welcome anywhere in the world, but Virginia's history drew him here. Peru was probably glad to let him go without an explosive scandal and trial."

"But if this is what Marilyn wanted to put into the last chapters, it can't be relevant now. You'd better talk to Alex about this."

"I want to. However, there was one other thing Marilyn told me that she'd set down in her notes. It seems that just before he died Juan Gabriel came out of his coma and managed to speak a few words. I've read the notes and they didn't make any sense to me, though Marilyn thought they were connected with Dolores's death in some way. With the manuscript missing, it never seemed important to do anything about the notes. But now Mrs. Montoro may want to see the book finished, and this could be important. I think she should see them before they are turned over to the police—if that's what is supposed to happen."

Peter looked doubtful. "I hate to see Alex upset all over again."

"Perhaps what Marilyn wrote in summing up might pull things together for her. I suspect that Marilyn's viewpoint might be slightly different from Mrs. Montoro's."

Priscilla was silent for a moment, finishing her coffee, crunching out her cigarette. Then she pushed back her chair and held out her hand to Susan.

"I'm very glad to know Mrs. Montoro's granddaughter. I must go now. Thanks for seeing me, Peter."

She seemed in a hurry, as though she'd said all she meant to say and wanted to be off.

Peter stood up as she left, and Susan watched her disappear through the gallery. Eric came to see her out, and Susan wondered about his always hovering presence. How much of their talk had he managed to hear? Not that it really mattered, she supposed.

"If you're finished, perhaps we'd better go, Susan." Peter sounded dispirited. The meeting with Priscilla must have brought too many things connected with Marilyn sharply into his mind.

As they drove back to the house, he was silent, lost in increasing gloom. Knowing so little, there was no way in which Susan could help, and she felt it was better to be quiet.

Not until they were nearly there did she ask a question. "Will you tell Alex about Priscilla and that she has Marilyn's notes?"

"Perhaps I'd better wait and see what Priscilla does. I can't be sure what's involved, or how much anything I might say would upset Alex."

A picture she didn't care for came into Susan's mind. She could imagine a stew coming to a boil. All those tiny, unrelated bits floating quietly on the surface, with the bubbling pressure underneath and out of sight. Then a bubble would break through here, and another one there, until the whole pot was a roiling mass—ready to spill over disastrously. That sort of boiling seemed to be going on right now beneath the surface of their lives. If it broke through, would there be any stopping it? Perhaps Marilyn's death had turned the heat down for a while, but now it was warming up again. Because someone was frightened about the truth coming out. *What* truth? And what role had the young Susan played?

Peter almost spoke her thoughts aloud. "Perhaps you're the catalyst, Susan. You were here when Dolores died. Alex has always believed that her death was no accident. You may have seen what happened. The child in you may know a great deal more than you realize. Marilyn did drop a hint or two that she was onto something.

But I don't think she'd worked it out and she never really talked to me about it."

"And you think I have blocked out of my memory something that might return at any moment and be a threat to someone?"

"It's possible. Some accidental stimulus could trigger a return of everything you've buried because it was too terrible for a small child to face."

"I don't seem to remember *anything,*" she told him, and heard a rising alarm in her own voice.

He took his hand from the wheel to touch her arm. "Don't try to force it, Susan. But if you do remember something about what happened, will you tell me right away? No matter how trivial it might seem, tell me before you talk to Alex."

She promised uneasily. Perhaps it would be best if she turned her back on remembering and let everything stay as it was.

When Peter pulled up in front of the house, Gracie was watching for them, and came running down the drive, excited and unlike her usual quiet self.

"Have you seen Miss Alex?" she cried. "Or heard from her?"

Peter got out of the car at once. "What's happened, Gracie?"

"We can't find her anywhere. She was going to have her lunch outdoors and then go upstairs for a nap. But she doesn't ever sleep so long, and

192 when I went to see, she'd never been down on her bed at all."

"Did she go out in her car?" Peter asked.

"That's what I don't like. Her car's in the garage. Besides, Miss Alex don't even go across the street without telling me where she's going. She isn't anywhere."

"We'll help you look for her," Susan said. "I suppose you've already tried the trunk room in the tower?"

"She's not there. I even went into that old shed where your papa used to work on stuff he liked to make. Of course we called and called, but nobody answered."

"What about Juan Gabriel's study?" Peter asked.

"George looked in there and shouted fit to wake the dead. But she's nowhere close by. I'm getting scared, Mr. Peter."

Pete evoked his bedside manner. "Don't worry, Gracie. We'll all look again."

Susan sensed concern under his quiet manner. The meeting at The Mulberry Tree with Priscilla Bates had not been reassuring.

"I'll look again in Juan Gabriel's study," she offered. "Alex mentioned a book of his she wanted me to read."

Gracie looked doubtful, but they separated to go in different directions.

Susan ran down to the boathouse and opened

the door to the study. The interior was dim and quiet. She spoke her grandmother's name tentatively, hesitating to raise echoes in this place. A lamp burned near the big desk, but the rest of the long room was filled with shadows.

For a moment she was held by a sense of awe. Juan Gabriel Montoro was a name she had heard since she was very young—a name that had never seemed related to her. Even her father, who had admired his writing, and used his books in his literature classes, never referred to him as her grandfather. So for her this room was a place where a legendary figure had written his distinguished novels. Alex had been famous for a time too, but now she was a living, fascinating woman to whom Susan had begun to feel close. Juan Gabriel was still remote.

She turned on more lamps, so that the shadows retreated to the far corners of the room. As she looked around the big room for some sign of her grandmother's presence, she saw the blue plate on the mahogany desk, with the sandwich Alex had not eaten. At least, she had come here. But why had she set down her food and gone away?

The stillness, with only the lapping sound of the creek beyond the far wall, seemed almost eerie—as though some presence lurked in the shadows. A sudden urge to escape from this place was

194 strong, but she refused the first prompting of panic and moved on to explore the room.

A great bank of books covered most of one wall. If Alex had come here for a copy of *The Black Swan,* she would have found it there. Susan moved toward the wall of books, and as she did so, a faint scent reached her. That was surely the Worth perfume her grandmother always wore. But if she had gone out of the room, would perfume have lingered so clearly on the air?

A long refectory table of heavy Spanish design stretched before the wall of books. Suddenly fearful of what she might find beyond the table, Susan walked around one end. Alex lay stretched on the floor. Her head rested on one crooked arm, as though she'd gone to sleep. But she was not asleep. One leg stretched out to its full length, while the other twisted out of sight between splintered boards in the floor, where she had fallen. Avoiding the broken board, Susan knelt to feel her grandmother's thready pulse, and saw the way her darkened lashes contrasted with her pallor.

When Alex did not respond to her name, or to Susan's touch, she ran outside, shouting for help. Gracie and Peter came from different directions, running down toward the boathouse. Susan led them to where Alex lay, and Peter worked gently to remove the sharp boards that held her leg in their vise. George was summoned, and he and Peter carried Alex into the house. As she was laid upon her bed, she moaned slightly and her eyelids fluttered open.

Seven

She could hear voices and knew that she lay on something soft. Her own bed? A distant pain throbbed somewhere in her body, but she couldn't identify it. She seemed to have been drifting in and out of consciousness ever since they'd found her and carried her into the house.

Perhaps she hadn't wanted to come back to the real world, preferring John Gower's arms. Of

course that was only a dream. Reality seemed un-
utterably depressing. It would be easy enough to
let her heart stop beating and just slip away. She
knew that something terrible awaited her if she
returned to full realization. Perhaps it was safer
to release her hold on life, since nothing really
mattered anymore. Where was that welcoming
tunnel of light they talked about?

"Come back, Alex. You're all right now.
You're not badly hurt. *Come back.*"

She could feel Peter's fingers on her pulse,
and suddenly her heartbeat steadied, and she
opened her eyes to see him bending over her.

"That's better," he told her. "I want you to
rest now. I'll give you something that will help."

She lacked the energy to respond, but he
seemed to understand that she'd heard.

On the other side of the bed a voice spoke
softly. "I'll be right here, Grandmother. Tell me
if you want anything."

That was Susan—Dolores's daughter. Perhaps there was something to come back for, after
all. She almost opened her eyes, but she'd felt the
prick of the injection Peter had given her, and
her lids felt too heavy to lift.

Another, harsher voice broke through to her.
"You should never have gone into that place
alone, Alex! All those rotten wooden floors! You
could have hurt yourself much more seriously."

She opened her eyes and stared at Theresa,

198 standing at the foot of her bed. This was what she had no wish to return to—the truth of that broken board. Even though she lacked the strength, that must be faced. Carefully, she tried out her voice. The sound was faint, rather tremulous—a voice she didn't know. Nevertheless, the room hushed, as everyone around her listened. Even Gracie, who was clearing away the bandages and syringe Peter had used, stopped near the door to listen.

"There were no rotten boards in Juan Gabriel's study. There was no reason for that board to break."

It took all her strength to say the words, and now there was just one more matter she must deal with before she could obey Peter and rest. She spoke the name that had come into her mind. "Tangier."

"It's all right," Theresa told her quickly. "I've phoned the island and they won't expect you. Emily sends her love."

John had known, Alex thought dreamily. John had come because she had needed him. She closed her eyes and went to sleep.

A soft stirring sounded in the room—an exodus, though Alex didn't hear. When Theresa followed Gracie out to the kitchen, Peter beckoned Susan and she came into the hall with him.

"Her heart is fine," he assured her. "The blackout probably came from a drop in blood sugar. That can happen with a fright. When she wakes up, give her something to eat. Perhaps toast and herb tea with a little honey. I've given her a very light sedative, so she won't be knocked out completely."

"I'll stay with her and be there when she wakes up."

"Good. I feel better with you here, Susan. You won't upset your grandmother as Theresa sometimes does. Theresa doesn't realize how abrasive she can be."

Susan suspected that Theresa realized very well. "Do you think that board Alex fell through could have been deliberately damaged?"

Peter looked so weary that Susan wished she could withdraw the question. He was already carrying a load he couldn't put down, and his meeting with his wife's friend hadn't helped.

She put her hand on his arm, longing to offer comfort. "Never mind, Peter. We can deal with all that later."

He touched her hand in quick thanks and went away.

When she turned to go back to Alex, she found Theresa blocking the hall door, her eyes dark with familiar malice.

"Wouldn't you like to remember what happened when your mother fell?" Theresa asked.

Susan stared at her uncertainly. Whatever was coming was sure to be unpleasant.

"Your grandmother doesn't want you to know, but *I* think you should be told the truth. *You* pushed Dolores down the stairs, Susan. You were to blame for her death."

Her defenses rose instantly. "I don't believe that! One thing I do remember is how much I loved my mother."

"Of course you did. That's what made it so terrible. You were too small to understand the result of the tantrum you threw."

Susan walked to the door and Theresa saw something in her face that made her step out of the way. Without speaking, Susan returned to her grandmother's room and sat down beside the bed, shaking. Theresa was making this up, of course. She had to be. Now, somehow, she must quiet the chatter of her own mind.

The copy of *The Black Swan* that had been found in the boathouse under Alex's hand, had been brought in and placed on Alex's bed table. Susan picked it up—the perfect distraction. This was an English translation, of course, since Juan Gabriel had written all his books in his native Spanish. His novels usually ran five hundred pages or more. Later perhaps she would read the entire book, but right now she wanted that special passage her grandmother had mentioned. She riffled through the pages, watching for a ballet sequence.

When she came to the place where the white swan danced, the words brought the scene vividly to life. The viewpoint was that of a man who watched from the wings as the dancer moved in the golden aura of the spotlight that followed her. In the background, the young swans of the *corps de ballet* held their motionless pose.

As she read, Susan could visualize the scene clearly. The dancer in the story had another name, of course—Tamara—and the man was apparently her lover. But it was Drina's dancing Juan Gabriel described. For this shining, immortalized scene in print, Drina danced again.

The words brought to life the long-limbed grace of the dancer, her marvelous control, the perfection of every classic step—yet all the while conveying to her audience a sense that every movement was the spontaneous embodiment of natural grace. The man who watched understood the emotion of the dancer and the love she felt for her human prince. For the prince, but not for the watcher? There seemed to be anger as well as love in the intensity of his watching.

Susan glanced toward the bed, and was startled to find Alex's eyes open. If Alexandrina Montoro chose not to succumb to a sedative, of course she would not. Her look was wide and very bright.

"You've seen Drina dance as Odette, haven't you? Juan Gabriel wrote of her so beautifully. Perhaps he understood her dancing in a way that Rudy never could. He knew the passion a dancer must bring to such a role. Once the technique is mastered, feeling is all that matters."

Susan sat very still, waiting for her to go on.

"Of course the music was my inspiration, guiding me. And I had wonderful partners who supported me and helped me to bring everything I could give to my white swan."

Alex had slipped from the third-person "Drina" into speaking of herself.

"Did you feel the same about dancing the black swan?" Susan asked.

A smile touched Alex's mouth—a small, wicked smile. "Oh, even more! Rudy always used the word 'evil' when he told me what he wanted from me, and I had a marvelous time in the *pas de deux* when Odile dances with the prince she is stealing from Odette. Black swan and white swan —evil against good. All embodied in Drina. And yet—" She paused as though she might have said more about the black swan.

Susan spoke softly. "How I wish I could have seen you."

"There are the photographs. But of course photographs stand still, while I was all movement on a stage. I could do those thirty-two *fouettés* to perfection—while now I have trouble crossing a street."

Susan marked the passage in the book so as not to lose it, as she listened. "Tell me more about that time."

"How Rudy used to torment me in rehearsals! He always wanted more of me than I could manage—or so I thought. He drew from me what I never believed I could give. It was his *belief* that filled me every time I danced. Only Juan Gabriel understood my lack of confidence—understood why I stopped dancing. At the time, I sometimes hated Rudy for his tyranny and wanted to escape—until it was all over and I was really free of him. Only then did I realize that a portion of myself disappeared when he died."

"You must have grieved for your lost ability to dance."

"Not as much as I might have expected, and only at intervals. When I stopped dancing I began to live. Drina disappeared when Juan Gabriel came into my life and turned me into someone new."

Susan puzzled aloud: "You sound as though you only became what someone else believed you to be. You sound as though there was no *you*."

"I suppose it was like that. For a time. Perhaps it takes us all a good many years to find out the real person we want to become. In the mean-

204 time we may even become a person we no longer care much about knowing."

"So which are you, Grandmother?"

Alex closed her eyes. "Sometimes I'm not sure. White swan? Black swan? Or neither?"

"Neither, I think. You are special—your own person. You are someone I want to know. And of course I don't know you at all yet."

Alex smiled sadly, and once more seemed to drowse off . . . Susan sat quietly, listening to the sound of her grandmother's even breathing, so that when Alex spoke suddenly, Susan started.

"*En pointe* I was nearly five feet, eight inches tall. It was hard to find partners for me, though Rudy said my height didn't matter. He said any dancer who partnered me would be raised to whatever height was required. I wonder what would have become of me if he had lived. But I must stop this and rest, Susan. I need to regain my strength. Tomorrow I will get up and try this damaged leg. Because soon, very soon, we must go to Tangier Island."

"Why?" Susan asked. "Why do you want to take me there so badly?"

"I think you'll see when we go. Be quiet now, my dear. Let me sleep."

She seemed to drop off instantly, as though still in command of her body, as she had been when she danced.

Susan noted the page numbers of the Swan

Queen's solo, so that she could find them again, and turned ahead, searching for that other passage she knew would be there.

The black swan's *pas de deux* with the prince came late in the novel, and again the man who loved the dancer stood in the wings, watching. Reading Juan Gabriel's passionate words, Susan sensed a difference in the writing. The description of the dancer in her black tutu, with black feathers crowning her dark hair, seemed to stir some new emotion in the writer. Anger, perhaps, at the betrayal of the prince by the black swan? That betrayal that would result in the swan queen's death. The man in the wings no longer watched with mixed feelings. He clearly hated the dancer, and Susan had a frightening feeling that when she came off the stage, he would treat her in some violent way.

Could this possibly be how the author of these words had felt about his wife—resenting, even hating the ambivalence of white swan–black swan in her character?

Suddenly Susan didn't want to know how the novel ended. Dark questions seemed to lie beneath words that almost sprang from the page in the angry power of the writing. Yet Peter had spoken of the devotion Juan Gabriel always felt for his wife. Perhaps this was the way he had kept himself sane—the therapy of writing out some hidden rage on paper?

A sound at the door made her look around, and she saw Theresa watching her. Susan went into the hall, drawing Theresa after her.

"Alex is sleeping—though only because she's chosen to sleep." Susan held up the book she'd been reading. "Have you read this, Theresa?"

"Of course. I have read all of Juan Gabriel's work."

Susan drew her still farther away from the bedroom door. "Tell me about the day when you came home and learned my mother was dead. I don't mean what you'd like to believe happened —but what you really know."

Theresa looked startled by her intensity. "What does it matter—since you don't believe me?"

"Because I *was* there. I must have seen her fall. Perhaps I know who really pushed her—if that's what happened. Perhaps something is imprinted on my memory somewhere. So tell me exactly what it was like when you came home that day, Theresa."

The other woman glanced toward the bedroom door and then crossed the hall to the living room. They sat together at each end of the wide sofa, and Susan could sense Theresa's tension as she spoke.

"That time was hard for me too. I was only twelve, and I'd never seen death before. I came home a little while after Alex found her, and it was terrible. Since she struck her head there was a scalp wound, and of course a great deal of blood. Alex was on the phone, and you were sitting there beside your mother's body. You were screaming hysterically and I think I slapped you, just to make you be still. You stopped right away, and then I could hear a soft moaning from up near the top of the stairs. I ran up to the second floor and found Juan Gabriel lying face down outside his bedroom door. He'd had a stroke awhile before, but he'd still managed to get out of his wheelchair. Perhaps he heard Dolores fall and tried to reach her. But he was unconscious when I found him—in a coma, so he couldn't tell anyone what happened. There—now you know everything I know."

"So you made up the part about my pushing my mother?"

"It's what *I* believe. It's what I think happened."

Susan stared at her, challenging, and Theresa looked away first. "Where was my father at that time?"

"He was out in his workshed, and Gilbert was with him. They were good friends, and Gilbert was interested in Lawrence's furniture-making. Because Lawrence was running a lathe, neither of them heard a sound from the house."

"Then what?"

"Your grandmother took charge of every-

208 thing. Even in her shock and grief, she was the strong one. There isn't anything else to tell." Suddenly Theresa's manner softened. "Don't torment yourself trying to remember. I shouldn't have urged you. I was just curious to find out what you knew about that time. Let it go—there's no use trying to relive it again."

"I don't believe I pushed her," Susan said. "It doesn't feel right that I could have. I wasn't here in Virginia much longer, was I?"

"No. Your father quarreled bitterly with your grandmother and took you away."

"To punish Alex, I'm sure. So that she lost not only her daughter, but her granddaughter as well."

For a little while Theresa had seemed almost open, relating her story without restraint. Now she withdrew, telling no more.

"That's all I know. Hadn't you better go back to your *patient?*" She emphasized the word, her resentment of Susan's presence sharpening again.

"I'll go back. I expect Peter wants us all to help. Perhaps you can spell me after awhile?"

"He put *you* in charge." Susan recognized the petulance from her long-ago experience of Theresa and knew that nothing she could say would ease her cousin's jealousy.

But why was it that she could remember so much about Theresa, and nothing at all about the day her mother had died?

Theresa escaped upstairs to her room and Susan returned to Alex's bedside.

Her grandmother had thrown back the light covering and was sitting up on the side of the bed in the flowered cotton robe Gracie had helped her into earlier. She'd extended her bandaged leg and was studying it in despair.

"How am I ever to walk on this? Help me, please, Susan. I want to see whether I can stand."

Clearly it would have taken a stronger sedative than Peter had cared to give to keep Alex Montoro down. Yet something had gone out of her. This was not the strong, determined woman Susan had met yesterday.

Susan had dealt with recalcitrant patients before, and she put gentle, persuasive hands on her grandmother's shoulders, easing her back against her pillow. Then she raised her legs, careful of the one that had been hurt as she lifted them onto the bed.

When her grandmother was comfortable, Susan remained standing beside the bed.

"I know you hate this, but you'll mend more quickly if you give your body time to recuperate. You've had a shock that was both physical and emotional." She left her hands on Alex's shoulders until she felt her body relax. "Peter said you were to have something to eat after you've rested. I can get tea and toast for you now, if you like."

"Presently. What were you talking to Theresa about?"

For a moment Susan hesitated, then decided it was better to tell her the truth. "I wanted Theresa to tell me what happened when she came home on the day my mother died. More than anything else, I want to remember."

Weariness sounded in her grandmother's sighing breath. "Perhaps it will all come back suddenly when something triggers your memory. Anything else?"

"Theresa believes that I pushed my mother, so that she fell on the stairs."

"I know what she thinks." Alex said with a dismissive wave of her hand. "I don't believe that for a moment. There was one very strange thing, however. When Theresa found Juan Gabriel he held a small ebony carving clasped in one hand. I don't know how he got it, or why he had it in his hand. It was something he had carved long ago and that I'd put away because I hated it. Something here has never been clear to me. Perhaps even something you saw and were too young to remember. Though I believe that such buried experiences are never really lost."

"If only I could remember."

"Never mind. What did you think of Juan Gabriel's description of the black swan? I'm sure you read that too, though I might have hoped you wouldn't."

"Why should you mind? It was your dancing he wrote about, not you. The disturbing implications only involve the viewpoint of the man in the wings."

"I doubt whether Juan Gabriel ever really knew where fiction ended and fact began. However, now that you've read the black swan scene, there's something else I want you to see—the carving he held in his hand that I've just mentioned. Remember the collection of wood carvings in the dining room?"

"Yes, I commented on them as soon as I noticed them. You said my grandfather had made them."

Alex's hesitation was long enough to seem odd. "Juan Gabriel loved to carve. When his hands were busy he could let a story soar in his mind until he was ready to set it down on paper. However, the carving I want you to see isn't kept with the collection."

Some memory seemed to be troubling her grandmother, and Susan waited uneasily.

After a moment Alex went on. "This particular carving was of the black swan. He worked in ebony, so it was truly black. When I first saw it, it wounded me deeply."

Tears glistened, edging Alex's closed lids, and Susan reached for one of her long-fingered hands on which the wedding band she still wore slipped loosely.

"Perhaps we shouldn't talk about these things now."

"Yes—we must! While there is still time. You are part of what happened, Susan, and before I die I want to know the answers. I believe you were sent—to help me find out."

Instinctively, Susan drew back. She didn't want to believe in some sort of fateful destiny that might force her into a path she would not want to follow.

Alex seemed to understand her hesitation. "It might be better never to know, never to look back over your shoulder. Still—there was your vision in the church today—of tombstones!"

"What did it mean? Please tell me."

"Some blood memory, perhaps. You'll understand soon enough. I'm torn between two opposites. Sometimes I think it's better to know all the truth, no matter how much it hurts, than to go on forever in ignorance. The truth might even free Peter."

"How could that be?"

"Marilyn Macklin believed that there was a strong connection between the present and what happened in the past. I think she may have discovered something that was dangerous for her to know. Though how this can be proved, I have no idea."

Perhaps it could be, Susan thought, remembering Priscilla Bates and the notes she held for the last chapters of Marilyn Macklin's book. But she didn't want to disturb Alex further right now and she let the matter go.

Past and present seemed to whirl suddenly into a vortex that drew her into its heart. Flashes of memory flared brightly, like streaks of lightning through her consciousness. Then everything settled, quieted, and she knew no more than she had before. She felt a little dazed and sat down beside the bed.

Alex seemed not to notice and she went on talking: "I've never shown the carving to anyone, but now I want you to see what Juan Gabriel made. I want you to tell me what you think of it. Sometimes I no longer know whether he loved or hated me at the end of his life."

"Did you love him?"

"Oh, yes! Not passionate young love, Susan. Perhaps that only happens once in a lifetime— something that is so strong that it sweeps everything else out of its way. What I felt for Juan Gabriel was steadier and went a good deal deeper. It grew stronger as I grew older. He was better for me than Rudy ever was. I was Rudy's creation. I had no life for him beyond being Drina. Juan Gabriel saw the woman I could become in my own right. He was kinder than Rudy, and a more loving teacher. And yet he wrote that scene of the black swan dancing, and

214   he carved the swan in ebony. If only I could understand!"

"Where is the carving now?"

"Remember that box in Dolores's trunk in the tower room? The one I wouldn't let you open? I had forgotten where it was and it startled me when I saw you pick it up. Go upstairs now and bring it to me."

There seemed no way to refuse, but before she could obey, the telephone rang in Alex's room, and Alex motioned for Susan to answer it.

It was Peter. "I've called Hallie Townsend, Susan. She's coming over to fill in and help you with Alex. Hallie's gentler than Theresa can be. She's on her way now by boat, so she'll be there any minute. How is Alex?"

"Wide awake and talking." Susan smiled at her grandmother.

"I might have known. Never mind. It's better to let her run the show, if that's what she wants. So long as she doesn't try anything strenuous. I'm glad you're there, Susan."

"Thank you, doctor." She put a hint of laughter into her words, and Peter picked up on it.

"Thank *you,* nurse," he said, and she knew he was smiling too.

"What did he want?" Alex asked.

"Peter has sent for Hallie Townsend to come over and sit with you—to spell me. He feels that

Hallie won't upset you as much as Theresa sometimes does."

"He didn't ask me if *I* want her here," Alex
said tartly. "I don't need anyone to sit with me
while I *sleep!*"

"Doctor's orders," Susan said lightly. "Maybe
he doesn't trust you to stay in bed. Before I go
upstairs for the carving, I'll ask Gracie to bring
you something to eat."

When she went out to the kitchen, Gracie
knew at once what to fix. "How is she, ma'am?"
she asked.

"She's a hard one to keep down."

Gracie's smile was fond. "I know. I sure do
know! It's good for your gramma to be ornery,
Miss Susan. Cheers her up to start telling everybody what to do. I'll take in her tea and toast in a
minute."

Susan returned to her grandmother. "Gracie
will be in soon. I'll go upstairs and look for the
carving now."

"Don't let Hallie see it, will you?"

"I won't," Susan promised.

Before she reached the stairs, Susan heard
Hallie's boat at the landing and went outside.
Hallie had on white pants and an oversized
denim shirt, and was looking more comfortable
than she had in the dress she'd worn earlier for
her work at the Reception Center.

When she saw Susan, she beckoned toward a

216 wooden bench set near the narrow strip of sandy beach.

She would talk to Hallie for just a moment, Susan decided, and went down to join her on the bench.

"Peter told me what happened to Alex," Hallie said. "I mean about her falling through a cracked board in Juan Gabriel's study. How is she?"

"Tired, I think, but not in much pain, and not ready to give in and rest."

Susan couldn't tell whether Hallie's nervousness was unusual or not, since she always seemed on edge.

"We need to talk, Susan," she said earnestly.

"Oh? What about?"

"Your mother. In some ways I think no one knew Dolores better than I did—though we made a strange pair. I was older, of course, and Dolores was so beautiful and gentle and graceful. She wasn't a dancer, but she was as graceful as Alex. I was the clumsy one who always knocked things over and fell over my feet. Dolores never seemed to mind, and she never criticized me. I might as well tell you, that there was a time when I was in love with your father. Foolishly, of course."

Susan said nothing. Hallie was the last woman her father would have been interested in —she knew him very well. Nevertheless, she felt sorry for Hallie, because, if her father had guessed, he would have been unkind.

"Of course he never knew—and he'd never have looked at me. Don't laugh, Susan, but when I was much younger I used to make up fantasies about Lawrence. Sometimes I even pretended I was Dolores!"

This was embarrassing, and Susan wanted to hear nothing more. "You might even have been my daughter," Hallie added wistfully.

Susan stood up, trying to find something kind to say. "Thank you for telling me all this, Hallie. We'll talk again, but I think we'd better check on my grandmother now."

Hallie jumped up at once, her movements as energetic as always, and started for the house with Susan.

When they entered Alex's bedroom, she was sitting up sipping tea from the bed tray Gracie had placed before her. Gracie nodded to them and slipped out the door.

"Susan, you look tired, why don't you take a break. I'll look after Alex," Hallie said, walking over to the bed. She reached behind Alex and began awkwardly to plump her pillows. "I hear you've been smashing yourself up."

Freed for her errand, Susan went up to her room and out on the circling balcony. She knew where Alex had left the key to the trunk room, but when she reached for it she found the place

218 empty. The doorknob turned under her hand, and when she stepped into the room, she saw why.

Theresa Montoro sat perched on Dolores's trunk, smoking a cigarette whose fumes added to the stuffy quality of the air in the room. She waved it carelessly at Susan.

"Don't tell Peter or Alex. I'm not supposed to smoke in the house. But who's to know up here?"

Theresa was the last person Susan wanted to see, and she went quickly to open a window, speaking over her shoulder. "What are you doing here?"

"I'm waiting for you. I didn't notice anything in Juan Gabriel's hand when I found him. I was too excited, so I didn't know about the carving until now."

"You were listening," Susan said.

"Of course. That's the only way to learn, isn't it? I always knew Juan Gabriel had something against his wife, but Alex is such a secretive person, I've never known what it was. You seem to have opened her up a little. Here's the box she wants you to look into. I got it out of the trunk while I was waiting. I wonder what Juan Gabriel intended when he carved this. Do tell me what you think."

Susan had no intention of opening the box with Theresa watching.

She accepted the small container impatiently. "I'll take this to my room, if you don't mind," she said.

"Don't bother. I'm leaving. I know what's in it, since Juan Gabriel showed me the carving after he finished it. But I don't know if Alex should ever see it again, Susan. It upsets her too much."

Theresa stubbed out her cigarette and left, looking pleased with herself.

Susan scanned the room—searching for something, though she wasn't sure what. So much of the mother she couldn't remember was here in her possessions—perhaps even a hint of her spirit. Was it a happy spirit? There had seemed to be hints that her mother had been far from happy. Perhaps her marriage was not all she had hoped. The stories she had written for her small daughter still waited in Susan's room, and she would get to them soon.

Now, whatever was in the box must be faced, and she couldn't open it downstairs with Hallie watching. The worn, dusty armchair where she had once sat on her mother's lap, while Dolores read aloud, was waiting. She lowered herself into a depth that no longer seemed as great as when she'd been little.

"Help me," she said aloud, not at all sure where she expected help to come from, but only knowing that she might be holding her own Pandora's box on her lap.

The container itself was beautiful, and she supposed her grandfather must have carved the decorations on the lid. It was made of a dark wood that was lighter than ebony, and tiny, stylized dogwood petals covered the lid. They had been rubbed with some essence of oil that gave them a sheen, and they were smooth to her touch. She raised the hinged lid.

The small treasure the box held had been packed carefully in cotton wool, and Susan lifted it out to unwrap the carving. At first glance, it was simply a beautifully carved black swan, its long proud neck extended forward so that the head rested upon outstretched human arms that seemed ready to flutter. This was both woman and swan, blended in the dance of wicked enchantment that Drina had once performed. This was Odile.

As Susan looked more closely she saw that a face was visible. The black swan's head was a woman's head turned so that the eyes looked up at whoever held her. Susan caught her breath.

The carver's artistry showed itself in the miniature work. Every stroke of the knife brought out the cunning quality of the face. Cunning and sly. The slant of the eyes reminded her of Alex's eyes. The mocking smile belonged to Alex. But there was something terribly malevolent about this tiny face, as though some monstrous wickedness lay beneath the creature's smile.

The effect on Susan was unexpected. She felt shaken by a distrust of her grandmother that she hadn't felt before. If this was Drina, it must also be a side of Alex Montoro that Juan Gabriel had seen all too clearly. But why had Alex been willing to let her granddaughter see this dreadful little carving? Susan had accepted the Odile scene in Juan Gabriel's book, but this seemed far worse.

Theresa was probably right, Alex shouldn't see this again, even though she had asked for it. Susan left the box behind and carried the ebony swan to her room, where she set it on the bureau. Later she would show it to Peter and ask him about it. He knew Alex as well as anyone, and even though he'd never known Drina, what mattered now was the essence of the woman Alex had become.

When Susan went downstairs to Alex's room, she found a new visitor sitting beside her bed. Hallie was there too, moving around in her nervous way, as though she couldn't sit still.

For an instant Susan met her grandmother's questioning look and understood that she wanted her reaction to the carving. This was something she wasn't ready to give, but she managed a smile that was probably not convincing.

Sitting up against her pillows, Alex introduced the stranger. "This is Emily Gower, Susan —Hallie's sister. A very old friend of mine from Tangier Island."

Eight

*A*lex looked intently at Susan's face the moment she walked into the room and recognized what her uncertain smile was meant to conceal. She had seen the carving and had reacted to it, just as Alex had feared. A new feeling of despair filled her. It had seemed necessary to test Susan by allowing her to see the ebony swan. A test that had obviously failed. Susan had been badly shaken by what she'd seen in Juan Gabriel's carving. Alex had carefully avoided bringing Susan too close to Juan Gabriel's memory. But what if his carving alienated her from her grandmother altogether?

A new visitor had arrived in Susan's absence, and somehow Alex managed to introduce Susan and Emily calmly, glad for a brief postponement in confronting her granddaughter. Emily, at least, had never been hurt by what had happened, and it must stay that way. Her hurt lay in the lapsing of an old friendship—something that was Alex's fault, not hers. Emily's pride would have kept her away. Alex knew she was here now only because John wished it.

Life on Tangier Island must have been hard, for Emily had aged and changed. The lively, eager young girl she had been had vanished. This might be the way Alex would have looked if she had become a waterman's wife.

At last Hallie showed signs of leaving, and that was a relief. "You don't really need us here," she told Alex cheerfully. "You need to sleep. Emily can visit with me for a while before she goes back to the island, so I'll take her home."

As she said good-bye, Emily avoided Alex's eyes, not ready yet to be friends again, and Alex couldn't blame her. If there were to be overtures, *she* must make them, and she thanked Emily warmly for coming.

"Be well soon," Emily said, "and let us know when you can come over and bring Susan. John told me to be sure and urge you to come."

Alex promised nothing. She had seesawed for too long. In her present discouraged state, with pain nagging at her leg, making all the effort it would take to visit the island seem impossible. If John wanted to see his granddaughter, let him come here. How could she have thought that she could endure seeing Tangier again with all its bittersweet memories? The fall that had weakened her had also jarred some sense into her.

When Hallie and her sister had gone, Alex closed her eyes and sank back in bed. By now she hoped that Susan would say nothing about the carving.

Susan sat down close to the bed and began lightly. "How are you feeling? Peter said your leg would hurt for a while, but I have some pain medication he prescribed that will help."

Alex waved that aside; physical pain was nothing. It was the inner pain she could no longer deal with.

But Susan was not ready to let everything go. "I saw the carving. What did it mean?"

Alex answered listlessly. "Fact and fiction always intermingled in his novels. For the sake of whatever story he was writing, he would do anything that served his purpose. His black swan was supposed to be evil, so he portrayed her that

way in his carving before he wrote about her in
the novel."

She had known without the slightest doubt
that her husband had loved her to the end of his
life. He had never been less than kind, never too
demanding, always showing her his gratitude
that she was his wife. The choice she had made
had been the right one. The wayward girl who
had loved John Gower was old now, too; something *she* had never quite accepted, and it was
about time she did.

Susan snatched at her words, looking relieved. "Of course! Juan Gabriel would have been
illustrating what he wanted to write when he
carved the swan."

To Alex her own voice seemed disembodied.
"Who else would he use for a model, since he
was basing his dancer on Drina?"

Clearly Susan was trying to dismiss whatever
disturbing emotion she'd felt when she first saw
the carving, but Alex had no strength to further
defend herself.

"Where is it now?" she asked.

"It's upstairs in my room."

"Then leave it there. I'll sleep now. I have a
handbell on my table, so I can ring if I want
anyone. I'll rest better with no one else in the
room."

For a moment she thought Susan might lean
over and kiss her cheek—perhaps guiltily, and

226 she was relieved when she merely reached for the copy of *The Black Swan.*

"I'll go across the hall and read for a while," Susan said. "Peter is going to stop by, so I can wait there for him."

Alex watched her go, knowing she would seek answers in the book—answers she would never find from the man she believed was her grandfather. There were too many questions that Alex herself had never found answers to. Why had Juan Gabriel been found in the upper hall? Had he been trying to reach Dolores? Had he managed, by sheer force of will, to stumble across the hall from his wheelchair in an effort to save Dolores from some danger he recognized?

Some months later, at the end of his life, Juan Gabriel had come out of his coma to speak those alarming words she had never understood. She had begged him to tell her what he wanted, but in the end he had flung out a hand as though to point, though all he'd managed to do was knock over a bowl of oranges beside his bed. She had told Marilyn what had happened, and everything had been set down in the notes for the book. Marilyn had been sure that he was trying desperately to tell Alex something he knew. But there had been no possible way to know if she was right.

There was one thing she did know—in the end, a trip to Tangier would be pointless, and she could give it up without regret. She'd sent Susan away so she could sleep, but her mind was wide awake, and memory was only a torment. Seeing Emily had brought the thought of John Gower back all the more sharply. The changes they would see in each other would be shocking. How could she ever have believed that she could see him again?

She had been disturbed by the weathered lines in Emily's face, the sadness in her eyes. She knew they had lost a seven-year-old son many years ago and had no other children.

There were other, unhappy memories she had always thrust away. At their last meeting, John Gower had been furious with her because she would not leave Juan Gabriel and run off with him. In those early days of the forties, Tangier men had been known for violence when duly aroused. So, she'd even been afraid for a little while.

But how could she have gone with John? Juan Gabriel had known her as Drina. Her dancer's life meant nothing to John Gower. By now, of course, he had long realized that his marriage to Emily had been the right choice. He would have forgiven and perhaps even forgotten. Or did one ever forget young love that was cut off and lost forever? Sometimes she wondered what would have happened if John had stood his ground and refused to accept her decision. Per-

228 haps it was fortunate for them all that he had let her go.

A tap sounded on the door, and she opened her eyes as Peter and Susan came into the room. Susan's radiance reminded her of herself as she'd once been. Peter's expression, however, was guarded, and Alex wondered if he noticed what Susan revealed when she looked at him.

"You're better," Peter said after examining her, "though Susan tells me you haven't done much sleeping."

"Sleeping is for old people!"

"That sounds more like you. If you're so wide awake, there's something you should know about, Alex. When Susan and I had lunch at The Mulberry Tree, Priscilla Bates met us there. Did you know Priscilla?"

"Marilyn's friend? Slightly."

"Marilyn intended to stay with her in Richmond for a while when she left Kilmarnock. They were old friends from university days in Charlottesville."

Alex had been sadly aware of the cooling of Peter's marriage. Marilyn's ambitions led in other directions than being a doctor's wife and the breakup was inevitable.

Peter explained about the last pages of notes that Marilyn had left with Priscilla, and which she still held. Priscilla had decided to do something about them when she learned of the manu-script's return.

"When you're feeling stronger, you may want to talk with Priscilla yourself, Alex," he suggested. "Perhaps you are the one who should finish Marilyn's book."

At the moment Alex had no heart for doing either. She had always been fearful about what Marilyn might choose to reveal in the conclusion of the book. Marilyn had asked for her help, but not her approval, refusing to write an *authorized* biography of Juan Gabriel's life. He held a place in world literature, she'd insisted, and even unpleasant truths should be told about him. Up to a point, Alex had agreed. Beyond that point might lie monsters, as old maps had used to designate unknown territories.

"I haven't the energy or the wish to see the book published," Alex told Peter.

Before she could say more, the screen door at the back of the house banged and Theresa burst into the room. She looked pale and frightened, and her heavy coil of hair had slipped untidily from its pins. To see Theresa disheveled was alarming in itself.

"I've just seen him!" she cried. "I've just seen Juan Gabriel!"

Alex sank back against her pillows and closed her eyes.

Peter said, "Hang on, Theresa. Sit down and catch your breath."

Susan poured a glass of water, and handed it to Theresa who just stared at it, as though she didn't know what it was.

Somehow Alex managed to speak patiently. "Where did you see him, Theresa? Upstairs in his old room?"

"No—no! He was in his study in the boathouse."

"Tell us the rest."

"After I left you I went outside, and I saw Hallie sitting near the dock with Emily. Emily was crying, and Hallie was trying to comfort her. When I asked what was the matter, Hallie said her sister was unhappy because her old friendship with Alex had been lost. She felt it was somehow her fault that it had been dropped over the years."

Alex sighed. There was no way to make Emily understand, and she didn't care whether Theresa did or not.

"I asked how I could help," Theresa went on. "Hallie got a very strange look in her eyes and said that something terrible was going on that Juan Gabriel had started. The way she spoke gave me the shivers. Hallie has a sixth sense sometimes, just the way I have. She stood up and ran toward the boathouse and Juan Gabriel's study. Emily and I followed her. Hallie went in

and just stood there looking around. Then, like a sleepwalker, she walked toward the wall of books at the end of the room. If I hadn't stopped her she might have stepped right through that broken place in the floor. I pulled her back in time and she seemed to wake up. I think she was really scared when she saw where she was, and she began to shake. Emily put an arm around her, but she went on shaking. Hallie believed there was *something* in the room with us. She thought it was Juan Gabriel's spirit come back to warn us about something that threatened you, Alex.

"Finally, Emily managed to get her out of that room and down to the boat. When they'd gone, I sat at Juan Gabriel's desk to try to collect myself."

Alex listened intently as Theresa went on. Was it possible that Juan Gabriel—his spirit, or whatever might be out there among his things—had a message for her? Of course it wasn't possible, but she listened.

"All of a sudden I knew he was there," Theresa said. "I knew I wasn't alone in that room, and I've never been more afraid."

"Did you actually see something in the room?" Peter asked.

"I'm not sure now." Dark hair tumbled over her face. "It was more like a feeling—a sort of pulsing in a far corner of the room. A thickening

232 in the air that I can't even describe. It made me want to run out of that place, just as Hallie had done. But I couldn't move. Then, as I watched, the pulsing grew fainter and was gone. If it was Juan Gabriel's spirit that Hallie thought she'd seen or felt, then it had brought some sort of warning with it."

Alex waited, not trusting Theresa. This could so easily be one of her performances.

Theresa went on from behind the cloud of her dark hair. "Perhaps Juan Gabriel's spirit is restless. His death couldn't have been peaceful. I had a strong sense of *warning*. It made me feel that there's something you haven't finished, Alex? Something you ought to do?"

Theresa pushed back her hair, and Alex saw the brightness of her eyes. If malevolence existed anywhere, it might easily come from Theresa herself. Besides, Juan Gabriel's death *had* been peaceful—she herself had made it so. Alex closed her eyes again.

"This is all too much! I don't know what to believe. Please go away and let me rest—all of you!"

For a moment no one moved. They were watching her—Susan and Peter anxiously, Theresa with a certain triumph, perhaps, because she knew how badly Alex had been disturbed by her words.

Theresa looked dreamily off into space.

"Lawrence belongs to the spirit world now too. What if it was *his* presence both Hallie and I sensed in that room? Lawrence was very angry after Dolores died. Angry with you, Alex. I was only twelve, but I remember that. If he never stopped being angry, he could be an angry spirit now. A spirit who wants to punish someone in this house."

The room was hushed for a moment.

When Theresa laughed, it was not a pleasant sound.

"You should all see your faces! The way you look! I've certainly given you something to think about, so now I have other things to do." Better things, seemed to be the implication.

No one tried to stop her, and when she'd gone, Peter said, "I think that's enough explosive emotion for now. You don't need this, Alex, and I hope you won't pay any attention to Theresa. Her imagination runs away with her."

That was true enough, but Alex was troubled by the effect upon Susan, who looked stricken and confused by this talk about her father.

"Aside from Theresa's nonsense—which Peter and I are accustomed to," she told Susan, "I'm sure Lawrence's spirit is not troubled and that he would have better things to do than stir us up. Hallie's notions can be as far out as Theresa's, and I don't think we should give serious attention to any of this."

234   Though she'd tried to sound matter-of-fact, she was aware of Peter's watchful look, and she couldn't be sure what he was thinking.

"If only I could remember what happened when my mother died," Susan said. "But no matter how hard I try—"

"Don't *try*," Peter said. "That will only drive it deeper. You can't force this, and you'll only torment yourself."

"But I *want* to remember! I don't think I can find any peace of mind until I do."

Alex spoke to Peter thoughtfully. "You've worked with patients who have needed to bring back forgotten episodes in their lives to help with present illness. Perhaps you could try that with Susan?"

Peter shook his head emphatically. "Susan isn't ill, and I don't want to tamper with her psyche. I'm not qualified."

"I don't want that either," Susan agreed.

Alex gave up. These two young people could only help themselves, and all she could hope for was that they might make better choices than she had.

She closed her eyes and waited for them to leave. The moment she was alone she sat up on the edge of her bed, moving her leg carefully. Dizziness and a stabbing of pain subsided after a moment, and when she could stand she hobbled across the room to her bureau and opened a drawer. She had hidden the sealed letter from Lawrence that had fallen out of Dolores's book of stories, and now she drew it out from beneath the nightgowns under which she'd tucked it. The time had come to learn what Lawrence had written—those words she'd been afraid to read so long ago.

Overhead a ceiling fan whirred softly at low speed, touching her with its gentle breeze as she sat in her armchair. The letter's creases had deepened with the passing years, but the ink was still clear in Lawrence's rather cramped handwriting.

Alex:

I am taking Susan away with me to my new teaching post in New Mexico. I do not wish her to grow up in that house of violence and depravity. I do not believe that my wife died a natural death, but to stay there in order to learn the truth would not bring her back. And, in any case, I think truth is something that you decided to live without long ago.

Any letters you send will be burned. Any effort to contact Susan will be refused. I will tell her nothing.

My only regret is that I injured Juan Gabriel, whom I have always admired. I shall see that Susan grows up without prejudice against him.

But, of course, with every prejudice against her grandmother.

Lawrence Prentice

Alex read the letter through twice, but it told her nothing new. She was still not sure of what Dolores might have revealed to her husband, though she could guess. Nor did she know for certain why Lawrence and Juan Gabriel had quarreled. She still could not face what she had feared at the time. Even now, so many years later, the pain of what she suspected struck too deeply to be faced. She could not endure the thought that in the very last months of his life Juan Gabriel had learned the truth. After the fight with Lawrence, he had refused to explain or discuss the matter. The next day a stroke had made speech so difficult for him that she would not urge him to say more about the incident.

The letter didn't matter, except that it had brought so much pain to the surface again. However, she could show it to Susan, and it would at least explain why her granddaughter had never heard from her.

All that mattered now was the present, not the past. She would go to sleep asking for help, and somehow she would be guided. Tomorrow she would know what to do.

Nine

$\mathcal{P}$eter drew Susan into the hall. "I'd like to talk to Hallie about what just happened. Sometimes Theresa goes off the deep end, but I'd like to hear Hallie's version of Theresa's story. It's too late now, but will you come with me in the morning and we'll visit the Townsends together? Perhaps we can catch Hallie off guard."

More had happened than Susan could digest.

238 She wanted to talk to Peter about so many things, and this would offer an opportunity.

"Of course I'll come with you, but not just to talk to Hallie. So much has occurred that I can't sort out, and I'd like to tell you something that has happened between Alex and me."

"I'll be happy to listen, Susan. The ride will give us a chance to discuss a lot of things."

"What if my worst nightmares are based on something that really happened—that I had a part in?"

"If that's true, you're carrying a heavy load. But Theresa can make up fantasies, so don't accept anything she says at face value. If you want to rest easier, Susan, you need to let that inner child come out. That's the only way you'll learn the truth."

He put an arm around her and kissed her cheek lightly before he went away. She was still his childhood friend and perhaps that was the way it ought to be.

For now it was good to have a few hours in which nothing of any consequence was likely to happen. Susan checked on Alex, who slept deeply, renewing herself physically, and probably emotionally.

When she went upstairs, even the tower room seemed a haven that held no threats. As she kicked off her shoes, she glanced at the bureau and saw that the carving of the ebony swan was gone. She knew only one person who might have taken it, but she had no wish to track it down now. Tomorrow would be time enough to have this out with Theresa.

For this little while she would relax and let everything drift away. Morning always brought new strength.

She awakened early, feeling refreshed. Not even Theresa was up when Susan went downstairs. She fixed herself toast and coffee and a soft-boiled egg, glad to have this time alone. Just as she finished eating she heard Peter's car and went out to the porch.

"I'm ready," she called to him.

"Wait," Peter said, coming up the steps. "There's something I want to do first—by daylight. Let's have a look at the board out in Juan Gabriel's study—the one that broke under your grandmother's light weight."

She went with him out the back door, steadying herself against facing her grandfather's study again. Finding Alex there had been a shock, and Theresa's dramatics hadn't helped her feeling about the place.

Early sunshine shone at the windows, sending long bars of light across the floor, driving all the shadows to the far corners of the room.

Peter knelt before the wall of books and ex-

240 amined the broken board carefully while Susan looked around. Nothing "pulsed" in any corner, and she had no sense of the "presence" Theresa claimed to have felt.

When Peter stood up, he spoke soberly. "Someone deliberately fixed this piece of flooring so it would break, intending injury. Who else could be expected to use this place but Alex? Only she might come in here. A good blow could have damaged the board so it would crack under her weight."

"But why? At worst, Alex might have broken a leg, but hardly anything more. So why was it done?"

"Who knows? The fall might have killed her if her heart had given out. Or perhaps it was a warning—though about what only Alex could tell us. Anyway, let's go talk to Hallie now."

As they settled into Peter's comfortable old car, Susan found herself remembering Colin Cheney's inevitable Mercedes. Peter's patients needed this concerned doctor who had helped them because he cared. She was no longer sure that *anyone* needed Colin's sort of doctor, who thought first of money and prestige.

As they traveled east, Peter explained where they were going. "Hallie uses her skiff when she visits Alex, since the creek is the best shortcut between their homes. The long way around is to follow the highway above where Sawmill Creek ends. We'll take a third way—the Merry Point ferry. The ferry is much shorter than going by the main road, and it's an experience in itself."

Susan watched the mostly empty countryside slip past. August corn had grown high enough to block the horizon where there were no trees. Here and there were small modern houses built in the economical ranch style, alternating occasionally with old white clapboards. More than once they passed some tumbledown dwelling, abandoned, but apparently not vandalized.

When the pale, rippled waters of the creek came into view and the road ended, Peter pulled the car to one side to wait for the ferry. A striped barrier protected cars from the water's edge where they would board the ferry. Susan could see the curiously-shaped little boat chugging toward them out in the middle of the creek. Space for two cars set bumper to bumper ran along one side of the boat, with a high, windowed structure for the "captain" to sit on the level above. The boat was attached to a steel cable, submerged out in the water, so boats lighter than the cable could pass over it. Only two cars were making the trip, and theirs was the only one waiting on this side to cross the creek.

"It will take a few minutes for the ferry to reach shore," Peter said. "Then we can board right away."

This was the opportunity Susan had waited

242 for, and she told him about the carving Juan Gabriel had created of the black swan from the ballet in which Drina had danced. As best she could, she described the wicked little face that had emerged from the wood—a face that clearly resembled Alex when she was young.

"My grandfather must have been fictionalizing when he carved the swan, just as he did with descriptions in his novels. But I'm not sure Alex believes that. The carving must have disturbed her a great deal, and it's my fault that it's been unearthed again. Have you read *The Black Swan?*"

"Alex never wanted me to, and I never questioned her, since it seemed a private matter. I've read most of the other novels. Have you read *The Black Swan?*"

"Only parts, because Alex wanted me to. That was the book she went to Juan Gabriel's study to get for me. She must have just taken it down from the shelf when she fell. Afterward, someone brought it into the house, and I've been dipping into it, reading the ballet scenes. Alex told me that the only time he described her dancing was in that book. She wanted me to read the passages about the white swan. They are beautiful—and written with such admiration and love. Not at all the way he described the black swan."

"Two sides of the same woman?"

Susan didn't want to believe that her grandmother was anything like what Juan Gabriel had seen in his black swan. She shook her head uncertainly.

"Alex put the box that contained the swan away in the tower room where she wouldn't see it. When I brought out the box, while we were going through a trunk, she stopped me from opening it. Later she changed her mind and sent me upstairs for it." Susan paused.

"I'm sorry you were upset," Peter said gently. "But this was long ago—it can't matter now."

"I'm not sure. My grandfather seemed to be saying something about Alex that I don't want to believe is true. Yet the carving almost convinced me for a little while. I left it in my room, meaning to put it away later on, but when I went upstairs last night, it was gone. Only Theresa could have taken it, but I have no idea why. Sometimes I wonder if she really cares about my grandmother. She's a very complicated woman and not always sensitive. She's told me that she thinks *I* pushed my mother on the stairs."

"Marilyn also believed that Dolores was pushed to her death. But not by you, Susan. Don't think that for a moment."

She wished she could take comfort from his words.

"But there were only two other people in the house—my grandfather and me."

"Marilyn thought there might have been

244 someone else. Someone who got away. I've wondered if she knew more than it was safe for her to know."

"Sometimes flashes come into my mind—almost giving me visual scenes. But they fade out before I can grasp them."

He put an arm around her, drawing her close. "Honey, I *wish* I could help." A deep tenderness sounded in his voice, and when he bent toward her she knew that in another moment he would kiss her in a far from brotherly fashion. Without hesitation she raised her head, knowing this was what she wanted more than anything else.

At that moment, however, something stopped him. He withdrew his arm abruptly, turning from the open invitation of her lips. When he began to speak, the words came rapidly, as though he needed to fill a dangerous silence—a silence in which he might have committed himself to too much?

Susan felt shaken and rejected, unable to understand the sudden change. He was talking about her grandfather now, and she tried to save her own pride by listening.

"I can remember watching Juan Gabriel when he was carving one of those little figures— sometimes human, sometimes animal. He would sit on that bench near the edge of the creek and work with wood almost as though it were clay. If

I was very quiet, he would let me stay. He told me once that he wasn't merely carving. He was freeing himself for the story forming in his mind. I'm not sure he always knew what he was creating from the wood. Some unconscious part of his mind seemed to guide his hands."

What hidden part of Juan Gabriel had told him to create that evil little ebony swan? But none of this seemed important to her now. The only thing that mattered was the way Peter had drawn back, as if from a perilous brink.

The ferry crossing toward them had reached the docking place, and a ramp led the two cars off the boat. When the ferry was ready, Peter drove aboard, and then got out to place chocks behind the back wheels of his car, so they wouldn't roll. He stood for a moment talking to the young man on his high perch above the engine, where he could view the creek. When the noisy machinery started up, Peter came back to the car, and they sat watching lightly rippled waters flow past. She was glad for time to raise her own defenses.

On the opposite bank, trees grew thickly down to the edge of the creek, and only an occasional roof could be seen. A strip of sand had collected in one place, forming a narrow beach. Farther downstream the creek curved out of sight on its way to the Chesapeake.

"Tidewater Virginia," Peter said, raising his

246 voice above the engine sound. "I've always been glad this is my bit of country."

It would have been her country too, Susan thought, if her mother hadn't died, if her father hadn't taken her away. Perhaps then she might have been the one to marry Peter.

He smiled, watching her. "You're a lot like your grandmother, Susan. I don't think you even guess how much you resemble her." He was friendly, as always, but it was as though that moment of tenderness had never existed.

"Is that good or bad?"

"I suppose it's a mixture. We're all mixtures, and somehow we have to make sense out of the conglomeration we've been handed."

"Alex seems very wise to me, and I haven't been very sensible about my life."

"Don't be too sure about Alex's wisdom. You seem to have a practical sort of good sense, with compassion behind it. I'm not sure how compassionate your grandmother is, except toward her family and close friends. And we certainly don't know how wise she was at your age."

As they talked, the little ferry reached the far bank of the creek. The docking arrangement was the same, and when they drove ashore, Peter took a side road that followed the water.

"It's only a short distance," he told her. "The Townsend house is older than the Montoros', and it has always been in their family."

After a few miles he drew into the foot of a short driveway, and Susan looked out at a house that was neither as eccentric and fanciful in its architecture, nor as elegant as Alex's home. A long straight porch ran across the front, with a slanted extension of overhanging roof. Azaleas that must have been glorious in the spring formed a bushy green line below the front edge of the porch. Above, set into white clapboards, were three windows with gray shutters.

Hallie must have heard the car, for she came to the front door to greet them quizzically. "Hello! I didn't expect to see you again so soon." She turned her head. "Gilbert, we have company."

As Susan and Peter left the car, Hallie crossed the porch. "Come on in," she invited, though her tone was less than welcoming.

Peter thanked her amiably. "We came early so we could catch you before you left for work."

"I'm off today," Hallie said. "How's Alex?"

"She's doing very well. May we talk to you for a few minutes, Hallie?"

If Hallie's nervous elbows had been wings, she would fly, Susan thought as she and Peter entered a parlor that emanated a faded Victorian flavor.

Whatnot tables abounded, crowded with miniature family pictures. There was a shell collection, and various china objects of no particular

248 distinction. Susan recognized some of Theresa's decorative eggs. The curved-back style of the sofa belonged to the last century, as did several cushioned chairs. Above the sofa, a bank of framed flower prints had been arranged on the wall.

Peter wasted no time. "While we were with Alex yesterday, Hallie, Theresa came in from Juan Gabriel's study in an upset state. She told us that you had sensed some sort of presence out there, and that you were so upset that you ran away. We all know that Theresa has a great imagination, but this seemed important, so we'd like you to tell us what happened."

Gilbert had come quietly to the door of the parlor and stood listening. He acknowledged Susan and Peter with a nod and then spoke sardonically to his sister. "Yes—do tell us what happened, Hallie."

Hallie looked even more flustered. "It's easy to stir Theresa up. Sometimes I can't help baiting her. That Incan princess bit of hers puts my teeth on edge. So I told her I could feel Juan Gabriel there in his study, and that's all there was to it."

One never knew when Hallie was telling the truth, and Susan asked her own question. "Was that really all there was to it, Hallie? Are you leaving anything out?"

Hallie fluttered her hands. "I was just making it up. Only—" she broke off and looked at her brother.

"Go on," he directed impatiently.

"I know you won't believe it, Gilbert," Hallie said, "but I think *Theresa* saw *something*. The way she looked scared me, and I ran out and went down to my boat, Emily followed me. We came home together, and a friend picked Emily up to take her back to the island. I don't know what Theresa saw."

A movement across the room caught Susan's attention, and for the first time she saw a man sitting quietly in the shadowed corner—Eric. He had probably kept still so he could listen unseen. Now he stood up and came into the light, his good looks making him almost a younger replica of his father.

Gilbert's exclamation was one of impatience. "Why aren't you at the restaurant? You should have been there for the breakfast hour."

"Why aren't *you* there?" Eric countered, and then spoke to Peter. "What happened with Theresa isn't unusual. She's had these tizzies before."

"This seemed different," Hallie said softly.

Apparently no one had told either Eric or Gilbert what had happened to Alex. Peter explained that a board had been deliberately damaged in Juan Gabriel's study, so that Alex had fallen through and hurt her leg.

Gilbert stiffened at the mention of Alex's injury, and Susan noted how sharp his features

250 could seem in profile, contradicting the more amiable mask he displayed full face.

"Probably a rotten board," he said.

"I don't think so," Peter began, but a telephone in the hall startled them with its sudden ring, and Hallie went to answer it. When she returned she looked worried.

"That was Theresa. She wants to speak to you, Peter. Alex seems to have disappeared again."

Susan followed Peter into the hall and listened anxiously as he spoke on the phone.

". . . I see. We'll be home as soon as possible. No—don't call the police. If she's gone off on some errand of her own, she'd only be annoyed. Don't worry, Theresa."

"If there's anything I can do—" Gilbert said, sounding anything but eager to help.

"There's nothing," Peter told him.

"Leave your car here, Peter," Hallie said. "I can take you more quickly in my boat."

For a moment Susan thought Eric might insist on coming with them, but a look from his father stopped him.

Hallie hurried toward the back of the house and Peter followed. Susan, however, stopped to look around the parlor one last time. She had a strange feeling that she'd missed something—something she ought to notice. When she studied the mantel again she realized with a shock what was there.

At the far end, where she hadn't seen it before, stood the ebony swan. The tiny, sly face, filled with wicked secrets, looked out over graceful arms, extended and crossed at the wrists. There was just one way it could have come here. Theresa had taken it and given it to Hallie. But why?

When she caught up with the others, waiting for her on the dock, Peter helped her onto a seat across the square end of the flat-bottomed skiff.

With the outboard motor running, there could be little talk, and Susan waited impatiently during the short time it took to reach the Montoro dock. Once ashore, she held Hallie back for a moment.

"I saw the carving of the ebony swan on your mantel, Hallie—how did it get there?"

"An ugly little thing, isn't it?" Hallie spoke carefully. "Theresa gave it to me yesterday when I was at your grandmother's house. She didn't want Alex to see it again and be upset."

The explanation was simple enough, yet Susan still felt uneasy.

Theresa came down to meet them, looking upset, and Peter spoke to her. "Let's go inside and you can tell us what's happened."

The light summer coverlet on Alex's bed had been thrown back, and her nightgown lay crum-

252 pled at the foot, as though she had dressed hurriedly.

Gracie had joined them, and she went to the closet to look along the hangers. "Only Miss Alex's blue slacks and one of her special jackets are gone—the pale violet one."

Theresa made a wailing sound, and this time Peter shook her gently by the arm. "Stop that! I doubt that Alex has had a second accident. Tell us whatever you know."

"I don't know anything! That's the trouble. I was upstairs dressing when I heard the phone ring. Somebody answered, and I didn't pay any attention. I assume Alex picked up the phone in her room."

Gracie spoke firmly, as though needing to convince herself. "I heard Miss Alex answer, but I waited till she hung up before I went in. She looked like she'd gone back to sleep, so I didn't think the call was anything that mattered. I went on back to the kitchen. You and Mr. Peter had already gone, Miss Susan."

"Who discovered that Alex wasn't in her bed?" Peter asked.

Gracie and Theresa looked at each other, and Theresa answered. "I suppose we both did. I came into her room from the hall, and Gracie came from the back of the house about the same time. And we saw just what you're seeing now

—an empty room. It's funny she'd go off without telling anybody."

"Maybe she thought you'd stop her, Miss Theresa."

There was something about the way Gracie's eyes seemed to avoid meeting Theresa's that gave Susan a sudden misgiving. It was possible that Gracie might connive with anything Alex wanted.

"How long ago did you find out she was missing?" Peter asked.

Again Gracie and Theresa looked at each other—perhaps guiltily.

"Maybe an hour or so, Mr. Peter," Gracie said.

"I don't like her running around on that leg until it heals. How did she leave?"

"She took her car," Theresa said. "The garage is on the other side of the house, so we never heard it start. Perhaps she just let it roll down the drive, if she didn't want us to see her."

"At least it's her left leg, so driving won't hurt too much. Though I don't understand her going off without a word to anyone."

Gracie's uneasiness was evident and she didn't meet Peter's eyes, either. He caught her evasiveness. "All right, Gracie—you'd better tell us what you know. No more covering up for Miss Alex, no matter what she told you."

Ten

*A*lex wished that her beastly leg would hurt a little less. At least she could deal with physical pain. Fear that had its roots in the past was something else. Marilyn's death was part of the present terrifying picture, and she'd grown sure that its source lay in events long past. Someone had been afraid of what Marilyn had unearthed in her research for Juan Gabriel's biography. The problem was that Alex had no idea what this might be. She had gone over and over everything she'd told Marilyn—but the missing piece didn't surface.

What she was doing now might help to answer the questions that had haunted her for all these years. Fortunately, she could drive, and she'd told no one but Gracie where she was going, and whom she intended to meet.

"Stall them as long as you can," she'd directed. "I need to see Priscilla Bates and find out what she can tell me. But she will never talk if anyone else is present."

This was all too true. Priscilla had opened up to Peter a little, but not completely. Last night before she went to sleep, she'd determined to see Priscilla, even if she had to drive to Richmond to accomplish this. There'd been no need for that, however, since Priscilla had phoned her this morning, sounding a bit paranoic. She'd explained where she was staying temporarily, and had agreed to meet her and begged her to come alone.

Alex's "escape" had been easy enough. She had taken her car and followed the road south toward Windmill Point at the very tip of the Northern Neck, where Chesapeake waters lapped this western shore.

She knew the area well. The rolling land around Kilmarnock had been replaced by flat, sandy ground, susceptible to flooding. Once all

256 this had been scrubby growth, but in recent years these acres had been turned into a resort with a fine marina and a number of two-storied condominiums to house guests. A good beach was one of the main attractions.

Alex parked beside the main building and got out of her car with some difficulty, using the cane she disdained. The hotel desk was at the end of a small lobby, and a young woman on duty recognized her.

"Good morning, Mrs. Montoro. Miss Bates said to give you a key, in case she wasn't in when you came."

Alex took the key and listened to the directions for finding Priscilla Bates's room.

The restaurant was open for breakfast, and she decided to eat something before the ordeal of meeting Priscilla.

She refused a table in the inner room and was given one on the level that overlooked the marina. There she sat before long glass windows beside the slip where several big boats were anchored. A channel from the bay had been deepened to accommodate larger boats.

As she ate breakfast and drank a cup of coffee, she could feel strength returning to her body. Even her leg felt better for a little food. When she returned to her car and drove along the sandy roads of the complex, she felt ready to hear whatever Priscilla might tell her. The room was on the ground floor, luckily, but no one answered her knock. When she went in and looked around, she wondered if Priscilla might already have left. No suitcases were in sight and the closet hangers were empty.

This was a corner room, generous in size. It extended from the front gallery to a small porch that opened onto the beach. Alex went through sliding doors and stepped outside. Sunlight, filtered by the branches of a nearby pine tree, sprinkled her with light. There was little wind, and waves washing to the edge of the sand caught the dazzle of a sun path over the water. Across the bay, where a lighthouse would flash its warning at night, were the adjacent shores of Delaware, Maryland, and Virginia. The three states came together to form the Delmar Peninsula, and the Eastern Shore of Virginia lay directly across the water from where she stood. Out there, a little to the north, floated the island of Tangier.

In her mind's eye she could see the island clearly, though it was invisible from here. It would lie low in the water. Its cluster of white buildings, which included two spired churches and a school, was located near the harbor. Homes were scattered sparsely a little farther afield. Now, after all her wavering and indecision, she *knew* that Susan must be taken to the island, no

258 matter what it might cost her grandmother. She must do this by tomorrow, if she was able.

No more excuses could be made because of her own reluctance to face John Gower. This morning's efforts proved that she could move around well enough. It was only the young Alexandrina who hated to have John see her old and crippled. But John would no longer be young either. After all, he was a few years older than she was, so time would have changed him as well. In any case, what did it matter? Emily had weathered badly from too much sun and the hard life of the island. Alex, at least, had escaped that.

How she wished she could run across the sandy ground at her feet—run through clumps of beach grass and feel the hard sand at the water's edge under her shoes. She moved away from the cement enclosure, using her cane for balance, but she was unable to go very far, thanks to her injured leg. What a mockery it would be, even if she reached the water! She could no longer run on the sand with her hair streaming behind her and John Gower running after her, his long stride purposeful. Yet they had not touched while Juan Gabriel sat watching them, and he could not hear their laughter from where he waited. Their words had been innocuous enough—then.

Ostensibly Juan Gabriel had sat in his folding chair making notes for his novel, and nothing in his manner had betrayed any knowledge of what was happening to his wife. Yet it must have hurt him to see them running together, just as her own inability to run hurt her now. At the time she hadn't cared—wanting only to run along the beach with John.

There had been a nobility about Juan Gabriel. If he had hated growing older, while his wife was still young, he had never given any indication. When he had carved her face in ebony, she had been shocked and fearful of what he might know. But he had seen her hurt and made her understand that this was his means of releasing the last traces of his jealousy of Rudy Folkes. As the years went by there had never been any lessening of his love, and she could thank God that he had never dreamed of the painful longing that existed in his wife.

Now, whether she liked to admit it or not, a trip to Tangier would serve a double purpose. It would allow John Gower to meet his granddaughter, even if Susan were never told of the relationship. But also it might answer a question that had haunted her over the years.

Why had John given her up so easily? Tangiermen were notably possessive of their women in those days. Why had he accepted her decision and never pursued her? If he had come after her, who could tell what changed course their lives might have taken? It had not been in character for John to give up, and perhaps some

260 wayward part of her had expected him not to. When he had let her go so easily she began to doubt the genuineness of his love, and she couldn't bear to think of that.

Her years with Juan Gabriel had brought her a deeper peace than she could ever have known with John. Perhaps even a more lasting love. In the end, Juan Gabriel had not been betrayed. All the years of their life together must weigh for more than that brief passionate episode of loving John. Yet her guilt remained. She had been bred to the standards of an earlier day.

She turned her back on the beach and the golden glaze of sun on the water, returning to the safety of smooth cement. In the shadow of the porch something moved and her heart leapt.

"I've been waiting for you," Priscilla Bates said from her corner chair. "You seemed deep in thought and I didn't want to interrupt your reverie. Thank you for coming, Mrs. Montoro." She stood up and held out her hand—a woman even taller than Alex.

Accepting the greeting, Alex spoke curtly. "Shall we go inside, and you can tell me why you wanted to see me in such a secretive way." She would say nothing yet of *her* own wish to talk with Priscilla Bates.

"Of course." Priscilla led the way into the room, and they sat in chairs on opposite sides of a round table, Alex alert and very much on guard.

She sensed that something was about to be asked of her—something she might choose to reject—and she studied the face of the woman who had brought her here. It seemed a good face, for all the evidence of inner tension.

Priscilla began, one hand fingering the clasp of the large bag she had not released from her shoulder. "Perhaps Peter told you that I have his wife's notes for the conclusion of your husband's biography. I know that Marilyn wasn't ready to show them to you at the time of her death. I felt undecided about what to do with them, since the rest of the manuscript had disappeared. Now that it has turned up, you should see them. Marilyn's book ought to be finished."

"That is for me to decide," Alex told her. "I would like to take her notes home with me so that I can study them. Though I don't understand why we had to meet in this extraordinary manner for them to be delivered. You could have brought them to my house."

"I didn't want anyone else to know I had them. Marilyn was murdered—perhaps because of something she knew—something in these notes? I don't want that to happen to me. Of course you may object to the revelation she intended to make about what happened before you left Peru—that your husband had killed a man and was wanted for murder."

"At this late date that could hardly matter.

262 Though I wanted to give my own view of those events."

Priscilla opened her shoulder bag and took out a folder, which she placed on the table between them.

"When you read what's here, there's something you should think about, Mrs. Montoro. During one of the interviews you gave Marilyn, you described an attempt your husband made to tell you something just before he died."

Aware of the sudden thumping of her heart, Alex listened intently.

"Marilyn told me that Mr. Montoro had been in a coma for several months after his daughter's death. I understand that before he died, he recovered the power of speech to some extent and tried desperately to tell you something. She said you wrote down the words you understood. They are here in these notes. Perhaps their existence has frightened someone."

Those four words Juan Gabriel had spoken were something Alex would never forget, though she could not explain their meaning. She had told Marilyn what they were, but she hadn't told her of Juan Gabriel's last desperate gesture. He had become terribly agitated, struggling with some word he couldn't manage. A bowl of fruit had stood on a low stand by his bed, and he'd reached toward it, knocking it over and dislodging an orange, so that it rolled across the floor. He had reached a trembling hand toward the piece of fruit as if pointing. There had been nothing more.

She was glad afterward that she hadn't pleaded with him to explain. She had simply held his hand and told him over and over how much she loved him and always would. She still believed that he'd understood, and she had felt a faint pressure of his fingers on her own.

Priscilla went on gently, seeming to understand her moment of remembered grief. "Marilyn believed that those words had to do with your daughter's death and that they indicated someone's guilt. It's possible that Marilyn talked to others about this, and someone was afraid of what her manuscript might reveal. Whoever removed the manuscript from her office at the time of her death didn't realize that her notes for the last chapters were with me. The only people to whom I've mentioned these notes are Peter Macklin and your granddaughter when I met them yesterday at The Mulberry Tree. Eric Townsend was hovering around a bit officiously, but I don't know that he was listening."

The Townsends again! Eric would eavesdrop if he possibly could, and he might have told his father and Hallie whatever he'd heard. Or even Theresa, for that matter. But where could that lead? There was no proof of anyone's involvement.

264   "I hope you will complete Marilyn's book, Mrs. Montoro. Both for your husband's sake and for Marilyn's. I have an appointment soon, but please feel free to rest here as long as you'd like." Priscilla stood up and held out her hand.

When she had gone, Alex picked up the folder from the table. However reluctant she felt, she knew she must read what Marilyn had written and come to some decision. She might as well read this now before she went home. Despite her intention, however, she sat for a little while without opening the folder, and when a knock sounded at the door of the room, she felt a certain relief. She knew who it would be and for now she could postpone this painful task. Peter and Susan had come for her, she was sure. At least Gracie had given her a good head start. She had no intention of explaining to anyone why she was here. Until she'd read these notes, she would consult no one.

When she opened the door she knew by Susan's face that something had happened between these two—something sad and disturbing. Peter's grave look told her nothing, but Susan was close to tears.

"You're an impossible woman," Peter told her. "Lie down on that bed and let me see what damage you've done to yourself."

She stretched out on the bed obediently, watching Susan as she went to look out at the bay through wide glass doors. Perhaps to hide her tears?

Peter took Alex's blood pressure and her temperature, and examined her leg. "You've come through a lot better than you deserve. You gave us all a scare—but thanks to Gracie—"

"That's why I told Gracie. I knew you'd break her down eventually. But you needn't ask questions, because I don't feel like answering them. Not yet. Perhaps Susan can drive me home now."

Susan turned around at once, clearly relieved to be given an assignment that would remove her from Peter's company. For the moment Alex wanted to think only of her granddaughter. If there'd been a breaking off of whatever tentative beginnings might have existed between these two, it was likely that Susan would want to leave Virginia soon. And that meant that Tangier Island and all it stood for must be faced at once. There had been too much vacillation—she would now do what must be done.

On the ride home, with Susan at the wheel, Alex leaned back in the front seat and closed her eyes, forestalling conversation. Neither she nor Susan wanted to talk.

As they approached the driveway of the Montoro house, Alex saw that a car blocked their way. Susan pulled over to the curb in front of the house and Peter pulled in behind them. Two peo-

266 ple stood on the porch—Theresa and Gilbert Townsend—and they were locked in some furious argument, oblivious to anything else.

"This looks like trouble," Susan said, and beeped the horn, leaning out the car window. "Can you pull into the turnaround in front of the garage, please?" she called to Gilbert. "I need to bring my grandmother close to the steps."

Gilbert threw her a spiteful look and turned back to Theresa. "I will not condone a marriage between you and my son. That's my final word. There's nothing you can do to change my mind."

Theresa answered him more quietly. "I think there is. I don't like threats."

Gilbert came abruptly down the steps, got into his car, and drove recklessly to the turnaround, recognizing Alex with a mere nod. There he waited impatiently for a chance to get away.

Alex watched absently. None of this touched her. Her only concern now was that Susan must at least be given a chance to know the truth before she went away.

When Susan pulled the car up to the front steps, Theresa came down to help Alex out, scolding all the while because she'd "run away." Probably she was only venting her irritation with Gilbert, who had never liked her, and whom Theresa detested.

Peter, who had followed them up the driveway on foot, shook his head at Theresa. "I think that's enough. Alex is not a prisoner in this house. She's perfectly fine—even though I don't approve of her running around on that leg. But she must make her own decisions."

Theresa scowled, but halted her outburst as she and Peter helped Alex up the steps. Alex was glad for strong arms to support her and for Peter's bracing words.

Susan came after them listlessly. "Do you mind if I go up to my room for a while?" she asked her grandmother. "I don't want any lunch."

So it was that bad? "Of course, my dear," Alex said. "We can talk later. And, Susan—everything *will* be better. It always is."

But she saw the brief look Susan exchanged with Peter, saw Peter turn away, and wondered if her words were true.

On her way to the foot of the stairs, Susan looked back at her grandmother. "There's something you should know. The carving of the ebony swan was missing from my room last night, when I went up to bed. When Peter took me to the Townsends' awhile ago I saw it on the mantel in their parlor. Theresa gave it to Hallie. But shouldn't it stay in this house with my grandfather's other carvings?"

Alex winced as she always did when Susan referred to Juan Gabriel as her grandfather. She

268 didn't want to think about the swan, but Theresa must be confronted. She took too much upon herself.

"Why did you give it to Hallie, Theresa?" she asked.

Theresa shrugged. "I didn't want to see you upset all over again by that ugly carving. I remember when Juan Gabriel showed it to you. Later you asked me if I knew anything about it."

"Do you remember what you said?" Alex asked.

"I've forgotten. Anyway, I was too young to have much sense."

She would not repeat what Theresa had said —not with Susan listening—though she remembered very well. Theresa, looking almost as sly as the swan, had suggested that this was the way Juan Gabriel must really have seen the inner Alex Montoro. She had been stunned by Theresa's words, even though Juan Gabriel himself had explained the source of his jealousy and it had all been forgiven. As Theresa said, she was older now, and a bit more considerate.

Though her legs no longer wanted to obey her, Alex walked into the living room and sat down beside the telephone. She spoke to Theresa and Peter with an assurance she didn't feel. "I will do whatever you want after I've called Tangier Island. I mean to take Susan there tomorrow, if Emily will have us."

"Why?" Theresa demanded. "Why must you go to Tangier?"

"That is my affair," Alex said. "Now I'd like to be alone."

Theresa looked as though she might object, but Peter led her firmly out to the kitchen.

Gracie passed them in the hall and looked in on Alex. "You doing all right, Miss Alex?"

Gracie was the one person Alex felt totally comfortable with at the moment. Probably Gracie knew her better than anyone else alive, and she could keep her own counsel. Alex had never been sure how much she might know or have guessed about the past, and it had never mattered. They had been young together, and a bond of affection and loyalty existed between them.

"I'm fine, Gracie. Thank you for—everything."

Gracie's smile was warm and understanding as she went away.

For a moment longer Alex sat with her hand on the telephone. What excuse was she to give Emily for this urgency she felt? How could she possibly pretend that this was a casual visit?

However, when Emily answered the phone she seemed to take it for granted that since John had wished this, of course they must please him, if it was possible.

"I'm glad you're feeling better," Emily said. "We've worried about you, Alex. Of course you

270 must come tomorrow. Fred Parks is here on a visit and has his plane with him. He'll be around for a few days. I'm sure he will fly over to pick you up. When would you like him to be there?"

Getting to the island wasn't easy, so this was a good solution. "Would ten o'clock in the morning be all right? I'll ask Peter Macklin to drive us over the bridge to the airport."

"That should be fine. If there's any hitch, I'll call you. We're looking forward to seeing you and Susan on our island, Alex."

Our island, she had said. And of course that was the way Emily Gower would feel about the place after living there with John for all these years.

Alex was about to hang up, when Emily continued, and Alex heard the change in her voice.

"You really can't postpone this any longer, Alex. The air needs to be cleared for all of us— while Susan is here. We'll be looking for you, so please don't cancel again. Good-bye for now."

Alex sat with the phone in her hand, as shocked as though an electric current had touched her. Emily's words could mean only one thing. At some time or other John must have told her. But Alex had always felt that what had existed between her and John had belonged in a secret compartment of time. All that young love they had shared! If Emily knew, the enchantment was tarnished, and she could hardly endure such a thought, however foolish she might be.

But she couldn't think about any of this now, and she called for Theresa to come and help her to bed. She wanted only to rest and forget all the disturbing elements of the day. Among them the disappearance from Susan's room of the ebony swan. She hated to think of it in Hallie's hands—on the Townsend mantel for everyone to see. She had dismissed this to Susan, but it was there at the back of her mind—a humiliation, because Juan Gabriel had chosen to carve her face as sly and wicked—evil.

Eleven

*F*or the first time since Susan had come to her grandmother's house, the stairs seemed steep and difficult to climb. For her these were haunted stairs, and she wanted only to be up them quickly and safely—in her room with the door closed. Whatever was happening to Alex seemed too distant at the moment for her to concentrate on. Only Peter filled her mind.

When she reached the tower room she sat down and closed her eyes, reliving those moments with Peter when he had come so close to kissing her. Now she knew why he had drawn back and removed himself from anything that might have developed between them. On the way to find Alex, he had managed his explanation with a gentleness that brought tears to her eyes, but which left her with no way to tell him how strongly she felt abc t him or how much she opposed what he planned to do.

As soon as possible, he'd told her, he was going away. He planned to move across Virginia and open a practice in a new place. Perhaps some country town in the foothills of the Blue Ridge where a doctor was needed. There were plenty of those, and perhaps he could make a difference.

"It's better for me to start over in a new place," he said.

"Just leave and let a murderer go free?" Susan said indignantly.

"I don't know who caused Marilyn's death. I wish I did, but I don't think that person will murder again. It wasn't that sort of crime."

"How do you know?" she asked.

He'd dismissed that. "Even though I was cleared, there will always be some doubt—whisperings. I don't want to live with that, and I won't draw anyone else into it." She sensed a steely resolve in him, and even though she longed

274 to say that *she* would want to be a part of anything that faced him, she did not dare. His moment of deliberate withdrawal on the ferry had indicated the finality of his decision. If he had felt as she did, perhaps he would never have chosen this course.

There was nothing left to say. An uncomfortable silence remained between them until they reached Windmill Point. There they found Alex in a strangely withdrawn state, in which she would tell them nothing. Alex had asked Susan to drive her home, and it had been a relief to be away from Peter for a little while. She was glad for the chance to be quiet, for she meant to betray nothing. Only a sharp look now and then from her grandmother suggested that she wasn't altogether successful.

When Alex suddenly spoke, it startled her. "Don't cry over him, Susan. You'll go on with your life to something better. Peter has his own wounds to deal with."

What could anyone as old as Alexandrina Montoro know about love, Susan wondered? Young love, first love! Even though she could never admit it to him, Peter had always been her first love, even though she'd been such a small girl when she had first known him. Alex was far too removed in years from what her granddaughter was experiencing now.

Susan looked about her room for something

to occupy her mind. The notebook of her mother's stories lay on the table where she'd left it. Perhaps reading them would distract her and carry her back to a more comforting time that was as lost in mist as all the rest.

She began with the last story in the notebook, since that was the last one her mother had written and the one she was most likely to remember. The handwriting was not always as clear as in the earlier tales, as though some disturbing emotion had driven her mother's hand.

Of course the story began with *Once upon a time*. A time when there had been a splendid and powerful king, married to a beautiful wife. His queen was a singer of songs and she played a mandolin. The king and queen had a daughter whom the king loved dearly—a daughter who worshiped her father. (Nothing about whether the mother and daughter had loved each other.)

All this was simple enough—a story by which a little girl could fall asleep. But then everything changed, and the writing grew harder to read, almost flying off the page. The queen, it turned out, had fallen in love with a groom in the king's stable. In a terrible revelation it developed that the princess had belonged to the groom and had not been the king's daughter after all.

Susan paused in her reading, feeling confused. What was truth and what was fiction? Susan read on feeling shaken and apprehensive.

The king was furiously angry, but instead of punishing the queen, or having the groom executed, he was angry with the daughter he had always loved—who was not his own child. He was so angry that he wrote a terrible song about the evil queen and gave it to his wife to sing, so she would understand his anger. He had forced the queen to sing the song, though it nearly broke her heart. Now he could no longer bear the sight of the princess, who became so sad she didn't want to live anymore.

Susan set the notebook down and spoke aloud to the vanished writer, "No, no, no! It couldn't have been like that. This is wrong! I know you were wrong!"

But the story had never been finished, and the lines remained on the paper with all their tragic overtones. Translated into life, would it mean that Susan's mother had taken her own life— flung herself down the stairs to her death? Was that the terrible act she herself had witnessed and wiped out of her memory? But if Dolores had wanted to die, surely she would have chosen a more certain means.

She longed to talk with someone about this, but there was no one she could talk to. Certainly not her grandmother, and now not even Peter. She felt too restless to sit here and think, and she went out to the top of the stairs to listen. A soft murmur of voices came from below. Theresa and

Gracie in the kitchen, perhaps? Or was Peter still here? She wanted to see none of them.

Outside on the deck that circled the tower, the August sun was hot. She went around to the outside stairs and ran down them to the ground. She hoped no one would see her, or note where she was going. Her goal was not Juan Gabriel's study—she wanted no more of that place. Instead, she crossed the lawn above the water to approach the more shabby structure of the shed where Lawrence Prentice had once worked. This was a part of her father she had never known. In their days in Santa Fe he had created nothing with his hands—perhaps he felt he must reject everything that had been part of his life in Virginia.

The door was unlocked and creaked on its hinges as she stepped into a large space that still smelled of sawdust and raw wood. Obviously no one had tended this place, apparently using it as a storeroom for discarded possessions. She moved carefully in thick, dusty shadows, searching for some evidence of the father she suddenly needed to find. Not the stern, remote man she had grown up with, but someone who might have been more loving when she was small.

What she saw told her that he must have walked out of this place for the last time without putting his tools away. They lay rusting upon a workbench, while the back of a chair he had been

278 working on rested across a sawhorse. So no one else had bothered to clear the place. Juan Gabriel had carved minutely, while Lawrence had built large, handsome pieces intended for practical use. Yet those two had once been friends. Her father had admired Juan Gabriel Montoro tremendously as a writer. He had collected all of his novels—except for *The Black Swan*. How significant was that omission? What had caused him to leave so soon after her mother's death, and why had he been so angry with her grandmother? There was also the unexplained fight between the two men.

Susan moved across the shed until she stumbled over some large, solid object in her path. When she bent to examine what it was, she saw that she had blundered into—a great brass pot. For an instant she recoiled, knowing that this was the instrument that had killed her mother. Yet a terrible fascination held her. She dropped to her knees and startled herself by circling the pot with her arms. She leaned her forehead against the cold, tarnished metal and began to cry.

Part of her adult brain knew what was happening. The child in her had gone back to the time of her mother's death, when she had kept vigil beside her body, perhaps leaning against this very piece of brass. There was nothing evil about a brass pot—not as there had been in Juan Gabriel's ebony carving of a swan. This was simply an inanimate object that had been in the wrong place at the wrong time. A fall had killed her mother—not this jardiniere.

With one arm resting on the circling brass lip, and her head upon her arm, she wept softly, making hardly a sound, releasing long pent-up emotions. Her tears were for her mother and Peter—grieving for lost companions whom she could never find again. Her tears were for her grandmother as well—a woman in whom she could never find again the loving presence she'd known as a child. There were even tears for her father from whom she'd wanted a love he'd never shown her, and with whom she'd been bitterly angry as she grew up. But most of all, at this moment, her grief was for the mother whose death she had witnessed, whose blood had stained her clothes—and who yet remained a veiled presence she could not recall.

Listening with some inner ear, she could almost hear angry voices at the top of the stairs, but they never came clear and she could not identify them. In her mother's story the king had been furiously angry and had rejected the queen's daughter, who was not his. Was there some hidden meaning here? Only her grandmother could tell her, and Susan wasn't sure she wanted to know.

Juan Gabriel Montoro, that brilliant, creative man, had been lovingly kind to his small grand-

280 daughter. Something in her remembered that and knew he would never have harmed her mother. Nor could she believe, as Theresa had claimed, that Susan herself might have pushed her mother in some moment of temper. There was more—something hidden that would not come clear.

Outside the windows of the shed, sunlight glared intermittently as clouds shifted in. This place was baking hot, and she could not stay here beside this instrument of death, however innocent the brass pot might be. Nothing had been solved by coming here. She got to her feet to stretch and became suddenly aware that a figure stood silhouetted in the open door of the shed. For an instant fear was colder than the touch of brass—appalling, unreasonable fear.

"Who is it?" she cried.

Gracie came toward her making sounds of reassurance. "I'm sorry, Miss Susan. I didn't mean to scare you. I saw you come out here awhile ago, and when you didn't come back for so long, I got worried. You all right?"

Susan moved toward her, weak with relief. Gracie saw the tear stains on her cheeks and opened her arms as she must have done long ago to a small child. Susan went into them, to be held and comforted.

"It's all right, honey. Good for you to cry.

Sometimes I wish Miss Alex would break down and bawl real hard."

But tears and being held were not enough. "I need to talk with you, Gracie. There's nobody I can talk to. Please help me," Susan pleaded.

"Sure enough—if I can. But let's get out of this hot, creepy place. It's getting cloudy and we can sit on the bench by the water. Out there we can talk all you want, and nobody but us can hear."

The house dreamed in summer warmth, normal and unthreatening. The tower poked into a cloudy sky—solid and steady, as it had stood since the last century. They sat together on the wooden bench with their feet near the creek's thin strip of sand.

"Miss Alex is asleep," Gracie said. "I looked in on her. And Miss Theresa's sitting nearby, in case your gramma wakes up and wants something. Mr. Peter's gone. I hear you're visiting Tangier Island tomorrow with your grandmother?"

"Am I? I don't know."

If she had any further thoughts on that subject, Gracie didn't express them. "You wanted to ask me something, child?"

Child! How good that word sounded—a word that encouraged her to give up her burden and place it in loving older hands. But she was no longer a child—or even a young girl. There were

282   some problems she could share with no one. What was it Peter had told her one time? That what he wanted was to make a difference? In her own way that was what she wanted as well. Not only as a nurse, but as a woman who refused to shrink from a past she had shut away as too terrible to contemplate.

She spoke hesitantly. "I don't know the right questions to ask, Gracie. So tell me whatever comes into your mind. Is there anything at all you can tell me that might help me now?"

Gracie didn't ask in what way Susan needed to be helped. She stared off toward the workshed they'd just left. "That place makes me remember the fight your daddy had out here with Mr. Juan Gabriel."

"Tell me about it, please."

"Trouble is, nobody knows what they fought about. Your granddaddy went out there where Mr. Lawrence was sawing up a piece of wood for a chair he was making. And I guess he told your granddaddy something that made him mad. I saw them both when they came through that door. Mr. Lawrence was cussing and yelling. I'm sorry, Miss Susan, but I never did like your daddy much. So I was glad when Mr. Juan Gabriel just up and punched him a good one in the mouth, so he flew out through the door. Your daddy was pretty surprised, I reckon. He never expected that from an old man, and he went down on his back right out there on the grass."

Gracie smiled at the picture in her mind, and then grew solemn.

"But Mr. Lawrence was a whole lot younger and stronger, so when he hit your granddaddy back real hard, he crumpled and just lay there. Mr. Lawrence didn't even care if he was hurt. He went back in the shed and banged the door. Mr. Peter was a young boy, and he saw what happened and called for help. George and him carried Mr. Juan Gabriel into the house. Old Doc Hazeltine came over when Miss Alex phoned him. The next day your granddaddy had a stroke.

"Your gramma was so mad at Mr. Lawrence that she hardly talked to him. After Miss Dolores was gone, she told him to get out of her house. She didn't want him around. So Mr. Lawrence fixed her real good. He went real far away and took you with him. Maybe your gramma never expected that to happen. Guess she always thought Miss Dolores's little girl belonged to her. When she woke up to not always getting her own way, it was too late. Mr. Lawrence hated everybody who was left in this house—even Miss Theresa, who was still a young girl and didn't do anything bad I know about. Though I don't much like what she's up to these days. But never mind that. Your gramma can handle her."

Gracie looked off toward where the clouds were piling up, black and threatening. "It's gonna rain pretty soon. We better get inside."

Susan put a hand on Gracie's arm. "You know something more about that fight—I have a feeling that you do. Will you tell me?"

Gracie patted her hand. "Some things I don't want to talk about. They'd only be guessing. You just go to Tangier Island with your gramma tomorrow. Maybe there's answers for you there."

This sounded all the more puzzling, but Susan knew Gracie's loyalties belonged first to Alex Montoro, and she would tell Alex's granddaughter nothing more on her own.

Susan allowed herself to be drawn toward the house as the first big splatters of hail came down.

Inside, Theresa sat at the kitchen table eating a late, pickup lunch. She looked at Susan coldly.

"What's all this about your going with Alex to Tangier tomorrow? She says I can't go with you."

Susan paid no attention to the question, her mind filled with new, disturbing images. She stood at a back window watching bits of ice clatter against the house, pebbling the creek's surface.

"Did you hear me?" Theresa demanded.

"What? Oh, I'm sorry. I don't know anything about a trip to Tangier." She spoke to Gracie. "Don't bother about lunch for me. I'll fix a sandwich and take it upstairs."

Gracie sliced cold chicken, telling Susan to sit down. She added buttered homemade bread, lettuce and tomato, and poured a thermos full of lemonade.

Climbing the stairs to her tower retreat, Susan was glad to be alone. She needed time to think, even if only to puzzle over the bits and pieces of information she'd collected since coming here.

The tower was still warm from the sun and she opened the windows that faced away from the slanting rain. The hail had stopped, but rain was driving hard against the closed windows and the tower roof. When she finished eating she sat listening to the rising storm. The afternoon had turned as dark as night, and lightning flashed almost continuously, bringing crashes of thunder that seemed to shake the tower. While the storm was exhilarating, it was also a bit frightening. After a loud boom and a zigzag of lightning that must have struck a nearby tree, the lights went out.

The storm drowned out any sounds from downstairs, and no one came to see how she was faring. She closed the windows she'd left open, but that shut out only a little of the storm's furious sounds, and the air in the tower room grew stifling. It was too dark now—except for sudden

286 flashes of light—to grope her way downstairs, and the storm would surely blow over before long. Already she could count a few heartbeats between lightning strikes and the boom of thunder, and the rain had slackened off a bit. She sat down to wait for it to be over.

As the storm grew quieter, she heard something move on the deck outside her room. In the next instant lightning flared across the sky, and she glimpsed a figure silhouetted against one of the tower windows. Alarmed, she began groping her way out of the room. But before she could move very far, the door was flung open with a crash, and a man in a dark slicker and fisherman's hat flung himself into the room.

Susan bumped into a table, losing her direction. He spoke to her across the room. It was Eric Townsend, and now no light mockery touched his voice, as a darker, more threatening note deepened it.

"Sit down, Susan. I want to talk to you."

Something told her that if she ran for the door, he would stop her. Nevertheless, it was safer to stay on her feet.

"What do you want, Eric?"

As lightning streaked the sky again, he took off his dripping rain gear and dropped it near the door. Then, without answering, he moved to the bureau and opened a drawer. His very silence was alarming as he drew out two candles and lighted them. He knew this room well enough to find the candles—whatever that meant. At once flickering shadows leaped around the room, and myriad lights danced, reflecting in the glass of windows. Candlelight revealed an expression on his face that frightened her even more.

"What I want is very simple." The softness of his tone carried its own threat. "I want you to pack up and leave, Susan. For your own safety you must go home as soon as you possibly can."

Or else?

An implied threat lay behind his words, and again she thought of escape. Now she could measure the distance to the door, but her knees were too weak to be trusted, and she stayed where she was, facing him.

"Maybe you'd better explain," she managed.

He came a step closer. "That's not necessary. Just *go* and you'll be all right."

She couldn't speak without revealing her fear. Perhaps he sensed that he'd gone too far.

"Relax, Susan. I wish you'd sit down. I have something to tell you."

Mirrored flame points dipped all around in a faint current of air, and Susan suppressed a shiver.

"Wow, it's hot in here!" He opened the door to fresh wet air. "The storm's moving away." Casual-sounding words that were meant to reassure, and failed completely.

She could see him clearly now. He wore jeans, soaked at the bottom, and his hair, usually carefully combed, had been roughed into untidy clumps, giving him a wilder look than she'd ever seen. There could be a serious instability in Eric that she'd never suspected before.

One side of the bed was nearer the door and she sat down on its edge, still not trusting her knees.

Eric roamed the room restlessly, pausing to look out into rainy darkness, speaking over his shoulder.

"It would have been a lot better for you if you'd never come here. Maybe you're beginning to realize that? There's still time to leave, you know."

It was best to seem agreeable to whatever was in his mind at the moment. "Just tell me why I should leave, Eric. I'd like to understand."

Her apparent acquiescence didn't fool him. "Let me tell you something you don't know. That accident of Alex's out in Juan Gabriel's study was never meant for her. I cracked that board so it would break and catch a different bird—you, Susan. Theresa knew, though she didn't think it was such a hot idea. But she'd told me that Alex never went out there anymore, and that you would probably go looking for a copy of *The Black Swan*. So I fixed a welcome for you. Just a bit of a warning. Of course somebody would find out about the deliberate damage, and you might be scared off. Then it all went wrong."

She kept her voice low, controlled. "Why would you want to injure me?"

"You wouldn't have been seriously hurt, but it might have been enough to make you feel you'd better not hang around. I could have followed up with a few other little scares, if you didn't take the hint right away."

"Like this one now?"

His eyes shone brightly with pinpoints of light, and she sensed inner debate. Would he carry out his threats now, or would he wait until another time?

Whatever happened, he mustn't guess how great her fear was. *"Why* don't you want me here, Eric? What difference can I make to you?"

He crossed the room to where she sat on the edge of the bed, and she forced herself not to shrink away. The change in him as he chose a more open attack alarmed her even more. He threw up his hands, laughing unpleasantly.

"Okay, Susan. You don't scare as easily as I expected. So I'll tell you. Then you'll understand how much I mean what I promise. Theresa and I want to be married. Oh, I know—there's a difference in our years, but with a woman like Theresa that hardly matters. This is what we both want."

She didn't feel surprised. Now she could

290 guess why he knew this room so well. She could easily imagine that Theresa would want this marriage. But why would a younger man like Eric even consider it?

"There's the matter of your grandmother's will," he said.

"What are you talking about?"

"The way Alex's will stands now, everything is left to Theresa. And believe me, she's earned every penny. We've had plans for that money but now that you've come into the picture, who knows what will happen? If we marry and you're here, Alex might even disinherit Theresa."

Understanding was suddenly clear. What predator did he remind her of? Perhaps a sleek, dangerous leopard? Or more likely a jackal?

He leaned forward without warning to where Susan sat rigidly on the edge of the bed. With a hand on each side of her and his weight on long arms, he leaned forward so that his face almost touched hers, cheekbone to cheekbone. Imprisoned, she couldn't move.

"*You* are going to help us," he said. "Then no one needs to get hurt. She's fond of you. So find a way to persuade her in our favor."

Her own rising anger betrayed her. She hated his closeness. He smelled of musty rain and his own high-pitched emotions. She could almost feel the pulsing in him—a fury that might go out of control.

In desperation she moved quickly, taking him by surprise. As she thrust outward with both arms, removing his support, he was forced to step backward to avoid falling. Freed of his arms, Susan ran toward the door, pulling it open. In a moment she was on the stairs.

"Wait!" he shouted after her. "Susan, wait!"

She went down recklessly, clinging to the rail. He didn't follow her except with words.

"Don't push me, Susan!"

For the moment she was safe—though perhaps only for the moment. Then, as she heard him go outside, slamming the tower door, everything around her changed, shifted in space, in time.

The stairs were steeper than ever—tricky. A death trap? Dream pictures illumined her mind, and she clung to the banister to slow her descent. There was no need for flight. It was too late.

Only one emotion was clear—the terror of a small child. An echo of old screaming filled her —and the memory of another anger, equal to Eric's. An anger strong enough to kill. The child had been deathly afraid. This was the fear her mother had experienced on these stairs when hands had thrust out to push her to her death.

Then time shifted back and she was herself again. Not until she reached Alex's room did she stop to breathe deeply. Her grandmother sat up in bed, with a book open on the coverlet beside

292 her. The lights were on again and she saw Susan's face.

"What was all that shouting about?"

Susan answered quickly. "I—I was scared. I nearly fell."

"Of course. I should have remembered how frightening that tower room can be in a storm. I should have sent Gracie up for you."

"I'm all right," Susan assured her. She couldn't talk about Eric now.

"I'm glad you came down, Susan. There's something I want you to read. Priscilla Bates gave me the notes Marilyn made for the last chapters of her biography. I'd like you to see them. Priscilla thinks they are important, but I seem to have lost my perspectives. Perhaps you can read them with a fresh eye."

"Of course." Susan took the folder of papers, her hands still unsteady, and settled down near a reading lamp. The storm sounds were far away, as Alex picked up her book again, and Susan started to read.

Marilyn had jotted her notes on the typewriter in outline form, with a few added details penciled in. She'd noted the political murder that had driven Juan Gabriel and his wife from their native country. She mentioned his obsession with the criminal mind, and gave the titles of several novels in which he had dealt with murder and crime. *The Ebony Swan* was among the titles listed.

However, it was the pages that dealt with Dolores's death that Susan found riveting, even though she knew most of the facts.

Juan Gabriel had suffered a stroke the day after a quarrel with Lawrence Prentice. He was in a wheelchair for some months before Dolores's death. Alex Montoro had been furious with Lawrence, but out of consideration for her daughter she did nothing.

Some months later, on the day of Dolores's death, Alex and Theresa were out of the house on separate errands. Alex had told Marilyn that Theresa was a precocious twelve-year-old whom Juan Gabriel had trusted to a greater extent than Alex thought wise. But as far as anyone knew, she had not been in the house when Dolores fell on the stairs.

No one could give an account of what happened that day. Juan Gabriel was in his wheelchair in the bedroom on the second floor, while Dolores and six-year-old Susan were in the playroom across the hall. Gracie was outdoors tending her vegetable garden. What brought Dolores out into the hall no one knew, but Susan must have come with her. Something so disturbed Juan Gabriel that he struggled out of his wheelchair, and Gracie reported that she heard him shouting, and that he sounded "real mad." When asked

294 why she didn't go inside to see what was the matter, she said she'd thought maybe Miss Dolores had better handle it. If she was needed, someone would call her. Mr. Lawrence was out in his workshed with a lathe going and he didn't hear anything, until somebody thought to fetch him. That was after Alex got home. Afterward, of course, Gracie blamed herself for not going inside right away.

Not until Alex came home, and Theresa a bit later, was Dolores found at the foot of the stairs, her small daughter beside her. Juan Gabriel had fallen out of his wheelchair near the top of the stairs and was unconscious when they found him. His coma had lasted until just before his death a few months later.

Susan stopped reading, aware that her grandmother had set down her book to watch her. Marilyn's account had pulled together the bits of information she'd heard since coming here and given her a sense of immediacy about what had happened. It was difficult to continue reading because of something nebulous that Susan had never been able to face. With an effort she read on.

Susan's father had claimed that Juan Gabriel must have pushed Dolores down the stairs in an uncontrollable rage. Rejecting his accusation, Alex had been so furious with Lawrence that she had ordered him out of her house. He had left, taking his small daughter with him.

It would be interesting, Marilyn had written, *to interview the daughter, who is now a grown woman living in Santa Fe.* Marilyn noted that she had tried to talk to Lawrence on the phone, but he had refused to see her, or allow her to talk with Susan, and had hung up when she persisted.

There were only a few more notes. Juan Gabriel remained in a coma for almost three months. Alex insisted upon caring for him up to the time he died. A few moments before the end, consciousness had returned and he had struggled to tell his wife something urgent. He had spoken four words that she was able to understand, and she had written them down and shown them to Marilyn: *Dolores. Never forgive. Murder.*

Below these lines Marilyn had written: *Does this mean there was something Juan Gabriel could never forgive his daughter? If Alex had any suspicion of what he meant, she isn't talking. I am not certain how much of this should be included in the book. I have a feeling that Alex is holding something back. The word "murder" is chilling, but Alex has no explanation for it.*

Susan returned the notes to their folder, aware of Alex watching her.

"Do Marilyn's words bring back anything, Susan?" Alex asked.

She could only shake her head. "Sometimes I

296 feel as though something is there, just at the edge of my mind, but it never comes clear. Perhaps it's time for me to talk to Theresa."

Alex looked surprised, but Susan had no wish to explain. Eric had gone, so she could go upstairs. She found Theresa in the workroom that had once been her own playroom, and when she looked in the doorway Theresa was doing something so astonishing that Susan could only gape in surprise.

Methodically, Theresa was dumping out the contents of containers and smashing her painted eggs one after another. Her worktable was covered with shells broken into colored bits. When she sensed Susan's presence and turned, her expression was bitter.

"A foolish occupation, don't you think, Susan? Painting eggs? I've had enough of it. Whatever talent I had as an artist has been wasted, lost. Dolores could always paint more beautifully than I could. She could always do everything better. Juan Gabriel may have treated me like his daughter, but I wasn't."

In this moment of revelation an unexpected feeling of sympathy for Theresa stirred in Susan. She spoke soothingly, as though to someone who had been ill.

"My mother was older than you were, Theresa. She'd had more time to develop her talents. So you shouldn't compare your work with hers."

Sympathy, however, was not what Theresa wanted. "Everything Dolores painted remains in this house—including that portrait of you. How I hated that picture when I was young. Even after your father took you away, I hated it. So I finally took to painting eggs—so I'd never have any competition. You can't compete with a ghost anyway."

"I hope you'll be happy if you marry Eric, Theresa."

Startled, Theresa swept the litter of shells into a wastebasket. "What do you know about that?"

"Eric came to the tower a little while ago, during the storm. He told me that he wants to marry you. But things are getting out of hand with Eric. He was angry—violent."

"What did he say?"

"He asked me to talk to my grandmother—plead in favor of your marriage. He is afraid she might cut you out of her will."

"That's foolish. Alex makes up her own mind."

"He also told me that he'd fixed that board out in Juan Gabriel's study so it would break under any weight. He did it because you'd said I would probably go out there for a copy of *The Black Swan*. The damage to the floor would be obvious, once it was carefully examined, and he

298 thought I would be so frightened that I'd leave. It all seems demented to me."

Theresa sat down stiffly on a stool near the worktable. "You have to remember that Eric is an actor first of all. He makes up scenes in his own mind and then lets his notions run away with him. Perhaps that's why I find him exciting —because he's never predictable. I'm sorry, Susan. I'll talk to him. You won't have any more trouble. I'm especially sorry about Alex's fall."

It was the first time Susan had ever heard Theresa sound contrite, and her feeling of sympathy returned.

"Is this marriage right for you, Theresa?"

Her answer came without hesitation. "Eric cares about me as much as he can care about anyone. Alex's will is a plus, but he will marry me even if she changes it. And Eric is what *I* want."

There seemed nothing more to be said on that subject, but Susan had come to talk with Theresa about something else.

"I've been reading the notes Marilyn made for the end of her biography of my grandfather. They were left with Priscilla Bates, who has just put them in Alex's hands."

"What did she write?"

"She set down the reason why Juan Gabriel left Peru. And also those strange words my grandfather spoke before he died. Something about Dolores—about never forgiving. He used the word 'murder.' Do you know about any of this?"

"Dolores's death wasn't murder," Theresa said sharply. "His mind was probably wandering. Even if you pushed her, it was hardly murder. The only person who's been murdered around here is Marilyn."

"No one ever told me the details of what happened to her. No one wants to talk about it. I know Peter was accused—but not why. Will you tell me?"

Theresa considered soberly. "In a way, I was to blame. An old friend was visiting me. I knew she was suffering from severe depression and her own doctor had prescribed a tricyclate drug."

"Tricyclates can be pretty toxic."

"That's why I wanted her to see Peter. I know he had helped some of his depressed patients by prescribing a careful, sugar-free diet and various supplementary nutrients. He was willing to treat her but didn't want to take her off the drug too suddenly. So he offered to refill her prescription at the drugstore and bring it here to the house the next morning. Did anyone tell you that tricyclates were found during Marilyn's autopsy?"

This was bewildering. "But how—"

Theresa went on, sounding grim. "He left the capsules in his office overnight along with some vitamins he'd picked up for Marilyn. They weren't living together by that time. But when he went to get the tricyclate prescription the next morning it was gone. At first he wondered if he could have misplaced it."

"And then his wife died?"

"Yes—of toxicity that resulted in coma and heart failure. She got the drug in her vitamin capsules. Someone must have broken into Peter's office—later they found an open window—and emptied the contents of the vitamin capsules, filling them with the distinctively marked tricyclate drug. She took three of the vitamin capsules— her usual amount—and it was enough to kill her."

For the first time the full horror of Peter's situation became clear, and Susan felt a little ill.

"But how could anyone have known that he had that prescription in his office?"

"That's what the police wanted to know. They were pretty skeptical. But someone did know, and Peter thinks that person must have been in the drugstore when he discussed the toxicity of tricyclates with the druggist and bought Marilyn's vitamins at the same time. Someone knew—and that could be how it happened. The police turned up no other suspect and it suited them to consider Peter guilty. At least the grand jury had the good sense to think otherwise. But the real murderer has never been found."

"So unless the truth comes out, Peter will always be under a cloud—is that it?"

"I'm afraid so."

She could understand his wanting to get away and leave all this suspicion behind him. Of course he would never drag anyone else into his troubles. She could understand but she couldn't accept.

"But why Marilyn?"

"Peter thinks she must have discovered something dangerous during her work on the book about Juan Gabriel. Something that shed light on Dolores's death. Perhaps something *you* know as well, Susan. So you'd better be careful."

The only way to be careful was to go back to Santa Fe, and she had no intention of doing that. Not now, not yet.

Theresa continued clearing her worktable, turning from Susan with an air of dismissal.

"Thank you for telling me," Susan said. On the way out she paused to look back. "You *can* still paint, Theresa. Why not try again? Something besides eggs."

Theresa didn't answer, and Susan returned to her grandmother's room. Gracie was just bringing in supper for them both on a tray, and as they ate together Susan told Alex about her talk with Theresa. Her grandmother listened sadly, but had nothing more to add.

The whole tangled skein was disturbing. Susan felt increasingly helpless and defeated. What could anyone do that hadn't been tried? But there must be *something*.

When they'd finished their light meal, Alex wanted to sit outside on the back porch. Their rockers creaked companionably while they watched a half moon sail through the few clouds left in a rain-washed sky.

"Tomorrow we'll go to Tangier," Alex said after a long silence. "I know it's time for me to take you there."

Susan sensed a note of reluctance in her voice. "Why is it important to make this trip to Tangier?"

"I can't explain, but it is important—maybe mostly to me. This is something we must play by ear. Whatever is meant to happen will happen."

Her grandmother's fatalistic note sounded ominous, but Susan asked nothing more. She tried to remember what she had heard about this island when she was small. That name she had never been able to get right was all that came to mind. She had always called it Tangerine.

Twelve

The small airport was across the Rappahannock River, and Alex hadn't flown out of it in years. Juan Gabriel had always preferred to go by boat when he ventured out on the Chesapeake. So did she. But for this trip she wanted to waste no time on the water. Tangier was no more than a few minutes away by air. The Gowers' friend Fred Parks had come to fly them over in his "Bamboo

Bomber." That had been the nickname for this particular type of plane when they'd flown in the war. Only a few were left in the country now, and Fred was enormously proud that this one had been completely restored, so that it was now state-of-the-art.

They were waiting for Fred to complete his flight briefing before boarding. Officials from Richmond were here with important visitors, and had preempted the runway.

To Alex any delay was welcome. She could feel tension in every muscle, and no effort of will lessened her anxiety.

Fred Parks, who had been born on Tangier, was busy telling Susan about the island as they waited in the airport building.

"The island is two and a half miles long and a mile wide," he informed her. "The inhabited parts are only seven feet above water. It was probably settled by members of Captain Smith's crew, who left ship while he was exploring the Chesapeake, though our favorite island storyteller claims that it was settled by criminals who were tossed out of England back in the 1600s—men who came from the Cornwall coast and brought their own manner of speech with them. You'll still find us hard to understand at times. We can run our words together, and there's a singsong quality. Tourists say, *What?* a lot."

"You talk like most Virginians," Susan said.

"I know." He sounded regretful. "The old speech is beautiful and it's a shame to lose it. But these days kids grow up and go away to college. Or sometimes off to war. And they come home—if they do come home—speaking in a different way, like the rest of the country. Those of us who use the old speech sometimes feel self-conscious about it, and we mostly use it among ourselves."

John Gower had gone to war, Alex remembered. She had watched the newspapers anxiously for news of his outfit. Oddly enough, it had been Juan Gabriel who told her that John had been wounded and shipped home. She hadn't wanted to care so much, but she hadn't breathed comfortably until she knew that his wound was minor and he had gone back to his island and crabbing.

Fred ran on. "Of course radio and television have changed everything. The whole world's more closely connected these days. Maybe that's good, but individuality can be lost. At least there's still an isolation about Tangier that sets it apart."

John Gower had spent his early life elsewhere, so he had no trace of the island speech by the time she'd met him. He had gone to the University of Virginia in Charlottesville, of course, and that too would have changed his manner of speaking.

How was she to deal with seeing him again? As the time drew near, she felt a tightening of the

306 anxiety that gripped her. The young girl, who remembered everything, was wide awake and all too eager to take over the older Alex's emotions. Alexandrina Montoro tried to ignore her. Only disappointment could result from too much remembering.

You're an old woman now, she told the girl. *Your young love is an old man. YOU don't exist anymore, and neither does he.*

She still felt concerned about Emily's words on the phone. How much did she know? How complete had John's betrayal been?

Never mind that. She couldn't deal with any of this ahead of time, and her thoughts drifted to Drina, who had once held the world's spotlight, and whom Juan Gabriel had tamed only partially. How frighteningly well he had understood the character he wrote about in *The Black Swan.* Understood out of his own creative genius. He had never known the truth about her love for John Gower. She'd been strong enough to conceal the pain of her loss. And she had recovered. The worst part had been having to live a lie when Dolores was born.

Outside on the ramp the people from Richmond were still bowing and waving and having their pictures taken. Alex stood at a window and watched absently, glad that Fred had found a willing listener in Susan.

Fred Parks was younger than John and Em-

ily—probably in his sixties—and he'd made flying the love of his life. In the old days he'd barn-
stormed from one country town to another all
over the South. Until flying became so common-
place that no one came out to watch, or to spend
money for rides in a small plane. Now he lived
with his wife in Florida, returning to Tangier
when the spirit moved him. Alex knew by heart
all the things he was telling Susan, and she listened with a sense of nostalgia. These matters
had appealed to her in the past, when she had
loved a waterman.

She remembered about the "cut" channel out
in the bay, which was the old Susquehanna
riverbed whose depth now offered the main ship-
ping lane between Norfolk and Baltimore. The
season started in May, depending on the whim of
the fish, and lasted until early December. Tangier
Island had always been a great center for crabbing as well as for fishing.

Reedsville, which had been a great fishing
center, had been one of the richest little towns in
Virginia. Captains' houses out of the past had
weathered the years with beauty and grace. Once
there had been widows' walks atop slanting roofs,
but most of these were gone because they cost
money to keep up, and captains' wives kept track
of their husbands more easily these days by radio.
Women's fears for their men at sea were as great
as ever, but news came more easily today.

"We can get on board now," Fred said, standing up. Susan offered her grandmother an arm, but Alex waved her off. She had sacrificed pride by bringing her cane, and it gave her a firm "third leg."

Boarding the plane wasn't difficult, since Alex hadn't lost all agility, and she could manage the few steps of a small stepladder Fred had brought to help her onto the wing. From there she stepped easily down into the cabin, managing to stay on her feet despite the pitch of the floor. Fred had explained that the old plane was what was called a tail-dragger, which accounted for the steep slant. The cabin was generous in size, and seated five comfortably. There was no aisle. A wide seat across the back would accommodate three if necessary, and there were two seats in front for pilot and passenger, or copilot. Alex lowered herself onto the rear seat and suggested that Susan sit beside Fred up in front, where she could view the approach to the island. Alex would look out the window beside her if she cared to, but there were clearer pictures in her memory of what lay down there on Chesapeake waters.

Revving up was noisy, and it was a relief when they sped down the runway and were quickly airborne. Fans and an air conditioner kept the cabin comfortable. The noise of the engines lessened, and now they could talk over the sound if they chose. Susan looked back now and then to make sure she was all right. Nurse and patient, Alex thought wryly. Yet she knew it was more than that. Susan's growing affection had become clear, though Alex couldn't decide whether this was good or bad. Since Marilyn's death, and since that damaged floorboard in Juan Gabriel's study, there were too many uncertainties, and perhaps Susan must be sent away before she could become too deeply involved. Gilbert had warned her about that in the first place.

From the plane the two shores of Virginia seemed separated by only a narrow strip of water, distances reduced from the air. Fred circled the island so that Susan could look down upon it before they descended.

Leaning close to the window, Alex saw again the little cluster of white houses, the spire of the Methodist church, the lacing of the island by canals. The few streets were narrow lanes running straight in grid fashion, except where inlets cut into the shore.

The entire island was at the mercy of sea and storm, and there had been serious hurricane damage in the past. Everyone prayed that the new seawall would protect the land from washing away completely.

In so many ways the island seemed worlds away from the rest of Virginia. Tourist boats could be used, but there had never been any easy visiting back and forth. In the past, women had remained behind their doors when strangers appeared. It was only in the sixties that changes began to take place.

Alex could still remember the names of various sections. She'd enjoyed the sound of them when she was young: Hog Ridge, Meatsoup, Sheep Hill, and Black Dye, among others. The Big Gut Canal split the island, and she could see it now below the plane—a straight, carved line from north to south.

Though the little airport building was at the north end of the island, the airstrip began at the south, so the plane came in over the beach, just below. Alex surprised herself by crying excitedly, "Look, look!" when she saw the strip of sand.

An older Alex could hardly bear to look, and she was glad when the beach vanished beneath the plane's tail as they touched down on a bumpy runway. They slowed, rolling along asphalt almost as choppy as the water of the bay, until Fred turned onto the ramp where two other planes were parked. He switched off the engines and got out to tether the plane and place chocks behind the wheels. Then he helped Susan out and came back for Alex.

When she got to her feet, she found her bad leg painful, but she took Fred's hand without letting anyone know of her discomfort. She crossed the wing as best she could and descended the small ladder.

On the ground the morning sun was bright and hot in this treeless space. The tiny airport building had been constructed since her day. It was only one room and "facilities" and was dwarfed by the hangar behind it. Emily Gower came out of the miniature waiting room that also served for air control, and walked toward them. Her smile seemed stiff and formal, and Alex knew this would not be an easy visit. But then, she'd never expected that it would be.

Fred Parks still had family on the island, and when Emily had thanked him, he told Alex he would see them later and went off. An island conveyance awaited them—one of the golf carts that served as public transportation. Cars were not allowed and most of the residents used bicycles or motor scooters. The golf carts served as taxis and took tourists around, as well as meeting incoming planes.

Emily introduced Ginny, their driver—a young woman in red shorts and a flowered shirt, an unheard-of costume in the early days Alex remembered. Alex was helped onto the front seat, while Emily and Susan sat behind. The cart could have carried several more passengers in its cross seats.

"We'll go straight to the house," Emily said. "John has been at the boatyard this morning.

312 Since he's no longer crabbing, he's part owner, and part boat builder as well. He'll join us for lunch."

Another respite, Alex thought gratefully. She'd begun to feel numb. Nothing she might do now would change anything. She had brought this visit about, but undoubtedly fate had its own plans, and she was no longer in charge. Emily seemed more like a stranger than her old friend, which was Alex's own fault.

Perhaps now, when they were both old, the rift could be mended. The past must no longer be allowed to matter. Perhaps that was what Emily had meant when she'd said that it "was time."

"This is a good day for you to come," Emily told Alex. "When the tourist boat is in, those of us who aren't needed go indoors and stay there until the crowd is gone. Not that we don't welcome our visitors—when they're friendly and well-behaved, as most of them are. And as we try to be. But this island is where we live and work, and sometimes we're stared at like creatures in a zoo. We do try to offer warm courtesy, and we want to receive the same."

By this time Emily was long an islander, and when an outsider became a native, she could show a special fervor about the place she'd adopted. Alex knew this from her own experience in being transplanted to Virginia. If a different choice had been made, she might have been a

Tangier Islander herself, and she no longer knew whether she had been right or wrong in her choosing. Perhaps today she would find out.

The cart rolled over what Emily called the "New Bridge" that crossed the canal—a long bridge that spanned swampy ground as well as water. On the other side it turned into a narrow lane that ran from north to south, with a single jog around the Methodist church.

Glancing over her shoulder, Alex saw Susan's lively interest in these surroundings. The graves hadn't come into view yet, and she wanted to see Susan's reaction when she got her first glimpse of them.

"We still live in John's old family home," Emily was explaining. "John wouldn't give it up for anything, though we've modernized a bit."

Listening to this narration, so formally given, Alex suddenly longed for the friend she'd loved and lost so long ago—not this stranger who was doing her best with Susan.

Along the lane that followed, the white picket fences she remembered had mostly been replaced by chain links. No doubt a protection against damage from golf carts and motor scooters, and certainly cheaper to maintain. Wild roses grew everywhere—she remembered those.

The first yard came into view. It was crowded with tombs, set aboveground and almost touching one another, and Alex turned again in

314 her seat to watch Susan. The shock of recognition that came into her face was evident, and she looked at her grandmother with amazement.

"This is what I saw when I was in the church!" she cried. "This was my vision!"

Alex spoke soothingly. "Yes—I knew what you were describing. This can happen, you know. It isn't necessary to understand."

The first time she'd come to the island Alex had been shocked by the crowded tombs in so many front and side yards. They had both fascinated and disturbed the young Alex. Since the island was water-logged, families had buried their dead in graves built aboveground in the only available space—their yards. Cremation was a modern solution that not everyone accepted.

Alex had been startled at the church when Susan had related her vision, but she had accepted the fact that not every experience could be explained by left-brain logic. Whimsically, she had wondered if some blood memory had been imprinted in a granddaughter, whose real heritage came not from Juan Gabriel, but from John Gower.

Emily was explaining casually. "John always says that it's comforting to have one's departed family members so close at hand. Though there are no graves in our yard, since his family used the small island cemetery. Now burials are often on the mainland. We islanders take our graves for granted and hardly notice them."

On either side of the lane stood handsome white clapboard houses of good size, all well kept and freshly painted. Many of the houses were built with a peaked front roof in an architectural style that had been adopted by early carpenters. Where there were no graves, small, neat yards lay open to the sun, with rare clumps of trees here and there. Once the entire island had been wooded, but over the centuries most of the trees had been cut down for building material and heating. Hurricanes had taken the rest.

Emily talked as the cart bumped along, and her words sounded faintly defensive. "I've come to love this island, Alex, though it frightened me at first. I wasn't used to such isolation—especially in winter. There's a wind they call the 'freezing fire' that comes off the bay. In the old days, when the bay froze, we could be cut off from the mainland for months at a time, since few boats could venture out. Now we have our small airport and there are always planes."

Susan shivered and Alex knew she hadn't fully recovered from having her vision connect with reality.

"It must be terribly lonely in the winter," Susan said.

"Oh, no! The men still sit around at the Double-Six—and talk man-talk. Women aren't

316 much welcome there. Did you know that islanders are called Tangiermen, but there's no name for the women? During the winter, we have lively parties and we do things we can't do when our lives are bounded by our husbands' work on the bay, and the regular visits of tourists. Of course, everyone on the island knows everyone else, and most of the islanders are related. You'll meet certain names over and over again." She broke off. "Look who's coming, Susan."

A young woman in shorts, riding a motor scooter marked POLICE, and with a small child perched on the seat in front of her, went slowly past. She smiled at Emily, who waved back.

"Our only police officer is a woman," Emily told Susan. "She does a very good job. In a small community like this we all keep an eye on our kids, and there's not much in the way of crime. Of course, we hold our breath over what can be brought back by young people who go off to school and come home with ideas that don't fit into our quiet life. It's a good life—better than you outlanders can imagine."

How thoroughly she had integrated herself, Alex thought. "There can't be many jobs for young people."

"That's the biggest problem. They can either become watermen or serve the tourists in some way. So a lot of kids grow up and move elsewhere. A number of babies were born this last year, so perhaps we're growing a little. We're about 750 in population at present."

"I admire you for adapting," Alex told her a little dryly.

Emily continued as though she hadn't spoken. "We'll drive you around, Susan, and show you some of our special sights. Then we'll have lunch at Hilda Crockett's Chesapeake House, where the food is good home cooking. Your grandmother and my John will want to talk about old times, so we'll leave them to that for a while. Here's the house now."

So this was what John had planned, Alex thought uneasily. There would be no respite, after all. The old woman and the young girl were once more at war, and the young girl had never had much sense. Panic and an urge to flee were in opposition with her foolish eagerness to see him again. Her knees felt weak, so that when Ginny helped her down from the cart, she leaned heavily on her cane.

"Just go on in," Emily directed. "If John's back, he'll be expecting you." Her voice seemed carefully neutral. As always, she would do what John wished. Could Alex Montoro ever have become so compliant?

The cart pulled away, but Alex did not go in at once. They had turned off the main road, and this was a parallel lane, with fewer houses and no graves. She stood on the walk inside a gate in the chain link fence and stared at the house she might have called her home.

A wide porch ran across the front. Above, set back from the porch roof, were three windows with dark green awnings. Over the center window rose the peaked roof common to the island. A red chimney stood up boldly on either side, promising warm fireplaces in winter.

Alex went up the steps and hesitated before the screened door. This was the moment for courage, for suppressing emotion of any kind. She tapped lightly, and when there was no response she obeyed Emily and stepped inside. A narrow hall ran toward the back, and a door opened on her right. After brilliant morning sunlight, Alex blinked in the dimness as she went through the parlor door.

For a moment she stood looking across a room in which the morning sun had been mostly closed out by shutters, so that the interior seemed cool and dim. A single reading lamp burned near the end of a couch where a man sat with a book in his hands. *An old man.* Her breath caught in her throat as he looked up and saw her. At once he set the book aside and got to his feet, moving far more easily than Alex was able to do.

She could only stand very still, staring at him, feeling more at a loss than she had in a long time. This man was as tall as the John she remembered, lean and wiry, not at all stooped, but with

a face that had been lined and weathered by his
trade on the bay. A stern face. This was no one
she knew, and she could think of nothing at all to
say.

When he spoke his voice sounded querulous
and not at all like the voice she remembered.
Had her own voice changed that much?

"Hello, Alex," he said. He turned on another
lamp, and his eyes seemed never to leave her face.
When he had looked for a time that seemed forever, his expression softened. "You're beautiful,"
he said in wonderment.

Beautiful? He was mocking her, of course.
She tried to remember how she had dressed that
morning. A bit much for a plane trip, perhaps,
but with a vanity she couldn't help indulging.
She had put on her favorite turquoise silk jacket
with embroidered white chrysanthemums. Slim
white trousers. Pearls in her ears—pearls Juan
Gabriel had given her, and that she'd put on as a
sort of protective charm. She stayed where she
was, stiffening in defense of that girl who had
begun to whimper inside.

"Come and sit down, Alex." John came to
take her hand, drawing her across the room. "I
know how strange this must be for you. For me
too."

She gave him another quick look as she sat
down, hardly touching his hand, holding herself
proudly erect. When she sat down carefully on

the sofa and set her cane aside, it promptly fell on the floor in its own perverse way. She ignored it and looked at this man whom she didn't know. Her eyes had adjusted from the outdoor glare, and now she could see him more clearly. He had been such a tenderly good-looking young man in those days when she'd loved every contour of his face. Now the myriad lines, even the weathering, expressed character and a quality of toughness she didn't recall. This was a far more interesting face than that of the boy she remembered—but it was the young face she had loved. Thick white hair gave him dignity, and he seemed far more assured and comfortable than she managed to feel.

He sat down beside her, though not close. "Tell me what you're thinking, Alex?" he said.

The question made her heart skip a beat because it came out of the past. That was a question he had often asked. She told the fool of a girl inside to be still, and managed an uncertain smile.

"I'm thinking right now that I'm two different women, and I don't know how to bring the two together."

"I know." The querulous note she'd first heard was gone, and the old resonance had returned. So he had been nervous too when he saw her. "I feel that in myself too, and it's not easy to deal with."

"But I don't want to be two people!" she cried, and now the querulous sound cracked in her own voice, undoing her further. "I've earned the right to be the woman I am. An old woman!" Her words defied him to contradict.

He turned his head away for a moment, so that she saw the carving of his profile, with all the young softness gone. He had, indeed, turned into a Tangierman, yet all those years away from the island still tempered him.

"We're both a lot more than two people, Alex. We can look back on an assortment of lives we've lived. More for you than for me. When I knew you, you were still very close to that young dancer you'd been. I'd never seen anyone so magical. When you moved you hardly touched the ground. You were vitally alive—and how could I not have been enchanted? But when you walked in just now I saw the woman you have become. You wear your years with grace, and there's still a magic about you. Somehow I knew there would be. An old man can remember, Alex."

Pain thrust deeply and suddenly, so that she could hardly endure what she felt. In that instant she could think only of all she had lost. He must have seen her betrayal of emotion, for he went on at once.

"When videos came in I bought one of *Swan Lake*. It wasn't *you* dancing, but I could half-close my eyes and see you on the screen. And I knew

322 —in spite of the anger I felt at the time—that we had been right to separate. No one can tether a swan. You'd have molted and lost your feathers. That long, proud neck would have bent in the winds of Tangier's freezing cold. Of course I raged at first because of the choice you made, though I knew later it was the right one."

You never came after me! The words sounded in her mind with remembered hurt, though she didn't speak them aloud.

"It took years to learn a little wisdom, Alex. Emily could turn herself into a waterman's wife, as you never could have."

Silence grew between them, as though there was no more to be said. Yet nothing had really been said, and she sat very still, waiting.

"You know why I wanted you to come here, don't you, Alex?"

"Of course," she said.

"Then will you tell me the answer? Is Susan my granddaughter? Was Dolores my daughter?"

Tears came so suddenly that she couldn't stop them. She felt the wetness on her cheeks and made no effort to conceal the emotion that shook her so unexpectedly. He touched a finger to one cheek, catching a shining wet drop. He had done that very thing before—when she was young and desperate. Even her cheek remembered. But tears could no longer be allowed, and she moved from his touch.

"Yes," she said. "Yes, to both your questions.
That's the reason I've come. Because you have a
right to see your granddaughter. I grieved for
you and Emily when I learned about your son's
death. I wished that you could know you had a
daughter, John."

"I felt a deep hurt when Dolores died. That is
the only time other than at my son's death that I
can remember crying real tears. In our day men
weren't allowed to cry. But I'd never known her
and when I knew I never would it broke my
heart."

There was too much emotion here—in both
of them. She tried to close herself against it.

"Does Emily know?"

"She knew what you and I meant to each
other before I married her. I'm not sure whether
she had ever guessed about Dolores."

Of course he'd had every right to tell Emily,
but she still wished he hadn't.

"Emily is strong and tough and capable," he
went on. "She didn't waste any time bleeding.
And after all, she is the one I married. She knows
that my loyalty to her has never wavered."

He didn't use the word "love," and it was
ridiculous to feel this surge of jealousy.

He had once been sensitive to her feelings,
and he startled her now by taking her hand and
holding it with a kindness, a tenderness that
could easily undo her all over again.

"We can never lose those two young people we used to be, Alex. Nothing like that has ever happened to me since. I've never run with Emily on the sand." He smiled faintly at the thought.

But he had lived with Emily in a house they shared, and all these years had been spent with her. Years that she had chosen to spend with Juan Gabriel. So who was to blame?

"You'd have been bored," he told her, the tenderness gone. "You'd have hated being a waterman's wife. I could never have given you a fraction of what your husband did. You were married to a distinguished, gifted man who adored you. I was wrong to ask you to leave him."

At this particular moment she no longer knew what was right or wrong. In her jacket pocket she found a handkerchief and dried her eyes, blew her nose.

"They'll be returning soon," he said. "I told Emily not to take too long. Are you going to tell Susan?"

His words recognized that the choice was hers.

She shook her head. "Not now. Perhaps never. I'm afraid to tell her because of what happened with Dolores." She paused and then went on, since he had a right to know. "Dolores was devoted to Juan Gabriel, who was the father she knew. And of course he was proud of her; she was his daughter. But the time came when I wanted her to know the truth. Perhaps I was blindly foolish, but I even felt that I owed it to you to tell her. I never expected her to go to pieces as she did. She was angry with me, and brokenhearted because Juan Gabriel was not her father. She even began to blame him and be angry with him as well. I'm still afraid that she may have exploded in Juan Gabriel's face that day she died. I don't know what happened, but I've always wished I could have talked to her again, made her understand what it was like when we were young—and—and—"

"Desperately in love? The way only thwarted young love can be desperate. But, Alex, it's different with Susan. She knew Juan Gabriel only as a small child. So perhaps—"

Alex caught the wistful note in his voice and went on. "She grew up out in Santa Fe knowing about Juan Gabriel Montoro only through his books. Probably feeling a little reflected glory at the fact that he was her grandfather. Her father never told her about us, though I know that Dolores told her husband before she died."

"Of course it would be hard for Susan to put me in his place."

"I don't know that. Susan is more like me than she's like her mother. Yet I'm still afraid to risk telling her at this late date. Susan and I have only just met. She hasn't even fully accepted me as yet."

John still held her hand and his fingers tightened on hers. "You'll know what to do when the time comes. *If* the time comes. For now, wait and see."

His understanding that put aside his own longing seemed more generous and giving than what she felt—more like the mother who had raised him. She had nothing to offer in return.

"I kept our secret," she told him. "I think my husband never suspected. He said nothing—ever. I do know how much I was loved and cherished."

John seemed to withdraw into himself. Clearly he didn't want to hear about Juan Gabriel, and it was a relief when the golf cart appeared outside.

Susan and Emily came in together, and Susan looked happy and interested.

"I'm glad you brought me here, Grandmother. This is a fascinating island. I almost feel that I have a connection with it. I've told Emily about my vision in the church."

Emily stood back a little, still wary and cautious, and Alex felt a sudden sympathy for her old friend. If Emily suspected that Susan was John's granddaughter, she might fear losing a little more of him to Alex.

"Susan," Alex said, "John Gower is an old

friend whom I knew when I first came to this country. Such English I spoke! He gave me a few lessons."

Susan held out her hand to John warmly. "Your wife has been telling me about the watermen of Chesapeake Bay. A life that sounds exciting, but dangerous as well."

"It can also be pretty dull at times," John told her, taking her hand.

Young hand in old hand, Alex thought. Blood speaking to blood. He held it for a moment and only friendship was offered.

The walk to the Chesapeake House was a short one, and they all went together under hot sun on this almost treeless island. The long dining room, with windows along both sides, was almost empty. Only a pair of flyers, father and son, had dropped in from the skies for lunch. When tourists were ashore these tables would be packed, and there would be an uproar of laughter and voices. John sat next to Susan, with his wife on his other side. Alex, next to Emily, felt grateful for the quiet room. Nothing was required of her now. She could listen to the talk and not even think. Susan and John seemed to hit it off well together, and she blessed him for the effort he was making. Even Emily seemed more relaxed now, reassured that nothing threatening would come of this visit, and that it would soon be over.

The service was family-style. Run now by her

328 daughter, Hilda Crockett's Chesapeake House was famous throughout the bay. Alex found her plate heaped with potato salad, cole slaw, crab cakes, Tangier Island's corn pudding, and pickled beets. They had all the coffee they cared to drink. The homemade rolls with preserves and butter were delicious. For dessert they were served pound cake and apple sauce—an island favorite.

Alex managed to eat a little, but refused second helpings. She was happy to see Susan hungry. John seemed more at ease now, amusing them all with stories of the bay. Emily had little to say, and Alex could find no way to get past the barrier her onetime friend had put up between them. This hardly mattered, since Alex would never return to Tangier again, and probably Emily would never again visit her. A halt was clearly being placed on their relationship, and Alex knew sadly that it would suit them both.

She was ready to leave as soon as they'd walked back to the Gower house. A golf cart would be called and they would be on their way. No need for John or Emily to see them back to the plane. John, however, sprang his own small surprise.

"I'd like to walk Susan down to the dock and show her the waterfront," he said. "Alex, I know you'll want some time with Emily, so why don't you wait for us at the house. I promise we won't take long."

So much for sensitivity! Alex suspected that Emily was no happier than she that they were to be left together. Though it would have been cooler inside, Emily sat down in one of the wicker rockers on the porch, while Alex chose the swing.

She tried vainly to think of some safe topic of conversation, but in the end there was only one thing she wanted to say. "I know we can't ever be friends again, the way we were when we were young, Emily. But perhaps we can clear the air a little. John hardly knew you at the time when I fell in love with him. So I never let you down. And of course John and I realized soon enough how foolish we were to think of any future between us. We broke off long before you and he came together."

Emily stared at her hands, clasped tightly in her lap. "I know that, but there's still Susan. Of course I know, Alex. How could I not guess? Women have instincts about such things, and this girl is Dolores's daughter. As she was John's. So what now? What is he telling her at this very moment?"

"He's not telling her anything, Emily. We've agreed on that. She need never learn about the past. We can let him have this time with her, so he can get to know her a little."

At least she had said the right thing. The relaxing of anxiety in Emily was evident.

330   "Thank you for talking to me, Alex," she said. "John has never given me any cause to worry about you. But Susan's coming brought everything I'd suppressed to the surface, and I could hardly stand having you come here. I didn't want to visit you when you were hurt, but John sent me."

If not everything of old pain could be mended, perhaps at least a better feeling between them would be possible.

"However—" Emily began and hesitated.

That could be one of the most ominous w 's in Alex's adopted language, and she stiffened, knowing something unpleasant was about to be said.

Emily collected herself and went on. "There is still something you don't know, Alex. John felt that you should never be told. But now I think you must be, whether he agrees or not. I feel that this is information long due you."

As Emily went on, Alex could feel all her defenses, her security—her very life—crumbling around her.

Thirteen

*J*ohn and Susan turned onto a wider lane of rough gravel and weedy grass that followed a slight slope down toward the water. She hurried to keep up with John's long, vigorous stride that gave no quarter to the noon heat.

She'd liked this man from their first meeting. In some ways he seemed younger than her grandmother. Not younger in appearance, perhaps, but

332 in youthful vigor. She suspected that he had lived exactly the right life for him, and she admired that, even though to her it seemed so restricted a life—though Alex's life was restricted too. Sometimes she felt that her grandmother was surrounded by high fences over which she could never climb. It would be good to know that she had kicked over the traces just once since she'd stopped dancing—instead of settling for the safety of marriage to a much older man. If only she could glimpse the young woman Alex had once been.

"Penny for your deep thoughts," John said.

"I was thinking about my grandmother. She's the most remarkable woman I've ever known, but she frightens me a little. I don't know how to get close to her."

He let that go without comment, gesturing toward the link fence that ran along beside them —a very long fence that reached from the water up to the cross lane they'd just left. Bits of paper seemed to be clipped to it, fluttering in the slight breeze.

"This is where people come in from the boats," he said. "So it's an old custom for Tangier women to clip their favorite recipes along this fence. There's an envelope attached for donations, if anyone wants to buy a recipe."

Susan had no interest in recipes at the moment. She walked at this tall man's side and listened while he talked about the island he loved. This was something she found difficult to understand. She hadn't been entirely truthful when she said she found the island fascinating. She couldn't understand why anyone would want to live out here on this bare, sunbaked spot of earth set barely above sea level. Nor could she understand why she had received a vision of what she would see when she visited the church. That was frightening to think about—dipping into realms she had no knowledge of.

"Who settled the island in the beginning?" she asked.

"There are various stories. Cornishmen? Or Londoners, whose speech from Elizabethan times you can still hear spoken? Or were there pirates, who mated with Indian women? Probably sailors jumped ship when Captain John Smith sailed up the bay. We have a colorful history. Francis Scott Key was imprisoned here during the War of 1812. When he was taken aboard ship as a prisoner in the attack on Baltimore, he wrote about those *bombs bursting in air* that he saw from the deck of a ship out of Tangier."

Interesting, but far too distant, Susan thought. "Tell me about my grandmother. You knew her when she was young."

He waited so long that she wasn't sure he would answer. They had reached the place where the boats came in, and when he gestured she

334 went with him to sit at the end of the empty dock, their legs dangling above the water. Susan breathed the salty, slightly fishy air and listened to the lapping of waves among the pilings beneath the dock. Out on a post in the harbor an osprey watched for fish.

After a time the man beside her began to talk, his voice low in its remembering. "Alex and her husband came to the island a few times. He was planning to write about what he saw here, though whether he ever did I don't know."

"I don't recall reading about Tangier in any of my grandfather's books. What do you remember about *him*. No one talks about him as a man —only as a famous author."

"He was a good deal older than Alex. I thought him distinguished-looking, and a strong personality."

"Did you like him?"

"I didn't know him, really. I was in awe of him—he seemed very stern and remote. Mostly off in some intellectual country of his own creation. No, I didn't like him."

For the first time Susan sensed that she might have stepped into deep waters. If John Gower had fallen in love with her young grandmother— which seemed possible—he would certainly have disliked Juan Gabriel. She moved to safer ground.

"I've seen pictures of him, of course. There

were always photographs on his book jackets. I used to think he looked like an eagle with that beaked nose and strong chin."

"I'm sure he could be like that. A man to reckon with. But when I saw them together he was always very gentle with your grandmother." John Gower paused, and when he went on something in his voice had changed—as though he smiled inwardly at some private joke. "I'm sure your—your *grandfather* was someone she loved very much."

"He has never seemed like a real person to me. Just a writer whose books I admire. I suppose that's why I keep asking questions. So I can find some connection between us."

"Perhaps you should tell your grandmother what you've just told me."

She'd said nothing of special significance, Susan thought, and decided to risk the real question in her mind.

"Were you in love with my grandmother in those days?"

He answered lightly. "Everybody loved her. But she was married, Susan."

She knew she'd been put off. "At least you can tell me what *she* was like when she was young. I can only see her as old."

He relented, smiling at her eagerness—a warm, almost affectionate smile.

"She's probably several times the woman now

336 that she was as a girl. But I can remember that she was filled with more vitality than anyone I'd ever known. She almost crackled with life—like a firewheel about to spin off into space. Or she could turn as cool as an ice queen and freeze whatever she touched."

As she had frozen him?

He went on, half-musing to himself. "Perhaps she's more human now—less like the swan queen who was out of the reach of mere mortals."

If he had loved her, how could he have married Emily, who seemed so much older than Alex, and rather dull? But of course Alex Montoro—Drina!—would never have looked at an impecunious young fisherman. He might have loved her, but he had been sensible enough to marry a woman who would make him a suitable wife. A woman willing to bury herself on Tangier Island. At the same time, some romantic part of Susan wished that Alex Montoro had defied society and run off with John Gower. And never mind that old eagle, Juan Gabriel!

John seemed to sense that she played a wistful game. He could be a thoughtful, perceptive man.

"Don't build fantasies around your grandmother, Susan. Perhaps sometime she'll tell you more about the days when she was young. She has become a private, rather secret person, so you'll need to wait until she can trust you."

"She can trust me now!"

"She doesn't know that. Give her time."

In a strange way time seemed to be rushing past. It wasn't a matter of waiting, but of reaching out to stop the flight of *minutes*.

"If she'd just talk to me! She's told me a little about her dancing, but not much else. There's so much I want to know."

He stood up from the dock, pulling her to her feet. He would never really discuss her grandmother—he was as bad as Alex was when it came to talking about the past.

"It's time to go back," he said. "I wanted to show you our harbor. There's so much you miss by coming in on a plane. Way out to your right on the bay is an old Liberty ship that floats above water in two broken pieces. It's been used as a target for bombing practice, though not with live ammunition."

Susan had the feeling that he held her there talking because he was reluctant to go back to the house.

"Perhaps I'll come again sometime," she told him. "If I stay."

Her words seemed to surprise him. "*If* you stay?"

"I don't know what I'm going to do. Sometimes I think that Alex just wants me to go away."

He spoke almost sadly. "I have the feeling

338 that your grandmother needs you. She hasn't anyone else."

"She has Theresa Montoro," Susan said flatly.

"I've never met Theresa, though I think my wife doesn't care for her. I meant only that you are Alex's one blood relative, and that counts for a lot."

Since Alex was often hard to read, Susan felt uncertain.

John Gower went on as they walked back up the lane. "I know very little about your grandmother's life at present. We've been out of touch for decades, and Tangier Island is isolated from the mainland in so many ways."

"Do you mind the isolation?"

"It's been my life—a good life. I've done what I most wanted to do."

They finished their walk in a silence that was not uncompanionable. In an odd way Susan had the feeling that she and John Gower had become friends, even though they might never see each other again.

When they reached the house, Alex and Emily sat on the porch waiting—one in a chair, one on the swing—yet they seemed miles apart. Susan sensed in an instant that something had happened to her grandmother—something devastating. The very droop of her shoulders was uncharacteristic, revealing dejection, hopelessness. New lines seemed to have appeared in her face, and her skin, always protected from the sun, looked even paler, as though she'd experienced some terrible shock.

Noting the signs with an experienced eye, Susan ran up the steps. "This trip has been a bit much for you, Grandmother. I expect we should start back."

Emily spoke calmly. "Your grandmother isn't as rugged as we islanders are, Susan. John, will you phone Chesapeake House? Somebody will send a cart over to take Alex and Susan to the airport."

Afterward, Susan remembered their leaving as a time of haste and confusion, with Alex behaving as though she'd removed herself from all reality. John Gower seemed bewildered, while his wife wore an air of complacency. Whatever had happened, Susan was sure, had stemmed from Emily Gower.

It was a relief when the Gowers decided not to come to the airport to see them off. All Susan wanted was to talk to Peter, who would know what to do. A phone call was made so that he would meet their plane. Susan spoke to him briefly, warning him about the change in Alex.

Fred Parks waited for them at the little Tangier flying field. This time getting aboard seemed more difficult for Alex. Earlier she had been

340 filled with anticipation and perhaps a little anxiety, both of which gave her energy. Now she had become indifferent, almost inert.

On the short flight home, Susan sat beside her grandmother on the cross seat, while Alex leaned back with her eyes closed. It would be useless to ask questions, Susan knew. When she and John had left to walk to the waterfront, Alex had seemed younger and happier than before. So sudden a change was frightening. Obviously she needed support, but how could anyone help in the face of this lassitude?

On the flight from the island Alex never looked out the window beside her, and Susan could only play the watchful nurse. She gave Alex aspirin for her probable headache and poured water from a thermos to help her swallow it. Afterward, unexpectedly, Alex reached for Susan's hand and held it tightly, as though she needed an anchor. Susan hoped that the pressure of her own fingers showed the love and tenderness she felt. With no understanding of what had happened, Susan was aware that a new bond had grown between them. For the moment her grandmother needed her, and with that Susan was content.

Peter was waiting when they landed, and he took over at once, accepting Alex's silence and asking no questions.

When they'd thanked Fred Parks, Peter led

the way to his car. But when he suggested that Alex lie down in the back seat on the drive home across the bridge, she looked at him from a remote distance that dismissed his concern.

"I'm perfectly all right," she said, and sat in the front seat beside him, looking weak and stricken. Her turquoise jacket that had seemed flattering and youthful this morning, had wilted, and Alex had turned into the old woman she'd always seemed to deny. What had Emily Gower said or done that had brought Alex to this alarming state?

There was little for anyone to talk about during the drive. Susan gave Peter a perfunctory account of their visit, and Alex said nothing at all.

Susan began to feel a new anger toward Emily Gower. If Alex had really had an affair with John Gower in the past, and Emily knew about it, perhaps she could have said something accusatory that had reduced Alex to a state of guilt. But somehow that didn't seem to be the answer. So ancient a happening could hardly affect either of them now.

When they reached the house Susan saw with annoyance that Hallie Townsend sat in the porch swing, creaking back and forth, obviously waiting for their return. She had a talent for turning up at inappropriate moments. At once she jumped up and hurried down to the car.

"Alex," she wailed, "you went to Tangier Is-

342 land! You went to see Emily and you didn't let me know. You could have taken me with you. You know I seldom get to see my sister!"

"Later, Hallie," Peter said. "Alex isn't feeling well just now."

He helped Alex from the car, and Susan put a hand beneath her grandmother's elbow. Alex, however, pushed them both away and faced Hallie.

"I'm sure you can visit your sister any time you wish, as she can visit you. There are always boats."

Hallie became suddenly aware of Alex's gray and fragile appearance. "What's happened to her?" she demanded of Peter. "What's wrong?"

No one answered, and they started up the steps.

Susan's concern was not for Hallie, and as she followed Peter and her grandmother into the house, Gracie came anxiously into the front hall and Peter spoke to her.

"Where is Theresa, Gracie? I'd like her to stay with Miss Alex for a little while."

Gracie hesitated. "She's left—gone with Mr. Eric, to be married, I guess. She left a letter on the hall table. I'll stay with Miss Alex, if you want."

If the news about Theresa and Eric meant anything to Peter he made no comment, and Alex seemed not to hear.

"That's even better, Gracie. Will you help Miss Alex to her room, please? I think she'll want to lie down." He kissed Alex's cheek and gently released her hand from his arm. "I'll look in on you soon, Alex. Let Gracie help you now."

Alex gave him a shaky smile and allowed Gracie to lead her away.

"Why shouldn't I stay with my grandmother?" Susan asked.

"Because I'd like you to do something for me—if you're willing, Susan. I've been turning this over and over in my mind and I think the time has come."

It was as though some inner alarm alerted her. Peter seemed grave and remote, and she felt suddenly afraid. She wanted only to resist whatever he had in mind.

"Let's go in here," he said and led the way into the long room that had once been a double parlor.

There was no longer any way to stop what was about to happen. She allowed him to lower her onto the couch, where he pushed her back gently, so that she stretched out full-length. He put a cushion under her head and pulled over a chair in order to sit beside her. She closed her eyes, knowing what he meant to do. Perhaps he was right, and the time to go back had arrived.

If only she didn't feel so nervous and uncooperative. Whatever had been buried in her mem-

344 ory for so long had been too terrible to recall, and she wasn't sure she could bear to remember now. At the same time she could no longer stop what was about to surface, whether Peter helped her or not.

Ever since she had come to Virginia, flashes had appeared in her mind. Sometimes she'd been aware of voices shouting angrily, though she could catch no words. Sometimes there were brief, terrifying explosions of color, with red predominating. Most of all there had been a sense of some terrible evil—something that might have come out of one of her mother's own dark fairy tales.

Peter began to speak soothing words meant to relax her, but this was not the way and she stopped him. Almost as though she sleep-walked she left the couch, pushing past his hands as she went into the hall. There she stood very still, focusing on a dim inner world of shadow and sound that belonged to very young memory.

"I must go back," she told Peter. "I think I can now, in my own way. I must go back to where it happened."

He nodded, understanding.

She put a hand on the banister and began to climb slowly—because the steps were high for six-year-old legs. The room where her grandfather sat helpless in his wheelchair, because of something called a stroke, was on her left. Down the hall on the opposite side was her own play-room. She went to the door and stepped inside, envisioning with an inner eye. Theresa's workta-ble and a few remaining eggshells were not what she saw. Instead, she was aware of her own small pieces of furniture and her playthings. No lights were on, but the room lighted itself in the mists of memory. Her mother sat in a big wing chair, reading aloud a fairy story she had written. Susan sat at a play table painting in watercolor, wholly concentrated.

Her grandfather's voice called out from his room. Though the sound was faint, it made her mother drop her pages and jump up. "That's your grandfather!" she cried and ran to the door. Susan knew that he had trouble speaking, so it was surprising that he could call out. She started to follow her mother but was pushed back at once.

"Go on with your painting, honey," her mother directed. "It's nothing."

Susan sat down again, but now she felt frightened. It was *not* nothing. Her grandfather was making angry, startled noises. She could hear him as he struggled from his chair, and she could hear her mother protesting. More than anything Susan wanted to shut out the upsetting sounds. She didn't want her grandfather to be mad at her mother, and she tried to pay attention to the watercolor that had turned very messy. She was

346 painting it for Grandma Alex, and now it had been spoiled.

When she heard her mother scream, she knocked over the water glass where she'd dipped her brush, and ran into the hall. Her grandfather had pushed himself up from his chair and for a moment she stood staring at him. He was holding some sort of carving and he put out his other hand to her. Then a terrible look came over his face, and while she watched, frozen, he fell full-length near the top of the stairs.

That was when she looked down and saw that her mother lay at the bottom of the steep flight, not moving. A terrible wetness of red seeped about her head. A red stronger than anything in Susan's paintbox.

She almost fell down the stairs herself in her hurry to reach her mother. A mother who didn't answer or move, even when her small daughter began to scream.

It must have been only a little while after that her grandmother came home and found them there. Only a little later Theresa came home too. But Susan couldn't tell them about the awful thing that had happened. She hadn't really seen her mother fall, but the way her grandfather had looked—she was afraid that he had pushed her down the stairs. Though she never told anyone that, and she never would.

The mists cleared and the years fled past to

the present. The grownup Susan sat on the bottom step of the stairs, with Peter's arm about her.
She leaned into his shoulder crying softly. That
day Susan's father had come in from outside with
his friend Gilbert Townsend. But she didn't want
to remember any more. All the rest was too painful, and she wanted only to forget.

Peter held her, and now he was saying all the
things she wanted most to hear. That he loved
her. That he wanted to keep her safe and never
let anything terrible happen to her ever again.
She turned her face for his kiss, and then pushed
herself away. Because it wasn't over. She knew
very well that there was more to come.

"I don't believe in what I thought happened,"
she told him. "My grandfather would never have
hurt his daughter. He was trying to *save* her. I
know that! Somehow I know, even though I
didn't understand anything at the time."

"You've remembered something more,
haven't you, Susan?"

"It's more a feeling than something I saw. A
sort of whoosh down the hall toward the upper
stairs. As though someone rushed away."

"Someone else was there?"

"I have a strong feeling that I heard someone.
All I could think of at the time was my mother
lying there—and the horror of what I thought I'd
seen. That my grandfather had pushed her. So I
had to put it all away from me. I had to shut it

348 out and forget in order to protect myself. But the terror has always been there deep down inside me, sometimes stirring about in my dreams. I've had an awful feeling that it was my fault, that I could have saved her."

"You know better now."

"Yes. And I know there's more."

She closed her eyes, trying to bring back that other something that hovered just out of sight. But it was all a blur. The blur of someone rushing away down the hall, making that whoosh of sound. Someone who knew about the outside stairs from the tower and could escape easily.

"I'm sure someone else was there. But what can I do about it?"

"When your grandmother is feeling better we must tell her," Peter said.

"Tell her what? That part of me believes that Juan Gabriel pushed my mother down the stairs? Even while I deny that, I'm afraid it might be true."

"Alex must be given a chance to think about this. The contradictory feeling that someone else was in the house may give her new hope."

Peter's arm tightened about her, and Susan tried to let everything else go.

Fourteen

*A*lex managed to smile at Gracie. "Don't worry about me. I'm perfectly all right. I'm not going to bed and I don't want to be fussed over. Visiting Tangier Island wasn't easy, and I need some time alone to think about it."

What Gracie might have known or guessed had never been apparent, but she knew when to

350   retreat. Once more she slipped away, keeping her own counsel.

When she was alone, Alex took off the turquoise jacket—a totally unsuitable choice for the trip!—and tossed it over a chair. Vanity had gotten the better of her because she'd wanted to look as well as it was possible for an old woman to look. Of course that had hardly proved to be important. After all, her only purpose in going to the island was to allow John to meet his granddaughter.

Nevertheless, it *had* mattered to look her best. She had felt as tremulous as a young girl when she'd stepped into that room and John had risen to greet her. He had looked at her in the old way and told her she was beautiful—so that for an instant she had felt young again.

She put on a dressing gown and went to stand before a pier glass in a corner of the room, trying to see what John had seen. But now she felt even older than when she had gone to Tangier and listened to what Emily had told her.

That was what she could hardly bear to face. In the glass Drina still looked out of eyes that had hollowed over the years, and somehow she recognized a comforting truth. She could recall John Gower's face in every detail, recall everything about him. But she was not remembering the old man she had just seen on the island. So that was probably the way he would think of her too—as that young girl only a few years removed from Drina. Only those who grew old together took the changes for granted and forgot the look of youth.

Since she would never see John Gower again, his memory would remain bright and young. Or that was the way it might have been if she had never gone to Tangier. But how could her memories remain untarnished after what Emily had told her? The frightful truth was what she had been trying to hold away because it was impossible to accept.

She sat down heavily in an armchair and leaned her head back, closing her eyes. She had never known, never suspected what had happened all those years before. In a sense, her entire life had been a sham, and how was she to live with that knowledge now?

Emily had told her, speaking quietly at first. They'd sat near each other on the porch almost companionably, while Emily destroyed the very fabric of her life. She could still hear her voice clearly—that older voice of a stranger.

"You never knew, did you, Alex, you never knew that your husband came here to the island to see John?"

Alex had looked off at the sunbaked, marshy brown stretches, visible where houses were sparse. She'd said nothing, suddenly tense.

Emily's smile was hardly friendly. "Did you

352 really think that your husband would never guess? He must have taken one look at you and known you for a young woman in love. And *not* with him. I doubt that you ever looked at him the way you must have looked at John. I remember there was a glow about you in those days that could only come from being in love. I wasn't close to John then and I didn't know who the look was for."

Alex couldn't bear to see the expression on Emily's face, and she closed her eyes.

"Mr. Montoro must have known that he needed to act to save his marriage. So he came to see John. Of course I knew about none of this until after John and I were married. I'm glad he could trust me enough to tell me."

John's trust had to be given to his wife, and the wound Alex felt was unjustified. The hurtful voice went on. "Your husband wasn't young then, but John was afraid of him. He knew about the rumors—that Mr. Montoro had killed a man in Peru. He brought a gun with him when he came to meet John—a Spanish gun with silver mountings. Perhaps the same one he'd used before? You would recognize it, wouldn't you, Alex? Of course, John was younger and stronger and swifter. He managed to take the pistol away from your husband. Mr. Montoro was a brave man, and an angry one. He stood his ground, even though he was disarmed. He told John never to see you again, or Juan Gabriel Montoro would kill him. John knew he spoke the truth. That fancy pistol is still on a shelf in our parlor, where John put it—though I've always wanted it out of the house."

Alex remembered the gun very well, though she had not seen it since that time when she'd found it in Juan Gabriel's safe. It had never turned up after his death, and now she knew why.

Emily was clearly enjoying this moment of malicious pleasure—the spilling of pain that had been contained over the years. "I always thought you ought to know, Alex, but John refused to tell you. He gave you up willingly, you know. But Tangiermen don't give up, and perhaps he was ashamed."

There was a new bleakness in this knowledge, and Alex held to her silence.

"Of course, no one else knew about any of this except Hallie." Emily spoke almost casually now. "Even though Hallie is the youngest, she always looked after Gilbert and me, so of course I had to tell her."

There'd been nothing to say. Even now, Alex didn't know how she could have responded to Emily's words. It had been safer to shrink into herself, to be very still and simply wait for John and Susan to return, so she could be taken home.

354 All she had wanted by that time was to leave Tangier Island forever.

The one comforting anchor she had clung to for all these years with Juan Gabriel had been her belief that he had never known, never been hurt. How foolish she had been to believe that! Still, she *had* chosen life with him over running away with John Gower. John had apparently chosen too. He had stayed away from her, rather than risk Juan Gabriel's anger. At least, her choosing had not been under threat.

Or had it? Had she carried some deep knowledge in her that if she had gone off with John, Juan Gabriel would have come after them and perhaps neither of them would have lived?

Yet he had forgiven her silently and continued to love her. Or pretended to love her? He had never let her guess what he had done, except, of course, that he had written *The Black Swan* and carved that wicked little face in ebony. At times she had been uneasy, wondering, but she had never accepted what he might know. Now the bitter truth left her feeling abandoned, unprotected. There seemed nothing left for her to nurture that was good about their life together.

How he had felt about Dolores was something else she could never know. Had he only pretended love for the daughter who belonged to another man? Had all his seeming tenderness toward Dolores, who thought him to be her father, been pretense? No! She would never believe that. He had secured his marriage in his own way, and if he had loved her more watchfully, she had never been aware. She had cheated Juan Gabriel of the full devotion she had owed him, even though she'd remained his wife and loved him in a different way.

No! No one could *owe* love. Love made its own rules. At least she remembered thankfully that when he was dying she had held his hand and told him over and over how much she loved him. Words that had been *true*. If he could hear her at all, he must have known that they were true. Their love had grown out of a long life together, had grown from the understanding they had given each other.

As a young man Juan Gabriel had surely known his own wild and passionate loves, though such experiences would never have made him tolerant toward a woman who belonged to him and was unfaithful. Or was it possible that he had arrived at a state of wisdom where he could forgive? How was she ever to know?

Confusion left her sadly helpless. Certainly she could never tell Susan the truth. When she had told her daughter that Juan Gabriel was not her father, Dolores had listened in white-lipped silence. Her only immediate response had been to write that terrible little allegory which Alex had not read until after her death. When Dolores had fallen on the stairs Alex had never stopped blaming herself.

Since Emily had told her, Hallie also knew what Juan Gabriel had done to prevent her from running off with John Gower. Alex could understand why Hallie sometimes looked at her with barely hidden disapproval. Hallie had never liked Dolores because of her own foolish crush on Lawrence Prentice. On the surface, Hallie had seemed to remain her friend, but who knew what she might have told others?

It would be necessary to talk to Hallie very soon and bring everything into the open. If she waited, Hallie might take the step Alex feared and tell Susan the truth.

Weariness of body and spirit swept through her. She longed to let everything float away from her. Now that it was far too late, she must let John Gower go—as she had never really done before.

When she stretched out on the bed, sleep came—though not dreamlessly. Just out of sight, on the edge of nightmare, something hovered waiting to destroy all that Alex Montoro cared about. Susan's happiness with Peter was at stake, and she must act to save her. In this half-conscious dreaming state she told herself that when she awoke she would know what to do.

Alex must have needed the rest because when she opened her eyes the sun had moved down the sky toward its late summer setting. Gracie had known better than to waken her for supper, and she didn't feel in the least hungry. She knew now what she must do—where she must go to find the help she needed. Somehow she must make peace with her own life, and somehow she must have the wisdom to know what to do about Susan.

She put on a pair of dark gray slacks, and a light cardigan against the chill she could expect in the place where she intended to go. Susan sat in the parlor, a book face down on her lap unread. At once Alex knew that her granddaughter and Peter had worked something out. That dreaming look on her face was recognizable, and a new happiness for Susan rose above her own pain. Peter was right for her. Susan's life would take a better turn than her grandmother's ever had.

"I've had a good rest," she told Susan, falsely brisk. "Now there's something I must do. Will you come with me?"

Susan rose eagerly to put her arms around her. "You're looking much better. I was worried about you. Something happened on the island—" But she knew better than to ask.

"Yes. I've had a shock I never expected. I'm still not sure how to deal with it. So I want to

358 return to the one place where I've sometimes been granted wisdom."

"To that special church?" Susan asked.

Alex nodded, and went to tell Gracie where they would be, in case anyone asked for them. Then they got into Alex's car, and she felt glad to be at the wheel, traveling familiar roads, taking some sort of action that might help her toward a resolution—a healing for her life.

When they reached the place, high billows of pinkening clouds floated above the dark grove of trees and the yew-lined walk to the door of the building. This was a structure that had seen centuries pass, and to which so much human grief, as well as joy, had been brought over the years.

Susan had asked no questions and had come with her willingly, but Alex sensed her concern. She paused on the walk and put a hand on Susan's arm.

"Allow me this. Long ago I lost all contact with formal religion. But something speaks to me here. I need a renewal of strength in order to deal with my life."

Susan nodded uncertainly, and Alex sensed by her look that she might be remembering her earlier vision that had proved prophetic on Tangier Island.

It was after hours and the church was locked, but Alex had brought the key she had acquired long ago as a trustee. She slipped it into the lock and the door swung open.

The great arched space with its high oxeye windows was alight with a rosy glow from rays that slanted across pews and aisles, otherwise lost in shadow. Alex raised her head to the benediction of light and moved slowly up the aisle. The stark beauty of vaulted spaces raised her spirit. In a little while the sky outside would darken, but she had come in time. The light blessed her, and the draining of courage ceased.

With Susan close beside her, she moved toward the chancel. No formal prayer rose to her lips. She had no need of such words. Whatever presence presided in this place knew why she had come, and a response seemed to echo through her consciousness. She needed only to listen.

You have the strength in yourself that you have always had. A strength that is greater now than when you were young. Accept and listen. Accept what your spirit already knows. If ordeal lies ahead, you will meet it, face it without faltering. The power you need is within you always. Use it.

"Grandmother!" Susan's whisper carried a warning and Alex turned to look toward the door they'd left open when they entered.

A figure stood silhouetted against the sunset light. As Alex tried to make out the face, she felt a sudden, almost superstitious fear of the past.

But it was only Hallie. She came up the aisle,

360 passing Susan. "You mustn't stay here!" she cried to Alex. "Get away before—"

But Alex was no longer afraid. Hallie was sometimes foolish but always harmless. She stopped her calmly. "We're perfectly safe in this place, Hallie. This is 'sanctuary.'"

"Not now!" Hallie cried. "Not anymore!"

If she was right, it was already too late. Someone had appeared behind her and stood at the foot of the aisle. The woman wore white pants and a white shirt, and had tied a white scarf over her head, so that she shone with false purity in the fading pink light. Emily Gower advanced up the aisle slowly, holding something balanced on the palms of her hands, as though she were a priestess making an offering.

In a flash of recognition, Alex understood everything clearly. The object Emily held was the ebony swan.

"I found this at my brother's house," Emily said. "I thought you should have it now. To remind you of what your husband believed you really were."

Hallie fluttered in apology. "Gracie told us where you'd gone, Alex. Emily felt there was still unfinished business between you, so when you left the island she came across the long way in one of John's boats."

Emily cut her off. "Never mind all that. Alex

knows why I'm here. She knows all the old scores that need to be settled."

Calmly Alex took the carving from her. She had asked for wisdom and courage and she still felt that unseen, protective support. Perhaps she could even give a name to it now. All that Juan Gabriel had felt when he had first known about John had indeed been vented, released into this carving and his writing. He had confronted John to preserve his marriage, and he had accomplished what he intended, even though the younger man had disarmed him. At least this was what she wanted to believe.

"It's time for you to know even more," Emily said. "To know everything. I've come to finish what you've started, and nothing else matters now."

Alex looked up at the fading radiance that filled the vaulted spaces overhead. "Not here," she said. "We will go outside and I will listen to whatever else you have to tell me."

Hallie cried out frantically. "No! *Don't* listen! I've listened too long. Too terribly long!"

Alex walked serenely down the aisle, and Susan, looking alarmed, came with her, a hand tight on her arm. There was no time to reassure her now, though Alex felt confident that Susan, at least, was protected.

Emily slipped past and ran ahead, moving with an agility Alex Montoro had long ago lost.

362 Hallie came last, haltingly, afraid to leave what had been called "sanctuary."

Outside, Alex led them away from the tombs of Carter and his wives and past the little collection of old gravestones. Twilight tinted the sky a rosy gray, and it was not yet entirely dark. Warmth from the day lingered, and fireflies danced among the bushes, offering false tranquility. Now and then a car sped by on the road, leaving the evening hushed when it was gone.

"We can sit here on the grass and talk, if you like," Alex said, as if this were a social occasion. When Susan helped her down and she had been settled with her back against a tree, she placed the swan beside her—almost companionably, since a sort of peace had been made between them.

"You've always known, haven't you?" she asked Hallie.

Hallie nodded miserably. "I blame myself. But how could I betray my sister? I know that what I did to protect her was wrong. *Now* I know!"

"Hush," Emily told her. "There was nothing you could do to stop anything. The blame lies with Alex. I want her to know all of it—so it can be ended. I can't live with this anymore. There was another time when I came to your house, Alex—when you were out."

Yes, this was the way it had to have been. "The day Dolores died?"

"Of course. This morning when I saw you and John together I knew you must hear the rest. I came over from the island that day to visit Hallie. I had found John looking at an old photograph of you, Alex. He never guessed that I saw him, but I wanted then to confront you. I was furious, jealous. I never intended anything else. When I came across from the island, Hallie was out, and Gilbert had left a note for her, saying he was going to see Lawrence. I borrowed his extra car and drove over. Then I crept around the house and climbed the tower stairs to let myself inside. I wanted to surprise you, catch you off guard."

Alex's heartbeat had quickened but she said nothing, waiting with a sense of the inevitable for whatever was to come.

"I ran down to the second floor in time to hear Mr. Montoro calling for Dolores. I stayed at the end of the hall and watched when she came out to see what was the matter. He was upset, almost choking over his effort to speak. I saw what he was grasping in his hands—that carving of the ebony swan. He asked Dolores why she had left it in his room, as he'd seen her do.

"She told him she'd found it in the tower room trunk when she was looking for something else, and it had shocked her. When he woke up,

364 she'd wanted to talk to him about the carving. She wanted to assure him that you weren't like that. She was sad that Juan Gabriel was not her father, but now she was trying to understand. She said that no matter what had happened in the past, she loved you both. Oh, it was a very pretty scene—except that he couldn't respond. He held the carving tightly in his hands and just stared at her."

Tears burned Alex's eyes. Emily, unwittingly, was giving Dolores back to her.

Once more, Hallie broke in weakly. "Please, Emily, don't say anything else."

If she heard her sister, Emily gave no sign. "Mr. Montoro was struggling to speak, but he couldn't get the words out. When I saw what was happening, all my hatred for you, Alex, turned into a rage against Dolores. *You* had a child—my son had died. Your child was also *my* husband's. And my husband still loved you, though he couldn't even admit it to himself."

Alex put out a hand toward Susan in apprehension, but Susan was too intent on Emily to notice.

Emily's tone became almost conversational, light and amused. "What could be a better revenge than to harm *your* child, Alex? Dolores was standing near the top of the stairs and I started toward her. Your husband tried to stop me. He struggled out of his wheelchair, but he was too late. I pushed her *hard*. I wanted to hurt her, to hurt you, but I never expected her to die. She screamed as she fell, and the child came running out of her playroom. Whether or not she saw me I don't know. I ran to the tower stairs and rushed down to my car. I guess Gilbert and Lawrence were in Lawrence's workshed, because I heard the sound of the lathe going.

"Back at the house where I was born—where I lived until I married John—I told Hallie what had happened, and what I knew. Gilbert arrived not long after, having left your house after I did, but before Dolores was found. We didn't learn until later that Dolores had died."

Hallie was crying softly. "We protected you, Gilbert and I. We knew you never meant to kill Dolores. But when Alex invited Susan to come here, we were both afraid of what she might remember."

Alex closed her eyes, painfully aware of Susan's state of shock and confusion. However, Emily was still willing to talk, and she must be encouraged to tell it all.

With an effort, Alex managed to contain her own grief and anger. "Marilyn Macklin had nothing to do with Tangier."

Again Emily's voice rose in pitch, though Alex could no longer see her face in the dimming light. "Marilyn was writing about Juan Gabriel Montoro. She was digging into the past to dis-

366 cover exactly what happened before he died. There were words he spoke to you. I was a friend of the family, and Marilyn was quite willing to talk to me, perhaps even pump me a little. She told me what Montoro had managed to say, and I knew how close she was getting to the truth. Closer than you'd ever realized, Alex. So I had to stop her, or what had happened to Dolores would come out for everyone to learn. I had to preserve my life with John."

"Luck played into your hands," Alex said.

"Not luck. Karma. It was all intended to happen, from the very beginning. Perhaps it could never have been stopped—and it can't be stopped now. I was with Hallie in the drugstore when Peter came to pick up a prescription for Theresa's friend. We were in another part of the store, but it was quiet, so we overheard the conversation. The druggist and Peter talked about what dangerous stuff this antidepressant was. In overdose it could kill. Peter said he was picking it up then, because he needed to deliver it to his patient early the next morning. So I suspected that he'd leave it in his office overnight. He was also picking up some special vitamins for Marilyn. He mentioned to the druggist that she took three of these a day."

"I drove Emily to Peter's office!" Hallie cried. "I thought she wanted to catch Peter to talk to him. I didn't know until afterward that she'd gone in a window, or what she'd done. It was horrible, but what could I do after Marilyn was dead?"

Emily spoke gently—a false sound that made Alex feel ill. "You couldn't do anything, Hallie. Because you love me and you had to think of me first. It was fated—even to Marilyn's vitamins waiting there for me. So now you can understand, Alex. Now you know that everything had to happen the way it did, every step of the way. Because of *you*."

They must get away from this place, away from Emily. There could be no "sanctuary" now, when she'd gone completely over the edge. But when Alex struggled to rise, Emily stopped her.

"Wait—there's something more you need to know. What happens to me now doesn't matter. I've set everything in motion. The whole story is in a letter to the police, with copies to local and Richmond papers. Letters that are in the mail now and can't be stopped. John's life is already destroyed, and so will yours be, Alex. Imagine what is going to happen to you when reporters and television people get hold of this and descend on you. What a shambles your nice, safe life will be!"

Alex could hardly absorb what she was saying. For all these years Emily had carried this terrible hidden rage, and now it was completely out of control. The dark evening, still warm from the heat of the day, carried its own threat. They were isolated here, helpless to stop whatever was about to happen. An early half moon turned the church roofs silver, and touched the silver mountings of the gun Emily held in her hand.

Hallie called out to Susan. "You must take your grandmother and go! Now! Emily, listen to me . . ."

But Emily was beyond listening to anyone. As Susan pulled Alex to her feet, she raised the Spanish pistol.

What happened next seemed to Alex to occur in slow motion—it was all so inevitable, so impossible to stop or change. Desperately, Susan tried to push her behind a nearby tree, but Alex found herself frozen in time, unable to escape. This moment was what she had been destined for, driven toward since the day of her birth. She faced John's wife calmly, without fear. Her death would be the ultimate expiation of guilt.

Emily, however, was laughing—an eerie sound that cracked the silence into splinters. "This isn't for you, Alex. You're an old woman, and it will be punishment enough to live out your years."

In the instant that she leveled the gun, Hallie flung herself in front of Susan. The sound of the shot crashed against the great brick building and died away until the night was silent. Hallie's soft cry roused no echoes as she slipped toward the ground.

In a long moment of horror, Emily stared at the bright red sheen on her sister's breast. Then she threw the pistol down and ran through the trees to where she'd left her car.

Strength returned in a surge and Alex found she could act again. There was no time to be surprised that she and Susan were still alive, and a lifetime of authority took hold as she spoke to Susan.

"Here's the key to the Reception Center—there's a telephone there. Call Peter. Get an ambulance. I'll stay here with Hallie."

Susan pulled off her thin cotton sweater and pressed it over the wound. "Hold this in place tightly," she told Alex, and ran off across the grass. Alex sat with Hallie's head in her lap, her hands pressed against the pulsing of blood.

Hallie looked up at her, whispering. "I had to make up for all the times I've protected her. I couldn't let her kill again."

"Hush," Alex told her gently. "Just be quiet until help comes."

"Poor Emily," Hallie murmured, paying no attention. "But she'll be all right now. She always loved the water, and there's peace for her out there in the bay. She told me that once."

Alex pressed harder against the wound. Suddenly she thought of sitting beside Juan Gabriel,

370 when he too was dying, and a strange clarity returned to her. He had tried to tell her. Perhaps he couldn't remember Emily's name, or perhaps he couldn't manage the name of the island. But he had knocked over the basket of fruit and pointed with a shaking hand toward an orange that had rolled away. Not an orange—a tangerine! The name young Susan had called Tangier Island.

Susan ran back across the grass. "Peter's on his way. He's calling an ambulance. I'll take over with Hallie now, Grandmother." She knelt beside them and lifted the sweater briefly. "I think the bleeding's lessening—we'll pull her through. We *must* pull her through."

If only she could cry, Alex thought. In some strange way she felt nothing—as though all emotion had been shocked out of her.

The smile that Susan leveled at her grandmother was filled with courage. With her special perception she seemed to understand. "It's all right, you know, Grandmother. No matter what happens now, the truth is better than not knowing."

If only she could believe that. But what if the truth wiped away too many comforting beliefs that had enabled Alex to live for all these years?

They could hear the sound of the ambulance coming from far down the highway.

Fifteen

Susan watched Peter supervising the paramedics as they put Hallie's stretcher into the ambulance. Alex had chosen not to stay. Once the ambulance arrived and she found out that Hallie would survive her wound, she turned oddly remote, insisting that she could drive herself home in her own car.

"Stay and help Peter, Susan," she'd directed, and walked away, limping only a little.

Now the ambulance was gone too, with lights flashing, and the grove of trees near the church seemed suddenly quiet—totally empty of sound. Susan touched the wet blood on her dress—blood that might so easily have been her own.

Peter walked toward her across the grass, his stride long and driven by new purpose. When he reached her he drew her into his arms so suddenly that she gasped for breath.

"You're alive—and you might not have been, if it hadn't been for Hallie." He pressed his face against her hair. "No more time wasted! I want you in my life. Will you come into it and stay there, Susan?"

The answer came easily. "Of course!"

He kissed her hungrily—an almost angry kiss that defied anyone to stop him. Then he held her face between his two hands and kissed her again, more gently.

Peter was all she wanted. They could share everything—work as well as love.

"Let's follow Hallie to the hospital," he said. "I have a lot to thank her for."

In the car Susan managed to tell Peter all that had happened—including the not-yet-fully-accepted fact that John Gower was her grandfather.

TWO MONTHS LATER

Peter had borrowed a boat from a friend in order to take Susan to the island. It was late afternoon when they docked. All the tourists were gone, so the islanders once more possessed their bit of land. Someone had said that in the hours after the boats were gone, Tangier came to life like Brigadoon. Susan found that it was like that now.

Children rode their bicycles freely along narrow lanes, and women strolled and talked together of island doings. The tourist shops had closed, and grocery stores were busy. With the sun no longer high, an October wind felt chill, hinting of what was to come. Susan had known she must make this trip before the "freezing fire" of the winter that still lay ahead.

The circus the media had made of the Montoro story had been as terrible as Emily had predicted. Alex had been besieged for weeks. Only recently had interest turned elsewhere, so they could breathe freely again. Susan had known then what she must do. Out of all the tumult and distress, one good thing had emerged. Peter had been completely cleared. He had reopened his office and was seeing the patients who needed him. Very soon Susan would begin working as his nurse—history repeating itself! While there were no longer barriers between them, she knew that Peter needed time to heal. That was fine—she wasn't going anywhere, and she could wait.

Hallie was at home—still recovering—and not yet her former self. Peter said this would take time—and a lot of forgiveness and affection.

Emily's body had been recovered on a Tidewater beach. And when that horror subsided, all Alex wanted was to shut out the painful past from her life.

Susan had said, "But John Gower is still part of the present."

"Not the John I knew." Her grandmother was curt. "If you want to see him, it's up to you."

For a time Susan had not been certain that she could risk such a meeting. John had disconnected his phone and cut himself off, protected by his island friends. He'd wanted to see no one, Fred Parks reported. She hadn't sent him word that she was coming, lest he refuse to see her.

The need in her to visit the island again and see this man who was her grandfather, had grown in determination. Tangier was part of her own heritage. She even had relatives there! All the island's strangeness was part of her own heritage, her very bloodline, and she knew it was time to establish contact.

When she left Peter with the boat at the dock, she'd taken one of the island golf carts. The driver's curiosity was evident, though no questions had been asked or answered. Near the house, Susan left the cart to approach on foot. John was sitting in a chair on the wide porch.

He bore little resemblance to the man she had met a few months earlier. His hair seemed even more white, and new, deep lines marked his face. When he heard her come through the gate and looked up, she managed a smile. He merely stared at her, as though he waited. For what? Blame? Rejection? But surely he knew she wouldn't have come for those!

She tried out the word tentatively. "Grandfather?"

Nothing changed in his face, and she went on matter-of-factly. "May I sit down for a minute?"

He nodded, all his defenses clearly in place. His wounding had gone deep—far deeper than Hallie's physical wound.

She had thought about what she wanted to tell him, but she began hesitantly. "When I was a little girl growing up in New Mexico I used to dream about boats. With desert and mountains all around, I had an obsession with water and boats. Where other kids wanted horses, I wanted my own boat. My father and stepmother thought I was a little touched. Perhaps I was. But something in me seemed to yearn for the freedom of water, being on water."

At least he was listening, though no line in his face had shifted.

Somehow she went on in spite of his impassive gaze. "Of course I don't really know anything about boats. But I must have loved them when I was very small."

The island silence seemed more complete than any she'd ever experienced—it was broken only by the occasional laughter of children from somewhere beyond those crowded tombstones. It seemed forever before he spoke.

"Can you ride a bicycle, Susan?"

"That I can manage."

"Good. Then let's go visit some boats."

He held out his hand and she felt the rough callouses from all his years of work around ropes and shipyards and fishing boats. As she moved beside him he seemed so much taller than when he'd slumped in his chair, and in a moment of perception she glimpsed something in this man that her grandmother must once have seen all those years ago when they were both young.

"First," she said, "can we go pick up Peter Macklin? He brought me here today. I'm going to marry him and I'd like you to meet him."

John Gower had the most wonderful, warming smile, and Susan knew that something had begun for her that had nothing to do with Alex Montoro.

Gracie and Alex were working late in the evening in the tower storeroom. Gracie had carried up box after box of photographs and other objects that Alex had decided to put away. Her dancing was history. Anyone who wanted to know about it could come up here and look through her collection if they wished.

The one bit of knowledge that might have comforted her was that the memory of Dolores as her own loving daughter had been restored. But that was not enough. Not even Dolores's daughter could bring Alex back to life. She had gone dutifully to see Hallie in the hospital and had only pretended to be alive. Emily's revenge had been far more complete than she could have dreamed.

What she really felt now was a chilling numbness. All power to feel any real emotion had been shattered as though by a storm of hurricane force. Only by doing active, seemingly purposeful tasks could she keep afloat for a little while longer. Nothing would ever be the same again since the firing of Juan Gabriel's silver pistol.

She had lost *him* forever—lost all that he had stood for in her life. For years she had lived in a swamp of lies. Even her youthful love was gone; she had seen John and he was an old man. She had been foolish to keep the young John alive in her heart.

Gracie's voice brought her out of her unhappy reverie.

"Do you want to keep these old dance shoes, Miss Alex?"

The box held two pairs of ballet slippers—one pair white satin, the other black. Both were frayed at the box tips, as could happen in a single performance. The last time she had danced *Swan Lake* she'd worn those shoes. She pulled out a white satin ribbon and wound it absently about one finger, then tucked it back into the box.

"Put the shoes away, Gracie. The girl they belonged to has been gone for a long time. I can hardly remember her."

Gracie looked sad, her eyes searching Alex's face. "Did you know Miss Susan went over to Tangier Island today? Mr. Peter got a boat and took her across."

That this had happened seemed no more real or significant than anything else. "I know, Gracie. It doesn't matter."

"It matters. You gotta come back, Miss Alex. That place you've dug for you ain't no good."

"There's no place else, Gracie."

Gracie looked about the storeroom, still searching. As her eyes lighted on something she had almost forgotten, she spoke with a new animation.

"You remember that old cape Mr. Juan Ga-

briel brought here when you first came? You remember how good he looked in it?"

"I remember." But she didn't want to remember.

"Bet you forgot that you didn't want to give
that cape away after Mr. Juan Gabriel died. You
told me to put it away up here. Somewhere that
moths wouldn't get to it."

Alex heard her with the same deep indiffer-
ence she gave to all matters these days. What did
the cape matter now?

Gracie went to a cedar chest that stood at the
far end of this quarter-moon room. She opened it
and took out the cape.

In spite of herself Alex's attention was
caught. She remembered too well, and remembrance stabbed deeply.

Juan Gabriel had possessed a theatrical side,
and he had reveled in that cape. Gracie held it up
so that its great folds floated free. It had been
woven from a special llama wool and dyed a rich,
soft gray. Its high-standing collar, buckled with
silver, had lent an impressive quality when his
strong chin jutted from its frame. The lining—of
his own choice—was a dark burgundy satin.
When Juan Gabriel had mounted the lecture
platform to read from his books, he always wore
that cape. As he approached the lectern he discarded it carelessly in ripples of gray and dark
red into the hands of some assistant. By the time

380 he stepped to the podium the audience was prepared for the drama of what would be a *performance.*

Suddenly she wanted to touch the cape. "Give it to me, Gracie."

Gracie went a step farther. She carried the heavy folds to place them around Alex's shoulders—and it was as though Juan Gabriel's arms once more supported her. She slipped her hands through the slanted openings and swung the cape around her, so that the folds swirled and settled.

Somewhere inside she heard a crackle of paper. When she reached into a concealed pocket she found something there—an envelope. She drew it out to examine—an addressed, stamped envelope that had never been mailed. With a gesture not unlike Juan Gabriel's she flung the cape into Gracie's quick hands and sat down in the old armchair.

"It's a letter to Juan Gabriel's editor in New York," she told Gracie.

When she slit open the flap, she drew out a page of her husband's strong handwriting and read the few lines—slightly stilted, as his letter-writing manner had always been.

My dear Frederick:

I very much appreciate your wanting to reissue a special edition of the American translation of The Black Swan. *I thank you most sincerely, but I fear I must oppose this.*

That is the one book of mine that I have been glad to see go out of print. It was written long ago in a time of anger and its publication may have hurt someone whom I hold very dear. I will not repeat that wounding. I believe that you understand, my good friend.

Yours,
Juan Gabriel Montoro

The date at the top of the letter was two days before Juan Gabriel's stroke.

Alex sat with the sheet in her hand while tears came into her eyes and spilled over her cheeks. The thawing had begun. With those few words Juan Gabriel had reached into her darkness with love and reassurance.

How ironic that after he was ill and couldn't talk with her, she had followed through on the reissuing of the new edition of *The Black Swan*—because she had believed this was what he would have wanted—no matter how much she'd hated that book.

She handed the letter to Gracie to read, and Gracie's hand shook as she followed the lines, understanding very well.

"We had to come up here today, didn't we, Miss Alex? It was time to take out that cape."

Yes—it was time.

A miracle had occurred. For the first time in months Alex felt wonderfully alive, filled with a new, astonishing energy.

"Can you finish up here, Gracie? I want to be ready when Susan returns."

As she reached the top of the stairs, the doorbell rang. That couldn't be Susan—she would let herself in.

Alex brushed back untidy locks of hair and untied her apron. She really didn't care whether she was suitably dressed for visitors or not, she was gowned in her own happy radiance. So let whoever it was take her unadorned. She turned on the outside lights and opened the door.

John Gower stood on the porch steps, with Susan and Peter on the walk below him. He spoke quickly, as though he feared she might close the door in his face.

"I've brought you something, Alex. A small gift."

On the palm of his extended hand rested a perfect little pink shell—from the beach on Tangier, she knew.

She hesitated only a moment, and then took the shell from him, understanding. This was a gift from a friend.

Dusty memories hadn't merely been swept away—they had been blown off in a storm that left a new clarity of vision that belonged to the present. Now the good memories were there to nurture and support.

She stepped back from the doorway, her smile young and beautiful to those who watched, and let the three of them in.

About the Author

PHYLLIS A. WHITNEY was born in Yokohama, Japan, of American parents, and also lived in the Philippines and China. After the death of her father in China, she and her mother returned to the United States, which she saw for the first time when she was fifteen. This early travel has exerted a strong influence on her work; many of her novels are set in areas she has visited in Europe, Africa, and the Orient, as well as in the places she has lived.

Phyllis A. Whitney is the author's maiden name. (The "A" stands for "Ayame," which is the Japanese word for "iris.") She is a widow, and lives near her daughter in Virginia. In 1975 she was elected President of the Mystery Writers of America, and in 1988 received the organization's Grand Master Award for lifetime achievement. She is also the recipient of the Agatha Award for lifetime achievement given by Malice Domestic.

Since 1941, when she attained her first hardcover publication, she has become an international success. Over forty million copies of her novels are in print in paperback editions. Her novels for adults now number thirty-six, and her devoted following has made bestsellers of most of these titles, including *Woman Without a Past, The Singing Stones, Rainbow in the Mist, Feather on the Moon, Silversword,* and *Dream of Orchids*.